A
Little BIT
YOURS

STARLA DEKRUYF

This book is a work of fiction. Names, characters, places, and incidents either are products of the author's imagination or are used fictitiously. Any resemblance to actual events or, places, living or dead, is entirely coincidental and not intended by the author.

A LITTLE BIT YOURS: A Small Town Fake Dating Romance—Pineridge Series-Book 3

STARLA DEKRUYF

Print Edition ISBN: 9798985626964

Digital ISBN: 9798985626971

A Little Bit YOURS

A Pineridge Novel

BOOK 3

STARLA DEKRUYF

For the dreamers who show up, work hard, and don't quit.

Content/Trigger Warnings

This book is intended for readers who are 17+. Please note that there may be content in this book that may be triggering for some readers. This list is not exclusive, so please proceed with caution.

- Cracked door—open w/ sexual content w/o graphic details
- Mild explicit language/cursing
- Alcohol consumption
- Talk of cheating (done in the past/off page)

CHAPTER 1

Norah

Everywhere Norah went, it looked as if Cupid had left his mark by shooting his arrow and causing a Valentine's Day eruption. An outbreak of pink and red, hearts, roses, and chocolate overtook the entire town of Pineridge, Colorado like a virus.

And Norah wanted no part of it.

Except that she'd agreed to help her sister, Isabella, plan a Valentine's Day party.

What had she been thinking? Was it too late to book a flight to Jamaica and get the heck out of Pineridge until the buzz of the holiday of love wore off? Maybe even longer. Maybe she could find a job there, make and sell beaded jewelry, meet a local named Philip, shack up with him, and never return.

Sadly, she wasn't very skilled in making jewelry, and too much sun caused her skin to get all blotchy, and she'd have to spend time getting to know Philip before moving in with him, wouldn't she? Besides, she'd really miss her family and her figure skating students.

Nope, she was stuck here through the dreadful holiday and beyond.

It didn't help that February in Pineridge was wet, cold, and downright miserable.

The towering piles of dirty snow cleared from streets and parking lots by the plow was another cursed reminder that the gloomy winter was here to stay for a few more months. Jamaica was sounding more appealing with each passing day she was stuck in this frozen wasteland.

Norah gave her Timberland boots a stomp before entering Tapp's Brewery.

Despite making good time, her bestie, Maddie was already there. She and Maddie had a recurring lunch date every Monday. Sometimes the location changed, but other than that, the day and time stayed the same. Having the repetition, the familiarity, the routine, kept Norah feeling like her life was normal.

And not like everything had flipped upside down.

Maddie waved from a two-seater table in the corner of the brewery, her long blonde hair pulled into a high topknot.

Norah weaved between crowded tables and busy servers. One would think by the amount of people inside Tapp's that it was the only place that served lunch in Pineridge. But since O'Henry's Bar and Grill closed last fall, the brewery had quickly become a local favorite.

"Hey," Maddie said. "I ordered you a Coke and the grilled cheese. But I wasn't sure if you wanted a beer or maybe something stronger?"

"Mads, it's barely noon." Norah shrugged out of her jacket, arranging it over the back of her chair before sitting down.

"It's five o'clock somewhere." Maddie grinned.

"True. But I better not, I've gotta get back to the rink after lunch. One of the other instructors is out sick so I said I'd fill in for her class."

"Suite yourself. But personally, I've been anxious to try out their new spring citrus IPA." Maddie picked up her glass of the hazy amber liquid.

"I bet it's delicious. Especially with Kelsey working her magic. Next time for sure."

And speaking of, when Norah glanced up, Kelsey was quickly approaching their table.

"Hey, ladies. I thought I saw you sneak in, Norah."

"Hey, Kels." Norah stood and gave her friend a hug.

"Kelsey, chef's kiss." Maddie kissed the tips of her fingers. "This spring IPA. Delicious."

"Thanks. I think this one's gonna become a favorite. Well, I gotta get back into the pit," Kelsey said, hiking a thumb over her shoulder. "The hops only have a few more minutes in the boiler. I just came out because it's been forever since I've seen you."

Norah sat back down and tried to push away the annoyance creeping in. Everyone was worried about her. Sure, she still got sad over her failed marriage, but she wasn't in a constant state of depression. Not anymore.

"Don't drop off the face of the earth like that again. Or next time, I'm hunting you down. I know where you live," Kelsey warned as she backed away, pointing at her.

Unfortunately, *everyone* knew where she lived. She'd moved back in with her parents after she and Landon separated. As grateful as she was for their support, she needed to get back on her own two feet.

"Sooooo?" Maddie said after Kelsey had left.

Norah picked up her glass and peered at her friend over the brim. "So what?"

Maddie groaned. "C'mon, Norah, the party is next week. What's the date situation?"

"Why am I the only one being interrogated? Last I checked, you didn't have a date either."

Maddie's eyes flitted away, and she smoothed her paper napkin over her lap.

Norah lifted her brows and leaned across the table. "Mads?"

"Hmm?"

"What aren't you telling me?"

Flicking her wrist, Maddie groaned. "Okay, fine. I kind of, sort of, might have a date."

Norah's mouth fell open and her eyes widened.

"Don't look at me like that."

"Like what? I'm not looking at you in any particular way," Norah teased. She played with her straw in the glass, pushing down the cubes of ice. "Well, don't leave me in suspense, who's the lucky guy?"

Maddie scrunched up her nose as she said, "Garrett Vance."

Norah let out a bark of laughter before clamping her mouth shut. "Sorry. I shouldn't laugh. Garrett is...he's a solid choice."

"Right," Maddie said flatly and rolled her eyes. "Now how about you try saying that again without wincing and raising the pitch of your voice."

Norah laughed again. "I'm sorry. I can't help it. But, Mads, you can't blame me for being surprised."

"Yeah, I know," she muttered.

"How did this even happen?"

Maddie fiddled with the silverware on the table, lining them up and then mixing them again. "He came into the gym and ordered a smoothie. We got to talking and he heard I didn't have a date to the party yet. We agreed the whole date thing was stupid, no offense," Maddie paused.

"None taken." Norah commiserated with them both.

The date thing *was* stupid. But arguing with Isabella was pointless. Once she'd changed her mind from a Galentine's party with only women to a couple's party, she had her mind set, and there was no changing it. Norah wasn't an idiot; she knew this was all part of Isabella's plan to force her to start dating again.

"And then Garrett mentioned we should just go together." Maddie shrugged her shoulders.

"Mads," Norah drew out her name. "You've been down this road before. Twice."

"Things are different now."

"How?"

A young server arrived at their table, two plates of grilled cheese and French fries in her arms. "Here ya go. Can I get you anything else?"

"No thanks, we're good." Norah's mouth watered at the sight of the greasy toasted bread.

The server nodded and moved to the next table, another set of full plates in her other arm.

Maddie pulled her sandwich apart, the cheese stretching perfectly, and she took a big bite.

Picking up half of her own sandwich, Norah pointed it at Maddie and said, "Don't think just because your mouth is full, you're off the hook."

"I'm a big girl. That childish crush I had on Garrett is history. And besides, I'm not looking for anything serious. So, Garrett is perfect."

Norah wanted to say something more. She wanted to object. Maddie hadn't just had a childish crush on Garrett. It was a full-blown infatuation. For three years. About a year into it, after she'd opened the smoothie bar at the gym, Garrett asked her out. They slept together and then he never called her again. He avoided her at the gym for months afterward. Until he needed a date to the couple's Halloween costume party last fall.

And the pattern had repeated itself.

Norah couldn't see her friend go through that again. But she also was in no place to give relationship advice. And Maddie was right about one thing—she was a big girl.

"Okay, okay. You're right, he sounds perfect."

"Now we just need to find you a date and we'll be all set." Maddie smiled wide and shoved a fry into her mouth.

Norah took a bite of her sandwich, the flavor combination of the gooey cheese, butter, and garlic exploded in her mouth. The worry over if Maddie would get her heart broken by Garrett again, if she'd find a date in time, or if Isabella would ever stop pestering her about the party planning, slipped away.

All Norah wanted to do was enjoy this sandwich. Heck, she wanted to marry this sandwich. She wanted to make sweet love to this sandwich and have its tiny grilled cheese babies.

"Norah?" Maddie called, interrupting her from her sandwich fantasy.

"Mmm?" Her eyes flittered open.

"Your phone has been dinging like crazy."

Norah glanced at the screen while it lay on the tabletop.

ISABELLA

Gina said you're all set to sample desserts next Tuesday at Sweet Cakes.

The champagne flutes I ordered from Amazon will be coming to Mom and Dad's on Friday.

Did you plan to pick up the rest of the party decorations from Dollar or Less?

Norah groaned. So much for forgetting about the party stress.

"Remind me again why I agreed to help plan this party for Isabella?"

"Because you love party planning."

"I do...or, I did. But I'm not so sure anymore."

"Hey, if you can't take directions or criticism from your sister, how are ya gonna take it from someone else?"

At this point, it would be easier to take directions from someone else. She really didn't want to let Isabella down. It was just a party, but to Izzy, this was so much more.

Not only did Izzy want everyone who attended to have a good time, but she also wanted to give Norah one night where she could kick back and relax and just have fun. Most importantly, she wanted her to not be alone on her first Valentine's Day since her split from Landon.

Norah exhaled a deep breath. "You're right."

But her shoulders tensed when her phone dinged again.

ISABELLA

Oh! And don't worry about finding a date. I think I've found the perfect person for you. Just trust me.

Norah gaped at the text on her phone.

"What is it?" Maddie asked around a mouthful of fries.

Norah gave a slow steady shake of her head, holding her phone out to Maddie.

"This is great. Now you don't have to worry about finding your own date," Maddie said.

"What kind of eligible bachelors does Izzy know in Pineridge?"

"Hmmm...good point."

Norah pointed a fry in Maddie's direction. "We should be *very* worried."

"It's just one date. If you don't like him, you never have to go out with him again."

True. And Isabella wouldn't set her up with some loser, would she? Norah was running out of time. The party was just over a week away. The countdown on Isabella's Instagram story reminding her was like a ticking time bomb.

Anxiety stirred in her stomach. If her knight in shining armor didn't walk through those doors any second, she very well could be attending the Galentine's party with some rando Pineridge loser that Isabella set her up with.

The door opened to Tapp's Brewery, and the tiny hairs on the back of Norah's neck stood at attention. Excitement pulsed through her. *Was her luck turning around? Was Cupid finally going to be on her side for once?*

Hope ballooned in her chest.

Maddie muttered a curse word under her breath before she said, "Don't. Turn. Around."

"Mhmm?" But it was too late. Norah was already turning around.

In an instant, the hope-balloon in her chest popped, expelling the air, and plummeting to the ground.

Landon Hoffman.

He made eye contact with her, only briefly, but long enough for her to see the guilt shining there. On his heels was none other than Mia Moseley. She slipped her arm around his waist. Instead of pressing a gentle kiss to her temple, like he used to do with Norah, he grabbed a handful of Mia's ass.

And just like that, Norah's body heated. Anger prickled her skin as the memories from the horrific night when she knew her marriage was over flashed into her mind. She'd spent weeks planning Landon's surprise birthday party. He hadn't had a big birthday since his mom was alive, so Norah wanted to make it extra special. She'd invited all their friends, had it catered, and she'd ordered his favorite treats from Sweet Cakes Bakery.

When Norah hid alongside the other guests in their darkened house, anticipating Landon's arrival, the last thing she expected was to be surprised herself. But when the keys sounded in the lock of the front door and Landon pushed inside, arms like octopus tentacles groping another woman, their lips interlocked, and their clothes being torn off, surprise was an understatement.

And now, he was parading Mia into Tapp's Brewery like they were officially announcing their relationship to the town.

It had been almost a year, so what did she expect?

"Hey, you okay? Do you wanna go?" Maddie asked, sliding a hand across the table to pat Norah's.

The touch brought her back to reality, and she returned her attention to her friend. "I'm fine. Or...I will be."

As much as she wanted to give in to her Jamaica fantasy, this wasn't a game of LIFE or Monopoly. There was no getting out of jail free card—or in her case, getting out of Pineridge.

Before Isabella's bright idea of having her host the party, Norah had planned to stay in her jammies all day, tucked underneath the safety of her covers, and binge Netflix until February 15th.

Attending the Galentine's party meant she'd have to actually acknowledge the holiday of love, and she didn't want to give Cupid the satisfaction. She and Cupid were currently in a middle school fight and no longer on speaking terms since her divorce.

But the party was only days away, and she still didn't have many prospects. There was Chad at the hardware store, except he'd been single and bitter since his longtime girlfriend left him for a tourist visiting from Chicago. Then there was Justin,

Norah's only other boyfriend in high school besides Landon, and she was fairly certain he had a secret significant other in Denver—and he wouldn't be showing his face in Pineridge anytime soon.

Isabella had said she'd found her a date and asked her to trust her, but Norah wasn't sure she could. She was probably better off taking charge of the date search herself. Because this couldn't be just *any* date. He had to be hot and successful. And definitely not a Pineridge resident. She needed a date that would make Landon lose his mind and second-guess all the horrible decisions he made the past year.

Her date had to be damn near close to God's gift to women.

Whether Norah liked it or not, she and Cupid were about to make amends.

CHAPTER 2

Todd

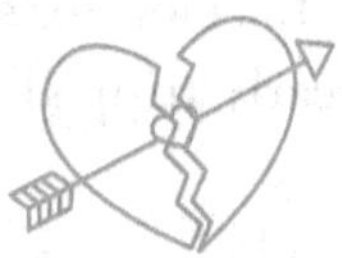

Working with your ex after you surprised her with a new puppy and a near-marriage proposal, and then she dumped you, felt like the absolute worst kind of corporal punishment. Margo was the very last person Todd Langston wanted to bump into as he slipped through the closing elevator doors just in time. He exhaled and smoothed down his tie, wishing he hadn't been running late today resulting in him being crammed like a sardine in the stuffy elevator with his ex.

But since he moved to his folks' house in Jersey a few months ago after the breakup, Todd had to get up at the butt crack of dawn to drive into the city. Today of all days, he couldn't afford to be late. He'd had this meeting with his boss, Jack Santos, on his calendar for weeks. It probably didn't help that he'd agreed to go out with his brother, Ryan the night before and had one too many drinks.

Okay, maybe two or three too many.

"Hey, Todd," Margo greeted, her voice too cheery for someone who'd just ripped his heart out.

He glanced over his shoulder and gave her a curt nod. "Margo."

He returned his attention back to the closed elevator door, wishing the thing would move through the floors faster.

Awkwardness filled the small, crowded space, heating it up to near-boiling temperature. He loosened the knotted tie at his constricted throat. When the elevator stopped abruptly and the doors slid open, Todd nearly tripped over his own feet in his attempt to escape.

It wasn't until he'd made it a few feet away that he finally allowed himself to exhale. Tomorrow, he'd take the stairs. No way would he willingly put himself through that suffocating, awkward-as-hell catastrophe again.

He passed a row of cubicles, mostly paralegals and associates, and slowed to nearly a stop when Scott, the biggest slacker of them all and one of Todd's closest friends at the firm, popped his head up.

"What's up?" Scott greeted him with a fist bump.

"Just on my way in to see Jack."

"Oh right, that's today. Good luck, bro."

Todd walked backward, continuing their conversation. "Thanks."

"We'll celebrate tonight. A beer at Marco's. You're buying."

"Sure—" his words died in his throat when Margo moved swiftly past him, her nose in the air.

Scott's eyes bulged. "Duuuuude," his voice hiked up several octaves. "What's going on?"

Todd furrowed his brows. "Uhhh...I'll get back to you on that." He hopped to a jog to catch up to Margo, keeping his stride at the same pace as her. From his peripheral, he caught her tracking him from the corner of her own eye.

She walked faster.

He walked faster.

When they came to a fork in the office—right would take them past another row of cubicles and left would lead them to Jack's office—they both turned left. Todd sucked in a breath, resisting the nagging urge to ask her what she was doing? And where was she going? And how could she walk so fast in those four-inch heels? He was practically speed-walking just to keep up with her and he'd always been told he had the legs of a gazelle.

Todd halted as soon as he reached the desk of Jack's secretary and Margo stopped as well. His breathing was so accelerated, that he had to take a moment to catch it before he could speak. Margo's chest rose and fell, but her breathing seemed level, normal even.

"I have a meeting with Jack at nine o'clock, is it okay if I go in?" Margo asked Jack's secretary, but she was already on the move, not waiting for a reply.

"Oh, um...but...I haven't buzzed him yet." His secretary looked frazzled.

But Todd was the most confused. "Wait." He exhaled, still panting. "I have..." *breathe*, "a meeting with..." *breathe*, "Jack at nine." He inhaled deeply, finally catching his breath.

Jack's secretary squinted at her computer screen. "You both have a meeting with him at nine, but—"

"Then I'm sure it's fine if I head in first, he is expecting me after all," Margo called over her shoulder while Todd rushed to catch up to her.

"But—" the secretary protested one more time before Margo pushed open Jack's door.

Todd followed behind her, slamming into her back when she stopped abruptly and causing her to choke on her greeting.

"Ja-aack." She shot a glare at Todd over her shoulder.

Todd took a step back and smoothed his tie again. The stupid thing was too long, constantly getting in the way. He didn't even know why he continued to wear it. He'd only kept it because it had been a gift from Margo, and he didn't want to hurt her feelings. But now, what did it matter?

Jack Santos pushed away from his desk and stood. "Margo. Todd." He glanced at his watch—a flashy Rolex. "I'm sorry, I must've missed Cindy's buzz."

"You know Cindy, such a chatterbox," Margo cooed.

Todd hated her butt-kisser voice. And her fake smile. Now that the two weren't dating, her habits and personality traits that he used to find quirky, now just annoyed him.

Jack rounded his desk and shook Margo's hand before presenting a chair for her to sit on. He shook Todd's hand and ushered him out the door.

"We'll be five minutes."

"Oh...yeah...sure, okay, Jack," he muttered.

He could take the hint; he wasn't wanted in this meeting. That was fine. He and Jack would have their own meeting next, and Margo wouldn't be privy to the words they exchanged either. Though he'd be lying if he didn't admit it bothered him.

Jack passed an infuriating look in his secretary's direction before he returned inside his office, closing the door behind him. Todd loosened his tie again and paced the floor, trying and failing to concentrate on the pattern in the linoleum.

There was one opening as a partner in their office. Todd had been working his ass off for the past two years, taking the crap cases, staying late, working weekends when Scott and the rest of his friends were going out for drinks, and attending baseball games, and concerts.

If Margo got offered the one open position as a partner, he'd lose it. He needed this promotion. His life was spiraling out of control, and he just needed one good thing.

One win.

After what felt like an eternity, Jack's office door swung

open and he escorted Margo out with a hand pressed to her back, the two of them laughing. Todd stiffened, his insides already wanting to sulk. Margo slid a confident smile in his direction as she passed him.

He swallowed.

Jack waved him inside and Todd took a seat in the same chair Margo had just been sitting in. Jack perched on the edge of his desk, stretching his legs out and crossing his ankles.

"Let's cut to the chase, shall we?"

Todd bounced his knee. This was it. Jack was about to offer him the promotion. He just knew it.

"As you're aware, we are looking to promote an associate from within the firm."

Todd nodded along, his heart hammering against his ribcage.

"Next month we'll be announcing the promotion of Santos and Cho's newest partner. Todd, you've been a valuable associate at our firm, so I feel like you deserve to hear it from me."

Todd rested a palm against his chest. "Jack, I'm flattered. You have no idea what this means to me."

"I'm afraid to say, it looks as if the promotion will be offered to Margo."

Todd opened his mouth to speak, but his words died in his throat. Blackness tunneled his vision.

Jack moved behind his desk, dropping into his chair. "You two are the best associates we have, but we can't promote both of you at this time." He paused, and propped his elbows on the mahogany desk, steepling his fingers. "There might be another opening soon, but—"

"I don't understand," Todd interrupted. "I've been working my ass off. I've taken every case dropped on my desk for the last two years."

"The other partners and I have recognized your workload. And how you've handled it. While we've been impressed in the past, lately...well, lately your work ethic has been questionable."

Todd deadpanned. "Pardon me, Jack, but what the hell does that mean? Questionable?"

It was unusual for Todd to curse in front of Jack—in front of any of his bosses here at Santos and Cho. But he'd never been this blindsided before. They'd always been an upstanding company to work for. A place he could be proud of when someone asked him which firm he worked for. Both immigrants, Santos and Cho started the firm nearly forty years ago, beginning with just the two of them and a single pro bono case, and grew into the company they are today.

"I'm aware of your recent breakup with Margo. And I feel for you, I really do. But we're an old-school firm. We pride ourselves in honor and respect." Jack stood again, sweeping his arm at the plaque on his wall with the company's motto engraved in it like an amendment or the Ten Commandments.

Todd slumped in his seat, rubbing a hand over the back of his neck while his mind raced. "I mean, yeah, my personal life has been a bit of a mess lately...but I don't see how that has affected my work."

Jack exhaled a long breath. "Todd, your social media accounts are public, and your content goes against what our firm stands for. You've been coming into the office late. Your attention to detail has suffered. Last week you turned in a case to your paralegal that wasn't even closed. Not to mention, your follow-through has been inadequate. You advised a client to take a deal without even going to pre-trial when you held concrete evidence of his company's innocence in your hands. And three weeks ago, one of your clients discharged you."

"That was one time. That's never happened before. And

the rest, Jack, I'm trying. I really think I've turned a corner. I've got six solid cases lined up. If you give me the chance, I'll prove it to you. I can do this."

He lifted his wiry brows. "And your personal life?"

At any other firm, his personal life wouldn't matter. But he didn't work at any other firm. He worked for Santos and Cho. A firm that prides itself on business integrity, following a moral and ethical framework. While his character typically aligned with those mentioned in the company's motto, lately his Instagram account hadn't reflected that.

But had Margo's been any different? She had all her socials public too. And she'd been posting pictures of her and Aaron Brown, another lawyer in their office.

"With all due respect, sir, I don't see how Margo has a leg up on me in that area."

"Margo's integrity hasn't wavered across all areas. Not her work, not her personal life, not even on her social media accounts. In fact, she seems to be handling her socials with dignity and respectability."

"And it doesn't raise any red flags that she's having an office fling?" he spit out.

"I know you don't want to hear this, but from the outside looking in, it doesn't appear to be a fling. She looks like an intelligent, successful young woman who is in a committed relationship. It's the exact business integrity our firm stands for."

What was Jack saying exactly? Because he went out for a drink with his brother or friends occasionally and didn't have a steady girlfriend, he wasn't *partner material*. That was BS.

Jack propped his hands on his hips. "Our decision has pretty much already been made. I'm sorry." He flattened his lips.

The room shrunk in on Todd. This couldn't be happening.

Not only was he losing out on the promotion, but he was also losing it to *Margo*.

"But I do have a proposition for you. One last Hail Mary, if you will."

Todd could hardly hear Jack. His voice sounded distorted through the thickness of the fog that enveloped the room.

His Apple Watch ticked against his wrist. Instinctively, he glanced at the screen. It was a text from Isabella.

> ISABELLA
>
> I need you. I'm desperate.

"The other partners and I have always been impressed by your diligence since you started your employment here at Santos and Cho. You've put in long hours, taking on more cases than any other associate, and you've done it with humility."

Todd's head swam with confusion. All this praise, for what? What was the point?

> ISABELLA
>
> Come to Pineridge and be my sister's date for the Galentine's party.
>
> Please!

Jack continued, "You haven't taken time off since you started here. That's a long time to go without taking a vacation. The partners and I think it would be not only beneficial for you but for the firm if you took some time off."

He couldn't be serious.

But by the look of Jack's raised eyebrows and tight jawline, he was dead serious.

"We're giving you four weeks off. With pay," Jack added, sweetening the offer.

"But, Jack, I have a caseload. I can't just abandon my clients."

"I'll have one of the paralegals reassign your cases," he countered.

Just the idea of taking a vacation made his skin buzz with anxiety. Jack was right, Todd hadn't taken time off since he started with Santos and Cho years ago. But that's what you did when you were trying to make partner by the age of thirty.

The reality of that dream being unlikely hit him like a Mac truck. His thirty-first birthday was quickly approaching. His vision tunneled and it suddenly felt like everything he'd worked so hard for was slipping through his fingers. He scrubbed a palm down his face and couldn't help releasing an audible groan.

"Todd, like I said, you're one of the best associates we have," Jack insisted.

But not *the* best.

"I don't know." Jack scratched at his head. "Maybe over the course of the next few weeks, you can somehow convince us to change our mind."

Wait. Was he serious? A tiny spark of hope bubbled inside of him.

And then something clicked in his brain. If being in a relationship made Margo a more appealing choice as the firm's next partner, maybe it would help him too. He read over Izzy's texts again. Her sister needed a date. He needed it to look like he'd settled down.

"You know, sir, this really couldn't have come at a better time," he began.

What the hell was he doing?

Jack lifted his brows curiously. "Yeah?"

"I was supposed to go visit my girlfriend in Colorado next week and take her to this fancy Valentine's party, but I didn't think I'd get the time off work."

"You have a new girlfriend? I had no idea."

Just the thought of Isabella's bratty little sister as his girlfriend caused acid to burn in his throat. Eight years ago, the girl had been responsible for his summer job at Imperial Theatre coming to an untimely demise. And he'd practically hated her since.

But she might be his last resort to becoming a partner.

"Not exactly. We've known each other since we were teens and recently rekindled our relationship," he lied, shaking his knee.

"I'm happy to hear it." Jack smiled wide.

"So don't go making your decision just yet," Todd quipped.

"Why didn't you mention anything sooner?" Jack questioned.

"To be honest, I didn't want to flaunt my relationship and make Margo uncomfortable. So I've been playing it cool, ya know, pretending as if I'm loving the single life. But I'm glad I don't have to keep my girlfriend a secret anymore. I'm glad I can finally make it Instagram official."

The lies wouldn't stop. He was throwing them up like a college student after a rager. What if Norah wouldn't agree to go along with this? How would he recover professionally? Not only could he lose the promotion, but his job altogether.

"This is great. I'm actually relieved. I've been rooting for you, son"

"That means a lot to me, sir."

"Okay." Jack stood.

Todd followed suit, standing with him.

Jack patted him on the back and ushered him toward the door. "Now, get out of my office. Go visit that girlfriend of yours. And I don't want to see you back here for four weeks."

"You got it, boss." Todd slipped out of the office, shaking his head in disbelief over what just happened.

Margo stood there, waiting for him like a circling crow,

ready to pick at his dead carcass. But he wasn't dead—close, but not yet. Except the look of pity on her face made him wish he were. It would be better if she did a victory dance instead of pouting her lips like that.

Because that was the truth. She'd won. And he'd lost. Again.

Todd rushed past her; relieved Scott wasn't at his desk because he had no idea how he'd explain what just went down in that meeting. There would be no celebrating over drinks at Marco's tonight. Instead, he needed to come up with a plan.

"Todd," Margo called, trying to catch up to him. "Would you wait a minute?"

He sighed and stopped, turning to face her. "I guess congratulations are in order."

A streak of pain flashed in her eyes. "Todd," she said on a breath, but the way she said it pinched in his chest and settled in an ache.

"Seriously, I'm happy for you. You deserve it." He flattened his hand over his tie.

"I'm sorry."

"Don't be. I got a pretty sick offer myself."

Margo's brows lifted, and a hopeful glow bloomed on her cheeks. "Yeah?"

Clearing his throat, he glanced over his shoulder. "Yeah. I get to take four weeks off. With pay. So..."

"Oh, Todd." If she hadn't already pitied him, she certainly did now.

"No, really this couldn't have come at a better time. I could really use the break. Plus, it will give me some time to bond with Samson."

"Right. The *dog*." She crinkled her nose when she said *dog*.

Heat expanded in his chest. It stirred up all the emotions from *that* day. When he'd surprised her with the puppy. When he'd planned on proposing to her. Until she'd blown up at him and confessed, they were going down two different paths.

"Yeah, that's right. The *dog*. Samson."

"I'm really sorry."

He tried to wave her off as if losing the promotion was no big deal. "It's fine. There's no need for an apology. I'll be okay. I'll take one of those vacation things that everyone seems to talk about, then come back in time for them to announce the newest partner. Hey, it isn't over yet. Guess I still have a shot."

The look of skepticism in her eyes at his optimism forced him to plant a fake smile on his face.

She crossed her arms and pursed her lips. "Todd Langston is going to take a vacation? I'll believe it when I see it."

She'd flown right over his comment about him still having a shot at partner.

"You're just jealous," he teased back and started heading toward the elevator.

He tugged his phone from his front pocket, preparing to respond to Isabella's text.

Margo walked alongside him. "Where're you going to go? And with a puppy?"

Todd couldn't risk Margo getting in the way of his plan. He needed to be careful. She and Izzy stayed in touch.

He shrugged. "I'll find somewhere. Maybe we'll just get in the Jeep and see where the road leads us."

"I've missed this spontaneous side of you," she said softly, a smile stretching on her lips.

The ache in his chest grew the longer this conversation lasted. There were a lot of things he missed too. He missed when the two of them were just starting out, both baby lawyers, learning together, staying up late, helping each other out with cases.

But as he gazed into her eyes and didn't find the same spark there that he always had before; realization set in that those days were long gone. Margo was right about one thing; they were on two different paths leading them to two very different futures.

Here goes nothing.

> Okay. I'll come. I'll be Norah's date.

> One condition. You can't tell Margo.

"Todd?" Margo called, holding the elevator door open while it released a continuous string of dings.

Todd took one long stride onto the elevator just before the door closed only realizing too late that he and Margo were alone.

"I gotta meet a client, but would you want to maybe grab lunch later? We could celebrate...talk?" Margo gazed up at him.

"No," he said sharply.

She lifted her brows at his bluntness.

He swallowed, his confidence draining, but pushed forward. "I don't think that's a good idea."

Margo flattened her lips and took a step toward him. She pressed her palm to his chest. She was so close. He tried to resist but failed and breathed in her familiar tropical scent.

She gazed into his eyes. "Listen, when you surprised me with the dog, and the insinuation of marriage, and then the mention of moving out of the city—it came from left field for me. I wasn't expecting it. I don't know if moving or the dog is something I can compromise on." She ran her hand up his chest. "But I do know I miss you."

His heartbeat quickened.

And he couldn't believe he was going to say what he was about to. But a lot had changed in the months since they'd separated. He saw things differently. Especially all the ways they were different and could never work.

"I miss you too," he began. "But you were right to say we needed a break. Margo," he said before exhaling, "we're not the same people we were ten years ago. Or four years ago. Or even two months ago."

She gave him a sad smile before slowly lifting her palm from his chest. "I guess. But are you sure this is what you want?"

"It is," he was quick to answer.

The elevator stopped and the doors slid open.

"Okay. Then I guess I have no choice but to let you go." She stepped off the elevator and stopped to glance over her shoulder at him. "I hope you know what you're doing." She spun and walked down the hall.

"Me too," he muttered to himself, watching her as she walked away.

It had been eight years since Isabella's sister, Norah pulled that little stunt, resulting in him getting fired from the theatre. He ended up not having enough money to purchase his books for the next semester of college and had to borrow money from his parents. But that was in the past. It was time he let go of the grudge and made amends with her.

The question was, was she over it?

CHAPTER 3
Norah

How many bottles of wine was too many? Was there a limit? Because as Norah perused the array of labels, a limit did not exist.

Not tonight.

It had been a rough day. Not only had she filled in as instructor for the class from hell, but she'd also had to watch Landon and Mia grope each other all through lunch at Tapp's like they were in an episode of Animals Gone Wild. She'd ended up ditching Maddie early because she couldn't witness the show any longer.

Not only that, following her awful day, Isabella had told her she'd be bringing her date by Tapp's later tonight for the two of them to meet. Honestly, all she wanted to do was get her wine, go back home, take a hot bubble bath, and binge her favorite comfort show: *F.R.I.E.N.D.S.*

With her hair piled in a messy topknot, a black fleece jacket zipped to her chin, and her feet stuffed inside a pair of Timberland boots, she trudged the wine aisles of Engelmann's, Pineridge, Colorado's largest grocery store.

She selected a bottle of red wine displaying a label she didn't recognize. Something from Napa Valley, California. At twenty-four years old, Norah wasn't an expert, but anything from wine country had to be good, right?

She gently set the bottle into the cart alongside the rest of her precious cargo. All the bottles lined up with their coordinating beige labels looked like attentive companions. A familiar voice caught her attention and caused her shoulders to stiffen. She'd recognize her ex's voice anywhere.

This was really not her lucky day.

The way she saw it, she had two choices. One: back out of the aisle and proceed to the checkout quickly and quietly. Or, two: turn the corner and be polite. Say *hello* and then proceed to the checkout quickly and quietly.

But when Mia's laugh erupted from the next aisle, the decision was easy.

Her heart rate picked up as she spun her cart around and headed to the end of the aisle. But when she whirled around the corner, her cart nearly bumped into someone. With little time to allow her brain time to register who the someone was, she jerked backward and tripped on the shoelace of one of her untied Timberland's. The next thing she knew, she was toppling backward, crashing into an endcap display of wine bottles.

Oh, please dear, God, nooooooo!

Norah pinched her eyes shut and held her breath until her butt hit the concrete floor with a *thud*. Thankfully, it was only a small display—of clearance wine. But as luck would have it, not only had the mysterious *someone* witness the entire, disastrous incident, but so had Landon and Mia.

Norah's breathing quickened and her face burned, the heat reaching all the way to the tips of her ears. She pinched her eyes shut and prayed this was all a horrifying nightmare. Much like her current life. Someone could smack her and wake her up at any moment.

As she felt the soft touch on her arm, and sensed the placid nearness of Landon, it hit her hard, deep in her gut, that she was not that fortunate.

She lifted her quivering chin and peered up at him with watering eyes from where she sat in a growing puddle of cheap reds and whites.

No. She could not cry.

Not here and not in front of Landon.

And certainly not in front of Mia Moseley.

"You okay?" Landon asked. "Are you hurt?"

There was sincerity in his gaze, but the blaring presence of Mia, his special someone, his new person, clouded any and all authenticity. All Norah could remember was the night everything went south. The night she knew without a doubt that her marriage of barely a year was over.

And the life they'd built together, *her life* would never be the same.

Norah did what any other respectable young woman would do in her situation; she faked it. She lifted her chin and cleared her throat, willing back the impending tears. "I'm fine."

"Hey, there you are, love muffin," a man's voice cut into the space between her and Landon.

The mystery man with whom she'd almost collided her cart, reached down and took her underneath the elbow, gently lifting her up. She pinched her brows as confusion swam while she tried to place him.

"Are you okay?" he asked, familiar brown eyes twinkling.

Todd Langston.

Norah couldn't find her voice. But she glared as all the old feelings surrounding Todd came rushing back at her. At one time, years ago, he'd been her childhood crush. Until he'd humiliated her after she'd poured her heart out to him and tried to kiss him.

And she'd hated him since.

"What are you doing here?" she grumbled under her breath, turning her backside away from Landon and Mia so they no longer had a front-row seat to her wet pants.

Todd shrugged out of his jacket and hung it over Norah's shoulders. "Coming to surprise my girl, of course."

Norah glared harder at him but tugged the jacket over her shoulders. She didn't know what kind of game Todd was playing, but she wanted no part in it. What she wanted was to crawl in a hole and die from embarrassment.

"Nor," Landon said softly.

"Don't," Norah warned. "Don't call me that. You lost that privilege."

A bit of hurt glazed over his eyes.

They had an audience now. Instead of requesting she pay for the damages, the Engelman's employees looked as if they preferred she save herself and just exit the store. Some locals she recognized, and others she didn't, stood by and caught the whole show. She was tired of being Pineridge's hottest topic of conversation. Tired of looking pathetic.

Poor girl, cheated on right under her nose. And after being married for barely a year. The poor, sweet child.

"Hey, I'm Todd Langston."

Landon shook his hand. "Landon," he mumbled, glancing back and forth between Norah and Todd.

"Ah, Landon, the ex. Nice to meet you, I'm the boyfriend."

Norah whipped her head up to look at Todd, her eyes bulging. *Boyfriend?* But her throat tightened, and all words disappeared.

Landon scratched at the back of his head. "Boyfriend? I had no idea you were dating anyone—"

"C'mon, sugar lips." Todd interrupted, wrapping an arm around her shoulder. "Let's get you home and cleaned up." He escorted her toward the door.

Regardless of the animosity she felt for Todd, having a sturdy frame to lean against wasn't the worst thing at this moment.

They passed by one of her old schoolteachers who saluted her. A mom of one of her students from the ice rink gave her a smile. And a young employee whispered, "Yessss, go, Norah. He's cuuuuute."

This treatment was far different than what she'd been receiving since word got out that she not only had been cheated on by Landon but that they were getting divorced fifteen months after saying *I do*. Typically, it was a lot of sad and pitiful looks from the locals. Friends who skirted around the topic. Family who continued to ask if she was okay.

Now there was the question of the year: *Was she okay?*

Not even a little.

As soon as they stepped outside into the parking lot, street-lamps shining down on the black asphalt, she shrugged off Todd's arm. "What was that?" she snapped. "And what are you doing here?"

The chilly night air whipped through the fabric of her wet pants.

Todd crossed his arms and sucked in a breath. "First of all, you're welcome."

She widened her eyes at him. "Excuse me?"

"I saved you back there."

"Ha," she scoffed. "Saved me? If I hadn't been trying to avoid running into you, I wouldn't *need* saving."

"And if I hadn't been there just now, you would've been humiliated in front of your ex and his smoking hot girlfriend." He threw out his arm.

Norah groaned, loudly. "I was *still* humiliated. And worse, now Landon, and the rest of the town, think you're my boyfriend."

"Again, you're welcome," he answered smugly.

"Ughhhhh." She rubbed at her forehead. "What are you even doing here? In Pineridge?"

"Izzy asked me to come."

It wasn't unbelievable that Izzy would invite Todd to visit. The two were close and had been friends for a long time. Since Izzy moved back to Pineridge, she'd been asking both Todd and Margo to visit.

"Okay, so why aren't you with Izzy? What are you doing at Engelman's, harassing me?"

Todd gestured his chin. "I have my puppy with me. I needed dog food."

At the mention of a puppy, Norah's heart softened. But only a little.

She backed up. "Well, okay then. I'd say it was good to see you, but I'm not a fan of lying."

He snickered at her, and she rolled her eyes as she turned around, stomping toward her car.

"Hey, sugar lips?" he called.

She stopped and her shoulders stiffened. This term of endearment already got under her skin. Turning to face him, she gritted her teeth. "What?"

"I'll catch your act later." He winked.

She wasn't sure if that was a threat or a promise. Either way, she wasn't about to stand around and find out. She had work to do.

WITH ONLY ONE WEEK LEFT UNTIL THE GALENTINE'S party—*could Norah even call it that anymore?*—she was beginning to stress. She'd been to six stores just today. If all the supplies she'd ordered online didn't arrive on time, she'd have to make a trip to Denver.

Party planning had always been something that interested her. Isabella had been nagging her for the past year to start her own business. But honestly, how would her business be successful with the lack of supplies in this town? Pineridge just wasn't equipped for parties of this caliber. And no, she wasn't going overboard like Mom had suggested.

But did Norah expect everything to be perfect? Yeah, she supposed she did. Because really, what else did she have going for her? After she moved out of the house she and Landon shared together, she'd moved back in with Mom and Dad and had been slumming it with them ever since.

Nothing says "starting over" quite like being back in your childhood bedroom complete with Jonas Brothers' posters on the walls and figure skating trophies collecting dust on the shelves.

Norah had sunk her teeth into the planning of this party. For the past month, it had consumed every aspect of her life. Which was fine. The distraction was good for her, and it kept her from buying a one-way ticket to Jamaica. Besides, she also really loved every part of the planning.

Okay, maybe not *every* part. She could do without Izzy's constant nagging.

Norah dragged herself into the house, with wet pants, and a

bruised ego. She kicked off her boots and hung her coat on the rack in the entryway.

"Hey, kiddo, that you?" Dad called from the kitchen.

"Yep," Norah hollered back before muttering under her breath, "Who else would it be?"

Mom gasped from behind her. "What on earth happened to you?"

Norah whirled around. "Hmm...and what exactly are you referring to? What happened to me tonight? Or what happened to my life? What happened to me that landed me back in my parents' house at the age of twenty-three?"

"Honey," Mom said, her voice soft. "I was only asking because your pants are soaked, and you reek of wine." She waved a hand to clear the air.

Dad stood by Norah's side now, an arm around her shoulder and pulling her into him. "Kiddo, you okay?"

Norah's throat tightened. There was that question again. She didn't want to take out her frustration on her parents. It wasn't their fault her life was a complete disaster. Tears pricked the corners of her eyes.

All her tears should've been cried out during her drive home from Engelman's.

"No. I'm not okay. None of this is okay." She stormed past them, stomping down the hall toward the kitchen. "I'm not supposed to be here. This was not supposed to be my life." She opened the cupboard where she kept her wine, snatching two bottles—because yes, this might very well be a multiple-bottle night—and she slammed the door shut.

When she whirled back around, a bottle in each hand, her parents both stood there, eyes sullen and their lips slanted in frowns.

"Don't look at me like that," Norah said.

Dad hunched his shoulders nearly to his ears. "Like what?"

Norah narrowed her eyes and brushed past them again, on a mission to get upstairs before she burst into tears.

"Sweets," Mom called. "We're just worried about you. And wondering if planning this Valentine's party is the best thing for you right now."

The party. She still had a trunk full of decorations she needed to drop off at Leo's studio.

There would be plenty of other nights for baths and wine and *F.R.I.E.N.D.S.* She exhaled a shaky sigh and let her shoulders fall before turning to face them. "I'm fine. Or...I will be fine." She forced a smile and handed the wine bottles to her mom. "I have to get cleaned up before I drop off some stuff for the party at the studio. Thanks for worrying about me."

Going up the stairs, she finally allowed the threatening tears to release. She didn't want to cry anymore. Especially not over Landon. He didn't deserve her tears.

But deep down, Norah knew she wasn't crying over Landon. They'd been divorced for six months and separated much longer. And she was fine with it. Okay, maybe not fine. But she was getting there. Err...she'd get there soon.

Just like she'd told her parents. Because she had to believe that. She had to think that things couldn't possibly get any worse. They had to go up from here.

She just needed to get through Valentine's Day.

Which reminded her that she owed Isabella a text.

Todd Langston? Really Izzy?

CHAPTER 4
Todd

This plan of convincing Norah to pretend to date him wasn't going to be as easy as he'd originally hoped. But Isabella's invitation for him to stay at her parent's house was genius. Forced proximity always worked in the romcoms he'd seen.

Norah and Isabella's parents had been nothing but pleasant and inviting, welcoming him and Samson into their home with very few questions asked. In fact, Jim Whitley was practically obsessed with Samson. He even offered to take the puppy outside and watch him while Todd got settled and showered.

The guest room the Whitleys set up for him was Isabella's childhood bedroom. The shag carpet was an awful shade of mauve and the day bed looked unsuitable for his over six-foot frame, but it was freshly made with a red and black plaid patterned comforter and coordinating pillows. After days on the road, it looked so comfortable and tempting.

But first, he needed a shower. He set up the kennel for Samson and headed down the hall and into the bathroom. His reflection revealed disheveled hair and extra-long facial hair. But he didn't want to waste time shaving tonight.

Isabella had promised she'd get Norah to Tapp's Brewery for him to casually "bump" into her. What he hadn't told Isabella yet, was that he'd already bumped into Norah. Almost literally. And she clearly still hated him.

It had been a pleasant surprise to find Norah all grown up. He wasn't sure what he'd expected. Obviously, she'd grown up. He'd seen her photos on Isabella's Instagram for years. But seeing her in person was different.

As much as he hated to admit, she looked sexy when she was angry. Those perfect lips twisted in a scowl. Those beautiful brown eyes in a glare.

He sighed, relaxing his tense shoulders. Thinking about her in any other way than with resentment was strange. Stripping off his dirty clothes, Todd stepped into the steamy shower. He was anxious to get the last couple hundred miles washed off him.

The scalding water hammered into his back, beading and rolling over his aching skin. He closed his eyes, attempting to clear his mind and soak up the few moments of solitude. No Margo. No Samson. Just him, alone, in the shower.

A shower. Where he was naked. And unable to keep his mind from traveling to a certain woman who had just popped into his life.

Norah.

She looked good. Better than he remembered her looking. And more grown up too. Pretending to date her would be easy.

But that was a bad train of thought, so he rinsed the shampoo from his hair and turned off the shower.

Drying himself, he wrapped the towel around his waist and ran his fingers through his wet hair. He glanced around the bathroom. Damn. He'd forgotten to grab his clothes from his bag. He dropped his head and groaned.

Cracking the door, he secured the towel at his waist and popped his head out. All clear. He quickly made a beeline to his bedroom, exhaling a shaky breath once he'd made it safely inside. He rummaged around his bag until he found a clean pair of boxer briefs. Dropping his towel to the floor, Todd proceeded to step into the briefs. But he froze midway when a loud gasp sounded behind him. He whipped around, tripping over the waistband of the briefs in the process.

Norah shrieked. "I'm so sorry!" She covered her eyes and spun around.

Todd wasn't sure if he was relieved it was Norah who caught him and not one of her parents or if he was mortified it was her. He yanked up his briefs and then chuckled, shaking his head. Because why should he be embarrassed? She'd been the one who barged into his room without knocking.

Besides, he didn't have anything to hide.

He rested his hands on his hips. "Alright, I'm decent."

She turned on her heel slowly and gazed up cautiously. After an obvious thorough examination, she whirled back around. "Ack! You said you were decent!"

"I mean, it's not like I'm naked. *Anymore.*" He found a pair of jeans in his bag and pulled them on.

"Technicalities," she muttered.

He zipped his jeans and bent to wrestle in his bag for a clean shirt. "Okay, now I'm decent."

"You sure this time?"

"Promise."

She reluctantly turned around. "Well," she paused, visibly sucking in a breath, "you're not completely decent, but I guess at least you have pants on."

"Why are you barging into my room anyway?"

Glaring, she stuffed her fists onto her hips. It was sort of adorable how her cheeks blushed.

"*Your* room? Since when is this *your* room?"

"Since Isabella asked your parents if I could stay here for the week."

She gasped. "Are you serious?"

"Dead serious," he quipped.

"But no one asked me if I was okay with you staying here. I live here too," she whined.

Unable to resist the satisfaction that weaved through him at being the cause of her annoyance, the corner of his lips tipped up. "Guess you're stuck with me, sugar lips."

She groaned. "Okay, fine. If this is true, we need to set some ground rules."

He didn't like the sound of this. Setting ground rules meant keeping them further apart. Which was the complete opposite of what he needed.

"First off, stop calling me sugar lips."

He chuckled, tugging a long-sleeved dark grey shirt over his head. "No guarantees. But what else?"

"Why *no guarantees*?" she grumbled.

"If you want people to believe I'm your boyfriend, don't you think I should have a nickname for you?"

"Ha!" she barked out, amusement lighting up her face. "Why would I want people to believe you're my boyfriend?"

"Maybe so they all stop thinking you've still got a boner for your ex?"

Norah opened her mouth and then clamped it shut.

"Maybe so they all stop feeling sorry for you?" I continue.

She narrowed her eyes. "They don't feel sorry for me."

"No? Because I've only been in this town for about three hours, sweetheart, and I can already see how they treat you."

"Sweetheart is off limits too," she muttered.

"How about you make a list for me," he replied with a grin.

She wasn't going to make anything about this easy, was she?

Leaning against the open doorway, she said, "I don't know what you and Izzy agreed on, but maybe you should've checked with me first before making me a little pawn in your game."

"So what are you saying? You *don't* need a date to this Valentine's party?"

There was hesitation in her response, and her eyes flitted away. "I do. But—"

"But nothing," Todd interrupted so she had less time to overthink this. "That's what I'm here for. Nothing else. Just to be your date for the party."

She frowned. "Then what was all that back there at Engelman's? You pretending to be my boyfriend in front of Landon?"

"I'm sorry." He shrugged. "I guess it just sucked the way he was parading that new girlfriend of his around like he was trying to rub it in your face."

She chewed on her lower lip.

It was cute. Sexy even.

But her feelings of animosity toward him were mutual. He couldn't stand her either.

"We can try to clear things up if you want?" he said, moving to the open doorway and resting a hand on the frame above her.

Blinking up at him, her brown eyes softened, and she swallowed so hard it was audible.

He leaned closer and gazed down at her, watching while she sucked in a breath. "Or we could let the rumor run its course. Have a little fun with it." He waggled his brows and smiled suggestively.

"And what would you get out of this?"

"I'd get to spend time with you." He winked.

She glared and punched a fist lightly into his stomach. She

ducked underneath his arm just before he retracted it and hunched over.

"Finish getting dressed, city boy," she called over her shoulder as she retreated down the hall. "We're going to meet Izzy at Tapp's, just as planned."

Yes! He pumped a celebratory fist into the air. He'd only been in Pineridge for a few hours and already he was making progress. Hopefully, by the end of the night, she'd be ready to agree to this ridiculous idea. The way he saw it, she might need this just as much as he did.

Once downstairs, he found both Norah and her dad, Jim Whitley on the floor on all fours playing with Samson. He cleared his throat when he entered the kitchen. Jim didn't even flinch, just continued to roughhouse with the dog.

But Norah glanced his way and slowly stood, giving Samson one last pat on his head. It was obvious she was checking him out, despite her effort in trying to hide it. Her typical "Resting B Face" whenever he was around quickly returned.

"Man, I love this dog," Jim said in between a chuckle. "He's an English Mastiff, right?"

"Yeah, that's right."

"Such cool dogs. I'd love to have one, but Sue is allergic. It's the hair. She says I can get a dog; it just can't shed. Do you know what that leaves me with? Golden doodles and poodles. How manly would I look walking through the neighborhood with a poodle?" He shot Todd an exasperated look.

Norah gasped. "Dad, you sound so sexist right now. Owning a poodle doesn't make you more feminine."

"You're right, you're right. I'm hip with the times." Jim raised his hands.

"Hey, there's always standard poodles," Todd suggested.

Norah rolled her eyes at him dramatically. "Don't encourage him. Please."

"Oh, Norah. The boys are just having fun," Sue said, picking up a cookie from a cooling rack. "Here, have a cookie. It looks like Samson wants one too."

"No cookies for him. But I think I can find some treats here somewhere." Todd stuffed his hands into the pockets of his jacket and found a couple small, sweet potato treats. He bent and gave them to the dog before petting the top of his head. "Who's a good boy?" he whispered, before straightening. "Thanks for the cookie. And thanks for letting me and Samson stay here for the week."

"Hey, if you let me hang out with your dog, consider us even." Jim resumed playing with Samson once again.

"Well, Dad, if you really mean that..." Norah's sugary voice trailed off in insinuation.

"What's up?" her dad asked from his perch on the floor.

"Todd and I were gonna run over to Tapp's and meet Izzy. Do you mind watching Samson?"

"Oh, they don't have to do that. I can bring him along."

"Mind? Of course we don't mind. It would be our pleasure." Jim scratched behind Samson's ears.

"Are you sure? You said Mrs. Whitley is allergic."

Samson was cute, sure. But he could be a handful. Todd had forgotten how much work puppies were. He hadn't had one since he was a kid. And even then, his parents and siblings helped. And don't even get him started on the slobber and shedding.

"He's sure. And don't worry about me, I'll survive. I'll just pop an allergy pill," Sue said, rounding the kitchen island and shooing him and Norah on their way. "You two kids go and have fun. We'll be fine here."

"Thanks, Mom." Norah gave her mother a kiss on the cheek. "Thanks, Dad." She squeezed his shoulder.

Todd hesitated, contemplating leaving the puppy.

Norah tugged on the sleeve of his shirt. "C'mon, I promise you, you couldn't be leaving him in more capable hands."

Her persistence drew him in, and he found himself mesmerized by her brown eyes as he shuffled his feet backward. Which made no sense. And was completely idiotic.

"Well, thank you. His kennel is upstairs. I'm still trying to potty train him so the crate will help."

"If it's anything like potty training children, then we're old pros. Done it three times. Not to mention helping with Finn's oldest, Ava."

"Dad," Norah said, "I'm sure it's completely different. But we have faith you'll be able to handle it."

Norah slid her hand into Todd's, the physical contact distracting him as she pulled him toward the front entryway.

Samson, who?

"Thanks...thanks again...for everything," Todd called over his shoulder in broken words.

She dropped his hand like it was nothing—nothing to hold it and nothing to let it go. And he wasn't sure how he felt about that.

Todd followed Norah down the hallway but stopped abruptly as a photo on the wall caught his attention. A wedding portrait. He spotted Isabella right away, wearing a frilly red dress. He recognized the dress from her Instagram. And then he looked at the bride. Reddish-brown hair, brown eyes, infectious smile. Norah.

He'd forgotten the whole reason Isabella had ended up back in Pineridge. She'd returned home one Christmas for Norah's wedding and made up with her high school sweetheart.

Isabella had filled him in about Norah's cheating ex-husband and her divorce. But he found it a bit surprising that her parents kept her wedding photos up on the wall. Every single time she walked down this hall, she was reminded of the failed marriage, the pain, the betrayal.

"You coming?" Norah called from the end of the hall where she waited for him.

"Huh?" His attention flickered back and forth between Norah in the flesh and Norah in the photo. "Yeah, yep...coming."

Norah had her attention fixated on her phone. He tried not to notice she'd changed into a pair of black worn jeans and a white cropped sweater with a jacket over the top. But she looked too good not to.

The air in the room felt stuffy suddenly. He pushed up his sleeves and sucked in a rumbled breath.

This was stupid. Before today, he'd never seen Norah as anything more than a kid. No more than a preteen with a silly crush on him. A kid who took her crush too far which resulted in him despising her.

But now that felt like a long time ago.

She lifted her gaze and luckily, instead of catching his eyes traveling too slowly over her midsection where a bit of her stomach was exposed, her focus landed on his forearm. More specifically, to the tattoo on his forearm.

She slipped her phone into her back pocket and caught him off guard when she wrapped a hand around his wrist and studied his tattoo.

"Um...whatcha doing?" he mumbled.

"I don't remember this. From when I saw you last, I mean."

"It's new. I got it a few weeks ago. After Margo and I broke up. She always said tattoos defiled your body, that you should only put clean things into your body."

Norah traced her fingertip over the black ink, causing a shiver to course through him. He rubbed at the back of his neck with his free hand.

"It's beautiful."

He swallowed. "Yeah?"

"Yeah." She smiled as she peered up at him and then in an instant, it vanished, almost as if she'd caught herself letting down her guard. She released his arm and flicked her attention away.

If she continued to smile at him like that or touch him like that or hell, touch him in *any way*, he wouldn't be able to go on hating her. Details regarding their arrangement could get blurry fast. But the fact was, all this would be—*could be*—was fake. The two of them didn't like each other. They were like night and day. Oil and water. And he was heading back to New York in ten days.

"Ya know how you can see a tattoo and you just know there's gotta be a good story behind it? I'm guessing that's the case with yours."

"You're right. This one actually has a great story. One that, let's say...a girlfriend would definitely know." He passed her a cheeky grin.

She rolled her eyes but smiled. "Well played, city boy."

Opening the front door of the house, she shoved him out onto the stoop.

"It was worth a try," he teased.

CHAPTER 5
Norah

It had been a year since Norah saw a naked man and you wouldn't hear her complaining. Sure, Landon had a nice body, but there was something about seeing a new one. Much like seeing a shiny sports car. Just thinking about Todd's smooth skin beneath his shirt and his narrow hips dipping into the waistband of his jeans was getting her engine revved up.

"So, what have you been up to these days? Ruin anyone else's life since I saw you last?" Todd asked, cutting into her fantasy as she drove them to Tapp's Brewery.

She flicked a glare his way. So much for thinking he was attractive. He was the same jerk she remembered. "As a matter of fact, no. I spend my days helping others."

"Right," he said, scratching at his chin, his eyes wandering like he was bored. "I think Izzy did mention something about you teaching kids how to skate."

"It's a bit more than that. But yeah, I'm a figure skating instructor at the big ice rink in town." She paused and tried to change the subject to him. "And what about you? I guess I didn't ruin your life too bad since you still became a lawyer."

"What you did caused a riff, that's for sure. But I'm resilient. I still put myself through school and now I'm one of the top lawyers at my firm."

If he was trying to impress her, it wasn't working. Or if this was his way of trying to make amends after "the incident", she wasn't ready to do that yet.

"Though the working with your ex-part—I don't recommend." He forced a laugh.

His comment rattled her for a moment. "I was really sorry to hear about you and Margo breaking up. You two were together a long time."

He shrugged off her words. "Not that long."

"You seemed perfect for each other."

"Perfect? Really?" He quirked a challenging brow at her.

Norah looked out the windshield for a moment before glancing back at him. "I mean, you were friends before you started dating, you're both lawyers, you're both driven."

"I guess..." his words trailed off while he peered down.

She didn't want to care. Not about his breakup. Not about him. But she knew what it felt like. To be the person who was left. "Do you miss her?"

"Honestly?"

"Of course."

"I miss the idea of her. I think maybe...I miss *us*, but not her. I don't know. Seems stupid I guess."

She shook her head slowly. "No, I get that. Believe me. It's not stupid."

They rode the rest of the way in silence, and she was grateful for the time to herself. Time to process the moments the two of them had shared already just today, process what had gone down between them all those years ago, and what would happen tonight if they spent any more time together.

As if it wasn't going to be bad enough entering Tapp's Brewery with a strange man at her side, but what if Landon was there? Norah had only been on two blind dates since they'd split, and she hardly went out anymore.

"We're here," she announced as she pulled into a parking spot in front of Tapp's.

The huge, metal brewery sign hanging on the side of the industrial building looked like it was showing off. Davis Vance designed the handcrafted sign for the local brewery. It had become a beloved piece by the Pineridge residents and Davis became inundated by project requests. As if his reality TV show on HGTV with his twin brother didn't keep him busy enough.

They climbed out of her car, the darkness creeping into the early evening sky and the air crisp. When they reached the front door of the building, Todd hurried and opened it to allow her to enter first. She gave him a skeptical look.

"What?" He shrugged. "I can be a gentleman.

She rolled her eyes at him. "Yeah? When?"

He ignored her question. "If we were dating, I'd always open the door for you."

"Whatever," she muttered, as she shuffled past him.

Inside, the warmth of too many bodies in one tight space enveloped Norah. Tapp's Brewery had a more modern vibe than O'Henry's Bar and Grill did. It was fresh and new. But since O'Henry's closed, it made Tapp's the most popular bar in town.

Norah took off her denim jacket and hung it on an empty peg by the door. She unraveled the scarf from around her neck and took the beanie hat off her head, shaking out her hair.

"You can hang your coat on any open hook."

Todd lifted his brows. "Really?"

"Uh, yeah."

He stepped closer to her and lowered his voice, "You expect me to leave my $300 jacket here? And trust that no one's gonna take it?"

She snorted a laugh and he looked at her—deadpanned. "Oh, you're serious. Um, yeah, people don't really do that here."

"They don't do what...steal?"

"Yeah." She shrugged as she backed away from him. "But whatever, it's your choice."

Todd stood there appearing conflicted, but since she continued walking backward, he reluctantly hung his coat on a peg next to hers and hurried to catch up to her. "You sure it's safe there?"

She patted his arm, the firmness felt underneath her fingertips. "Relax. These people have seen a Patagonia jacket before. And," she mocked a look of horror, cupping a hand over her mouth, "some of them even own one."

"Ha ha," he said sarcastically. "Very funny. But you don't

just leave stuff hanging by a door in New York. It wouldn't last twenty seconds."

Norah bowed and grinned. "Welcome to Pineridge. Now, if I'm going to survive this night, I need a drink."

She spun around and as Todd followed behind her, he placed his hand on the small of her back while they weaved between the crowd. It sent a shiver racing through her, and she couldn't decide if she liked it or hated it. It had been a while since a man touched her there.

It had been a while since a man touched her *anywhere*.

Norah's phone vibrated in the back pocket of her jeans, and she slid it out.

> **MADDIE**
>
> Dang! Is that him? I don't remember him looking so delicious.

Norah's cheeks went hot, and she glanced around the bar, rocking back and forth on her toes to see above the heads of everyone. She spotted Maddie propped on a bar stool at a high table in the corner. She grinned, ignoring Maddie's text, and slipping her phone back into her pocket.

Norah gave a head nod to Todd, and grumbled, "C'mon."

As she made her way toward Maddie, she couldn't help but notice the intrusive eyes of everyone on her. Her prior assumption was right; showing up at the most popular bar in town with a stranger would cause an uprise in the Pineridge rumor mill.

"Hey, Maddie. You didn't tell me you'd be here tonight."

Maddie slid off the bar stool and wrapped Norah in a hug. "And you didn't tell me *you'd* be here. You never come out at night." Maddie held onto her for a beat. "You've hardly been out in months," she whispered.

Norah didn't want to get into it with Maddie. Since she'd bumped into Todd earlier at Engelman's, she'd hardly thought about Landon. So the last thing she wanted to do was talk about him now.

"Maddie, this is Todd, Izzy's friend from New York. Todd, this is my best friend, Madison."

Maddie blinked her eyes rapidly, smiling wide and shaking Todd's hand. "Maddie."

"Nice to meet you." Todd smiled.

Still holding onto his hand, Maddie said, "Todd...as in Todd Langston?"

Todd's brows pinched together, and he glanced over at Norah. "Um...yeah. Should I know you?"

Norah elbowed Maddie and she widened her eyes at her. She'd told Maddie all about Izzy's college roommate, the really smart and tall guy who was studying to be a lawyer. The one who she gushed over because he once had glasses like Harry Potter and wavy hair like Henry Cavill that he tried to tame, and it made him look even more like Superman.

A best friend always knew about your childhood crush. Even if they were farfetched like the one she'd had on Todd. Best friends also knew when your childhood crush turned you down and humiliated you.

Maddie finally let go of Todd's hand.

Norah had to change the subject before Maddie got all best-friendish and started threatening the guy.

She scanned the crowd, going on tiptoe. "Hey, is Izzy around? She was supposed to be here."

"Oh, yeah, she's here." Maddie gazed in the direction of the tables situated near the karaoke stage. "There." She pointed.

Norah and Todd peered in the same direction. There she was, with Leo next to her, his arm draped over her shoulder. They looked so happy.

Norah's heart swelled seeing the joy radiating off her sister's face.

"Okay, let's go." She pinched Todd's sleeve and tugged him along with her. "See you in a bit, Mads," she called over her shoulder.

"Norah, wait," Maddie called.

But Norah was on a mission to get to her big sis. Izzy had some explaining to do. And as they drew closer to her sister's table, Norah's smile slipped, and she stiffened. She spotted the reason for Maddie's attempted warning. Across the table from Izzy and Leo—familiar long legs stretched out.

Landon.

And he wasn't alone.

CHAPTER 6

Todd

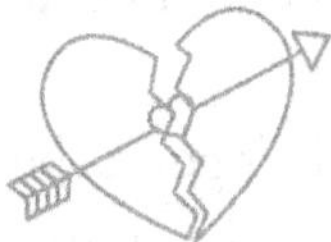

I t didn't take long to recognize Norah's ex. Todd caught his arrogant presence almost as soon as his eyes landed on Isabella. This prick had some nerve. Hanging out with Isabella when he probably knew Norah would be coming to meet her.

Todd's gut pinched. He involuntarily reached for Norah's hand and tugged her backward before they arrived at the table.

"Hey," he whispered, "do you wanna get out of here?"

Her eyes went round, and sadness shimmered in them as she met his gaze. A pang of distress punched his heart. And even more so when her lips pulled to one side in a sober smile.

"It's okay. It's a small town, it's impossible to avoid him."

"Okay, but my offer still stands?"

Her brows pinched together.

"You know, we could pretend we're dating?"

She chewed on her bottom lip.

"I've already come all this way. And I'm already planning on being your date to the Valentine's party. I mean, why not, right?"

Norah narrowed her eyes at him, but she hadn't let go of his hand. "Why are you so persistent? What's in it for you?"

"We can talk about it later. But that guy—your ex—he knew you were going to be here tonight and he's hanging out with your sister? That's a jackass move."

She pursed her lips and shuffled her feet. "Well...I guess it would be kinda nice to see him get a little rattled because I'm here with a guy."

"Rattled? Sugar lips, he's gonna be more than rattled."

She rolled her eyes but the smirk that appeared on her lips made him feel like he'd won a prize at a carnival.

"Are you sure about this? We can't stand each other. We can barely tolerate each other. And I can't have you changing your mind halfway through the week and ditch me come the night of the party and I end up standing there not only dateless but dumped."

All valid points.

But she needed this. She needed him. And in return, he needed *her*.

"I can set aside my loathing for you if you can?"

"Loathing? You loathe me?" She wrinkled her nose.

"Fine, my dislike. Is that better? Besides, you hate me," he reminded her.

A tall, muscular guy bumped into Todd's back, pushing the two of them closer.

"I don't hate you. I...I guess I've just held onto a grudge."

"So, what do you say? Are we doing this?"

Staring at him for too long without speaking caused his anxiety to spiral. "Fine. But I have a feeling when I learn your terms of the deal, I'm going to regret this."

He grinned. "Maybe. Maybe not."

"Norah?" Isabella's voice yelled above the sound of the live music streaming from the stage.

They'd been spotted.

Todd gripped Norah's hand and leaned into her, whispering, "Showtime."

"Oh my goodness, Todd!" Isabella shouted louder. "You're here. You're really here!"

They reached Isabella's table and Todd squeezed Norah's hand.

Isabella jumped up and squealed in delight as she wrapped him in a hug, tearing his hand free from Norah's. "I've missed you," she whispered into his shoulder.

"Me too. But c'mon, you were just in New York a few months ago."

She pulled back but kept her hands cupped to his shoulders. "Suddenly that feels like a lifetime ago now that you're here." Her eyes watered as she looked him over. Then she shook him before letting go. "I've bugged you for over a year to come visit me in Pineridge. I guess all I had to do was set you up with my sister."

He chuckled nervously. *Was Isabella going to ruin this for them?*

Leo stood and reached his hand out to Todd, giving his arm a pat in the process. "Hey, man. Good to see you again."

"Yeah, you too," Todd said and meant it.

Leo was a good guy. Even if he was the reason Isabella had moved away from New York. At least they'd been back to the city a few times just that year.

"I'm sorry, Norah, I didn't think you'd be coming tonight... what with all the party planning and stuff."

"I guess no one expected me to be here tonight." Norah narrowed her eyes at her ex who sat across the table.

The tension filled the space between them.

"Norah," her ex greeted her.

"What is this?" Norah's voice wavered. "A double date or something?"

"No," Isabella blurted, shaking her head.

Norah crossed her arms. "Well, that's what it looks like."

"We were sitting here and happened to bump into Landon and Mia. We started talking and then they sat down."

"C'mon, Nor, you can't expect us to never hang out. Leo's my brother," her ex muttered.

"Don't call me that," she bit out.

Her ex shrugged off her comment.

Instinctively, Todd moved closer to Norah. He had the urge to reach for her hand again but resisted. He had no place in Norah's business, much less her former marital business, but since he was posing as her boyfriend, he felt a need to protect her, to shield her from the sharp looks coming from her douche ex-husband. Possibly it was because he still pictured her as the young, naive kid sister of Isabella's.

She lifted her gaze to meet his, and the sadness conveyed in those deep brown eyes had his chest aching without permission. Maybe her eyes were the same, but she wasn't young anymore. She was tough and she just needed someone to stand by her side.

There was no one else to do it so he supposed he'd have to. He was her fake boyfriend after all.

"All I'm saying is, we're family. Don't you think it's about time we figure out how to move on? I mean, it looks like you have." He gestured his chin in Todd's direction.

It felt as if they had the attention of everyone in the brewery.

"You're right. I have moved on. But it doesn't mean we have to spend time together. Because we're not family." She took a step backward and tugged Todd's sleeve. "We're going outside to the beer garden. You guys enjoy your evening."

"Norah, wait," Isabella called. "Please don't go." She started after her sister, but Todd stopped her.

"Just give her a few minutes," he said. "Let me talk to her."

"You sure?"

"You asked me to come be her date. And I don't mind spending time with her. Once you get past the hard-shell exterior, she's not so bad."

Isabella laughed. "You're the best."

"Just remember, you owe me." He pointed at her as he walked backward before turning around to rush after Norah.

"Hey, wait up. Would you hold up for a second?" He reached out and touched her arm, but she yanked it away.

"You don't have to hold my hand anymore. They can't see us over here." She stuffed her arms into her jacket.

"Yeah, that might be true, but we're not doing this for just them." He glanced around the room, insinuating the others who were watching them.

Her gaze followed his.

"Let's go outside and get a beer. Or maybe two. It might take longer to convince you to agree to the terms of our deal."

Whipping her head in his direction, she narrowed her eyes at him. "Just what have you roped me into?"

"It's not that bad." He hunched his shoulders. "I swear."

She blew out a breath and relented. "Fine."

He quickly reached for his jacket by the door before she could change her mind. He was so close to getting that promotion.

"Would ya look at that, your jacket was still there after all," Norah teased.

A snappy comeback entered his mind, but he didn't say it out loud. He needed to play nice.

They slipped outside into the chilly night air. Todd followed close behind Norah, so he didn't lose her in the crowd.

With a jacket on, the outdoor gas fire pit lit, and the heat lamps, it was surprisingly cozy.

"Let's go order that beer?" She nudged her chin in the direction of a small opening in the side of the building with a counter and a large sign above that read: BAR. The brewery offered several choices of beer on tap. A cute, dark-haired woman he recognized, but had never met in person, stood behind the counter.

"Hi, Kels," Norah said.

The woman's blue eyes went huge. "Hey! I know you." She smiled at Todd.

"And I think I know you, too. Kelsey?" He leaned against the counter.

"In the flesh." She squealed and surprised him when she reached across the bar's counter and wrapped him in a quick hug. "It's about time you came to slum it with us commoners."

"Ha, you have no idea," Norah chimed in, "he was afraid to leave his precious Patagonia jacket hung by the door."

Kelsey snorted a laugh. "Let me grab you a beer. I bet you need it after your flight."

"Sounds great. But I actually didn't fly. I drove the whole way here."

Kelsey's attention snapped up to him. "You serious?"

"Yeah. I have a puppy, and well, apparently large breed dogs like him can't be boarded on a plane. So, I had to drive."

"How far is that?"

"About 1,800 miles."

"You drove 1,800 miles on impulse?" Kelsey set two beers on the bar countertop. "That's ballsy."

"I mean, no, not on impulse. I was invited."

She narrowed her eyes at him. "You trying to weasel your way into the position of Izzy's best friend? Because I will fight you for it."

"She's not lying, she will," Norah said.

Todd threw up his palms in surrender. "No way."

Setting the filled pint glasses onto the bar top, Kelsey said, "Okay, just so we're clear."

"Crystal." Todd held out his credit card and she waved him off.

"I gotta get back into the pit. If you need anything else, Davis and Kai are around here somewhere. But I wanna catch up with you later, Norah. It's so good to see you out and about," she called over her shoulder as she started her way back into the brewery.

"Thanks," Norah called, as she picked up both glasses and Todd followed her to a picnic table near one of the fire pits.

"And Davis and Kai are?"

"Kai and Davis own Tapp's. And Davis is Kelsey's boyfriend."

"My guess is, if I don't meet them tonight, I'll meet them at the party." Todd sat on the bench, pulled his long legs up, and tucked them underneath the picnic table.

Norah set his glass in front of him before she sat across from him.

He took a sip of the beer. The hoppy flavor burst in his mouth, but it had enough of a hint of sweet citrus on his tongue to complement the bitterness. He licked the beer from his lips and found Norah staring at him.

"You sure you're up for this? You know, you and I?" she asked, her thick brows raised.

"Yeah. I mean, how bad can it be?" He shrugged a shoulder.

Leaning her elbows on the table, she said, "I think you've forgotten how bad it was the last time we saw each other."

Her eyes revealed a challenging sparkle but in a cute way.

He remembered her being stubborn as a teenager. It didn't seem as if she'd outgrown that as an adult.

"It did get a little ugly, didn't it?" Dismissing the way things went down all those years ago was pointless. Perhaps facing it head-on was the way to go.

"You humiliated me in front of your coworkers. But what was worse; you made me question my self-worth. I was a confused, vulnerable fifteen-year-old girl. You were my first kiss," she said, the last of her words coming out sounding scratchy. "When you turned me down, it hurt me. And it may not have been right, but I guess I just wanted you to hurt, too."

Her eyes glossed over, and for the first time since that incident, he got a small view into what she might've gone through that day. All he'd cared about was losing his job. He hadn't given her feelings much consideration.

"Mission accomplished. You definitely hurt me. I was the one who did you a favor by getting you into the musical for free. Then you used my generosity against me. Getting fired from that summer job affected my income and buying books for college the next fall."

Norah's eyes flittered away for a moment. "You knew I had a crush on you. When you offered to take me to the musical and get me in free—just the two of us—I guess I thought you liked me. We talked a lot and laughed a lot together."

"Norah," he said with a sigh, "you were fifteen."

"So?" She stuck her lower lip out in a defiant pout.

"*So?* I was what? Twenty-two, twenty-three?"

"So you turned me down and made fun of me to your coworkers because of my age?"

"No. Yes...ugh," he groaned. "I don't know, I was a stupid kid myself back then."

"Ya know? It seems like nothing has changed. You're still a stupid kid." She sniffed and rubbed a hand over her nose.

Her comment stung, no matter how much he was trying to play it off.

"Just sitting here with you makes me irritated, I don't know how we're gonna pull this off."

"Well, we better figure it out real quick because there are already a lot of eyes on us." He ran a hand over the back of his neck while he nonchalantly glanced around.

Norah tracked his vision.

"Listen," he lowered her voice, leaning closer. "If you want to do this, I'm all in, but you're gonna have to cooperate and play the part or no one's gonna buy it. Then what's the point?"

"Fine," she said in an exaggerated groan. "But no more stalling, I need to know what's in it for you. What do you need from me?"

Watching his thumb as he traced it over the condensation rolling down the side of his glass, he blew out an elongated breath. "Margo and I are both up for the same promotion at work," he began.

"And?"

"I've worked my ass off for that promotion," he blurted and looked at her finally. The sincerity he found in her eyes was enough to encourage him to continue. "Not that Margo hasn't, but I guess I feel like I've wanted it more. It's been a dream of mine to make partner at the age of thirty. And I know I was their top choice."

Norah furrowed her brows. "So, what happened?"

"After Margo and I broke up, I lost my focus. My attention to detail plummeted. I don't really know." He shook his head and took a sip of his beer.

"You don't have to explain it to me; I get it. When Landon and I first separated, I couldn't teach my classes at the rink. My body was there but my brain wasn't. And to be honest, my heart wasn't there either."

"Yeah? Did you start going out every night, hooking up with random people, and showing up to the rink late for your classes and hungover?"

The pause of her response and the purse of her lips gave him comfort. Like maybe she wasn't going to judge him like he'd felt so many others had. His bosses, his parents, Margo, hell everyone other than his brother, Ryan it seemed.

"Nothing like that. Though I have become a pro at deciphering different wines, and I've binged every TV show on Netflix."

He deadpanned. That was hardly the same thing. Though at least she wasn't looking at him any differently. She already had a distaste for him, it couldn't get much worse he supposed.

"My boss doesn't think I'm *partner material*," he said, using air quotes.

She frowned. "I'm confused. How does all of this have anything to do with me?"

"My company is old school. They have a pretty high standard of a business motto that they want their employees to adhere to. They pride themselves on values and such." He sucked in a breath, looking at her as he finished, "Margo has since moved on and apparently is in a committed relationship which is exactly what my boss expects from me."

"Oh." Norah nodded and then her lips went into an O shape while she repeated the word, realization setting in. "That's where I come in?"

His heart hammered in his chest. "Exactly."

"So if I agree to this, how long would we need to fake this relationship?"

"I'm not sure."

She pursed her lips as she considered his offer.

Was it even an offer? Because what was he doing in return? Escorting her to a Valentine's party? That didn't feel like a fair trade. He was potentially asking of more of her time. Maybe even for a trip to New York.

"Are we talking like a few weeks? A few months? Or a few years? Because I'm not going to be in this charade with you where next we have to get married and then have a couple of kids to seal the deal."

"I promise, it's nothing like that. A few weeks to a month—tops. Maybe one trip to New York, paid by me, of course," he said, his words rushing out, so afraid she was going to say no.

"Of course. Because you can bet your little behind, I wouldn't be footing that bill."

"I wouldn't expect you to." He leaned in further. "And I can assure you my behind isn't little. It's perfect."

She rolled her eyes but couldn't hide the smirk of amusement on her lips. "I've got one more condition."

"What is it?" he grumbled.

He knew this was going too easily.

"I need some help finishing up the party planning. You help me with that—AND—not only be my date to this party but also continue with pretending you're my boyfriend, then you've got yourself a deal."

"Really?"

She nodded. "But if we expect people to believe this, we should probably start getting along."

"Deal." He held out his hand.

She picked up her nearly empty glass and held it out to him. "Deal." Mischief shined in her eyes.

He responded with a clink of his glass into hers.

There was no turning back now. They were doing this.

CHAPTER 7
Norah

Had she given in too easily? Maybe she should've held out for more. Played "hard to get". Except there would be no "getting". Because this was all fake.

If fifteen-year-old Norah could see her now. Out with Todd Langston, her childhood crush. Planning a fake relationship with him like they were the stars in an early 2000s rom-com. Those never ended well. So why did she think they could actually pull this off?

Were people going to buy this "relationship"? Friends and family who had known her forever or Todd's bosses? Would Landon and Margo believe it?

She and Todd practically lived on opposite sides of the country from one another. He was a successful lawyer who had turned into a playboy the last few months and she was a newly divorced woman who lived with her parents and who had been attempting to dodge the entire social scene of Pineridge for the last year.

"I guess in an attempt to get along, we should probably find out a little bit more about each other.

"Okay, let's start with which nickname you like best?" He waggled his brows.

She groaned. This was a terrible mistake.

"Why are you so set on giving me a nickname?"

He shrugged a shoulder. "Girls like that sort of thing, don't they? I saw it as a headline on the cover of Cosmo while I was in line at the grocery store."

Nicknames were a favorite trope in all the popular romance books. But the only nickname Landon had ever called her was "Nor", and she cringed at that now.

"Fine," she muttered and gave a flick of her wrist before picking up her beer. "I don't care what you pick. Just don't make it cringey."

His lips twisted while he gazed past her like he was giving this some serious thought. She wasn't sure why it mattered; he'd only have to use it for a couple weeks. Then he'd forget all about "sugar lips", or whatever he chose, and go back to his regular life.

"I've got it. Buttercup."

"What? Why?"

"Because you remind me of that character, Princess Buttercup in the movie A Princess Bride. You're cute and sweet but you're also stubborn and a little spicy, too. Like her."

Her heartbeat picked up, thumping against her ribs. Don't get her wrong, the idea of him choosing a nickname for her—this nickname—was intriguing. And a little sweet. But she had to remind herself that this wasn't real.

He grinned. And as much as she didn't want it to affect her, it was too late. His wobbly, adorable smile sent a twinge of excitement low in her belly.

"What do you think?" He continued smiling at her and she continued to pretend she didn't notice.

"Whatever. It's fine, I guess." She waved off the impending attraction drawing her to him.

"Hey, you two," Izzy interrupted. "I'm so sorry, Nor. How are you?"

"I'm fine." But that wasn't entirely true.

Truthfully, she was annoyed with Izzy for hanging out with her ex-husband so casually and not as if he'd ripped out her heart and stomped all over it. But mostly, she was confused. She hadn't expected to find it this easy to hang out with Todd.

Sure, his teasing and now the nickname was annoying. Yet with him, she didn't have to try so hard at being *okay*. Everyone in her life expected her to be *okay* and with him, she didn't have to pretend. He knew she was a little bit messed up. Because so was he.

And since this relationship was fake and strictly platonic, there was no pressure. No expectations.

Except if she was being honest, there was some temptation. That messy hair of his that kept sticking up made her want to reach out and push it back with her fingers.

Besides that, strictly platonic.

"I'm so sorry again about Landon and Mia." Izzy squeezed in close to Norah on the end of the bench despite there being plenty of room on the other side of her. She wrapped her arm around Norah's shoulder and gave her a side hug. "You know we'd never double date with those two."

Logically, Norah did know that. Or at least, she hoped Izzy and Leo wouldn't do that to her. Not yet anyway.

But Landon *was* Leo's brother. Whether she liked it or not, eventually Landon would probably settle down and get married again. And Izzy would have to spend time with them.

"Don't sweat it, Norah. I give it another month—tops—till

they break up," Leo said, as he sat across from Izzy and took a swig of his beer.

Norah felt the eyes of everyone on her and she shrugged a shoulder. "What do I care if they break up or not?"

But the thing was, Landon and Mia had already been together for almost a year. Maybe even longer. After they got caught in the act at Landon's surprise birthday party last year, Norah hadn't really been privy to the specifics of their "relationship" or timeline. Though they were coming up on a year since Landon's birthday.

At this point, it was probably safe to assume that this thing —this *relationship*—was more than a fling. But that was fine. Norah was over Landon. The humiliation and loneliness were something entirely different though.

"One day Landon will realize he made a horrible mistake, and it will be too late. By then, Norah will have snagged herself the best guy who treats her like the fabulous woman she is." Isabella held her glass out to cheers with Norah.

Satisfying her sister, Norah clinked her glass against Izzy's, but as she sipped her beer, she couldn't help but let her gaze travel to Todd. And when she found him staring back at her she choked on her beer.

"You okay?" Izzy patted Norah's back lightly.

Norah coughed into her closed fist a few times. "I'm fine."

"You sure?" Todd asked, a subtle smirk on his lips.

Just lovely, he'd caught her.

"Went down the wrong pipe, I guess." Her face heated.

The two hadn't discussed the details of this plan of theirs. Would they fill in Izzy and Leo? Or would they lead them to believe the two of them were dating for real? Izzy had asked him to come be Norah's date for the party, but maybe she'd believe the two of them hit it off.

"So, Langston," Izzy began, "how was your trip? How'd Samson do with that long of a drive?"

"Surprisingly, really well. I think he just might be in training for the best road trip companion there ever was."

It was sweet, the way Todd talked about Samson. It was clear he should've always been a dog guy. How had Margo never noticed this?

"I got the best photos of him riding shotgun, staring out the windshield like he'd never seen anything so beautiful as the Rockies."

"Ohh, let me see the pics." Isabella swiped Todd's phone off the tabletop. But after looking at the screen for a few moments in silence, she hurried to shove the phone back in his direction. "Sorry. You have an Instagram notification."

"What?" Confusion swam in his expression until he glanced at his phone. His jaw popped. "Oh, right. Did Margo not tell you about her new boyfriend?" He handed the phone back to Izzy.

"She told me. But I guess I didn't realize she'd announced it to Instagram."

He shrugged. "No big deal."

Unable to refrain, Norah peered at Todd's phone screen while Izzy held it. Margo's most recent post was a photo of her and a broad-shouldered man dressed in a business suit with dark clean-cut hair. She had her arm looped around his neck while they kissed.

Norah knew exactly what Margo was doing. She was playing hardball. Margo was a genius. She was making it obvious to not only her followers, but the partners at the firm that these two were in a relationship.

Izzy looked as if she was going to press the issue, but instead, she swiped the Instagram app away and opened Todd's photos. Norah looked over Izzy's shoulder while she scrolled through pictures of Samson. Some by himself and some selfies with Todd. They'd had quite the adventure.

"Looks like Samson is going to be the perfect dog for you," Izzy said, handing Todd back his phone.

"I think so too." Todd smiled.

"Sooo?" Izzy dragged out the word, brows raised. "You wanna talk about it? About Margo?"

And there it is.

Norah tried not to watch the expressions play out on Todd's face while he considered a response. She rubbed at the back of her neck, eyes flittering up to his.

"Hell no. I'm on vacation. Besides, there's nothing to talk about. We broke up. It happens. End of story."

"But you guys were such good friends. And I gotta admit, when I go back to New York, I'm gonna miss our little trio."

"We were good friends. And I'm sure, in time, we'll find a way to be friends again."

The air felt awkward between them. Norah's only respite was to remove herself from the space altogether. And maybe Todd needed saving too.

Norah climbed off the bench and stood near Todd. "Hey, what do you say we go grab another drink?"

He jumped at the opportunity. "I'd love to."

"We'll be back." She gave a wave to Izzy and Leo.

Resting his hand on her lower back, she held her breath while Todd guided her toward the outdoor bar. This was part of the show, part of the act they needed to put on. And yet, it gave her feelings she shouldn't be feeling.

On their way, she caught sight of Landon in her peripheral. He and Mia stood near a gas firepit talking to a few other people. But he spotted her too. And when their eyes locked, she felt a pinch of guilt. It was hard to forget that she didn't belong to Landon anymore.

She and Todd reached the bar and waited their turn. Norah hoped she wouldn't bump into anyone who would want to talk. She had only been to Tapp's a handful of times in the past year.

"You okay?" Todd asked, leaning closer to her. "I see your ex is keeping a close eye on you."

"Yep, fine," she blurted.

"I'm just trying to make this thing look real. But if you would feel more comfortable, I can move my hand?"

"No, it's fine. It's good." She pinched her eyes shut and sighed. Spilling her guts to Todd Langston was not something she'd planned on doing tonight. Or ever if she was being honest. "Ugh," she groaned and opened her eyes. "I just hate feeling like he still has a say in what I do and who I see, who touches me, ya know? Like he somehow still owns me." Just saying the words aloud caused an acidic taste to burn in her throat.

Todd moved even closer next to her, close enough that the heat radiated from him, rushing onto the bare skin of her face.

"You're joking, right? I hope he never made you feel like that," he mumbled, peering into her eyes, while his hand remained on her back.

There was sincerity shining in his gaze. But maybe this was all part of the act.

She pulled her lower lip in between her teeth and shrugged off his question.

But while they waited for their next round of drinks, Todd pressed the subject further. "Did your ex really make you feel like that?"

"I mean, sometimes. But that's marriage, right?"

"I hope not," he said.

The bartender set their drinks down, and Todd nodded his thanks.

"Have you ever been married?" she asked.

"Uh, no."

Norah tilted her head to the side and hunched a shoulder as if saying, *point proven*. Then she took a sip of her wine. Her throat puckered. Maybe switching from beer to wine wasn't such a good idea. She nudged her chin in the direction that was opposite from the table Izzy and Leo sat at, and away from the crowds and he followed her.

"But I still don't think marriage is about ownership. Sure, compromise. Communication. But it should be a partnership," he said from behind her.

What Todd said made perfect sense. But that didn't mean that's how it was. At least that's not how her marriage had been.

They reached a small table near a game of cornhole, and she set her wine glass down. "You're saying all the right things, believe me. But you're preaching to the choir. I love the idea, it's just not plausible. Just wait until you get married."

Todd's facial expression went stony. "Yeah, you're probably right." He waved her off and took a drink of his beer.

A sense of dread filled her. Maybe she'd said the wrong thing. But since he'd never been married, what experience did he have? Sure, he'd been serious with Margo, but dating for a couple years was different than being married.

Unless...damn. All Izzy had told her was that they'd broken up. But maybe they'd been engaged? Or he'd proposed and she turned him down?

She was a jerk.

"Want to tell me what happened? With Margo?"

Without making eye contact, he said, "She wanted to break up. Right after I surprised her with Samson and right before I was going to propose."

"Whoa," Norah said, exhaling a deep sigh.

"Yeah." He took a sip of his beer. "But do you want to hear the craziest thing out of everything?"

Norah nodded.

"I wasn't surprised by her reaction—disappointed—but not surprised. Each time I mentioned anything about moving out of the city, marriage, the K-word, she got all weird."

She quirked a brow. "The K-word?"

"Kids." He shrugged. "It was all too much of a commitment for her. She wants to stay in the city, and focus on her career."

"You say it so nonchalantly," she said.

He didn't reply, only stared into his glass.

"It sucks when they move on so quickly, huh?" When he glanced up at her she elaborated. "The suit in her photo."

"Aaron," he provided.

Norah puffed air into her cheeks before releasing it on a slow exhale. She shook her head. "It's rough when they make it Instagram official, too. Though better than walking in on them in the middle of the act."

"No," he gasped.

"And in front of all your friends and family while they hid, waiting to jump out and shout *surprise* at his birthday party."

"Seriously?"

"Planned the entire surprise party myself."

"Okay, you win. That's worse."

She held her wine glass out to him, and he clinked his against it in a *cheers*.

"But explain women to me, because why only a few weeks after Margo wanted to break up because," he used air quotes, "*she isn't ready to make a commitment*, she's now got her arms wrapped around a new guy?"

"Well, that guy clearly isn't commitment material. He's the rebound guy. He's the *safe-need-the-promotion-guy*."

"I guess," Todd agreed. "I just hope she knows what she's doing."

"I think it's sweet you still care about her."

He shrugged. "We were friends before anything else."

"I also think that your heart needs a jumpstart. So you can get back to loving what you did before it became jaded."

"What do you mean?"

"After Landon and I separated and I moved back in with my parents, all I wanted to do was run away. There was too much of a connection between the Hoffman's and the Whitley's. I wanted to get out of Pineridge. And fast. But here's the thing, Pineridge is my home. There's so much to love. So much history here. I had to remind myself what I loved about it. So, I visited places in town that hold meaning to me. And I did certain things that made me appreciate Pineridge again. It was a way for me to jumpstart my heart."

"I guess that makes sense. But what kind of things are we talking about?"

She swirled the wine in her glass. "Some things were simple. Like getting my favorite cup of coffee at the Daily Grind. Or my favorite beer at my local brewery. And visiting the Love Lock Bridge. Did you know people travel here from all over the U.S. just to put a lock on the bridge? And I just take it for granted."

Todd quirked a brow. "People come here to see a bridge?"

"It's not just *any* bridge." She took a sip of her wine. "But these are just examples. For you, it could be contacting a past client you helped to win their case, visiting your college, opening those old textbooks, grabbing food from your favorite place that you used to during late night study sessions."

He nodded. "That makes sense. Guess it's worked out pretty well for you," he said, gesturing his chin in her direction.

"Ha. Don't be fooled, my heart is not completely healed by

any means. Otherwise, I wouldn't have panicked back there around my ex." She exhaled a light laugh. "I'm not sure a heart is ever completely healed after it's been put through trauma like that. It's like a brain. It learns how to function after being injured. And hopefully, it will find love again."

"I don't even know if I'm hoping for that."

Her heart stalled in her chest. "What do you mean? You don't want to fall in love again?"

With a shake of his head, he said, "I don't know. Love kinda sucks."

A bubble of laughter came out of her. "You're right. It does. Sometimes. But then it doesn't. I guess I'm hoping if you're lucky enough to find that right person, it won't suck."

"Yeah, maybe."

They were quiet for a moment. Until Todd finally said, "So I'm guessing this is a place on your list? Ya know when your heart needs a jumpstart?"

She nodded, a small smile pulling at her lips. "It is."

"Okay, I'll bite. What qualifies it as having a place on *Norah's Heart Needs a Jumpstart* list?"

"Great question. For starters, it has Kelsey. Her presence alone makes any place better. And besides having great beer, it has a local feel. This place is about community. It reminds me how much I love this town."

When she finished talking, her eyes flittered up to meet his and she found his lips tugged at the corners. "What?"

"Nothing. You just get this adorably excited look on your face when you talk about this town."

She tucked her chin to her chest. *Did he just call her adorable?*

"Yeah, well, I guess it has its moments."

Todd's phone buzzed on the table between them. Norah

couldn't help but allow her eyes to wander to the screen. Another Instagram notification. Margo had made another post.

Dang, Margo, two posts in one night.

Todd stared at the screen for a moment until he flipped his phone over and chose to ignore it.

"You gonna look?"

"Nah, what's the point? She's just trying to rub it in that she's in a committed relationship."

Hesitating, she finally said, "Okay, but aren't you, too?"

He knitted his brows together, looking clueless.

"Not only should you show her that you're not fazed by her new relationship, but you should also be showing her you've moved on."

"Yeah?"

She rolled her eyes. "Don't make me change my mind." Before she second-guessed herself, she snatched his phone out of his hand. "Let's take a selfie of the two of us and then you can post it to your Instagram story."

"Now?"

"Why not?"

He wavered, running a hand through his hair and glancing over his shoulders.

"It's not an engagement announcement, Langston. It's just a photo."

"Okay, yeah. But are you sure? There's no going back after we do this."

He was right. Once their picture was out there, they were committed to seeing this fake relationship through until its fake demise. She swallowed and nodded once. "Let's do it. Besides, we've already told Landon. And as much as I don't want to admit it, seeing his reaction to you holding my hand was priceless."

"Well, no offense, but your ex is a real piece of work. Someone had to remind him what he's missing."

Warmth bloomed in her chest. It was nice having someone who hadn't been privy to the whole incident still see the situation for what it was. But more than that, in a matter of a few words, Todd Langston made her feel like she wasn't invisible.

Just like he had when she'd been fifteen. At first, he'd been her hero. She'd gotten mixed up on the subway and ended up being nearly two hours late to Les Misérables. She was devastated to miss it. While Izzy had given her a hard time, Todd not only got her in free the next day, but he'd also accompanied her. If she hadn't already had a crush on him, that act of kindness would've sealed the deal.

Then he ruined everything.

But that was in the past. She'd told him she could get over it. She could forgive him so the two of them could pull off this scam. A fake relationship. And they were about to announce it to the world. Or at least, a small corner of it by posting a pic of them on Instagram.

Unraveling the scarf from her neck, she stood and tossed it onto the table. With his phone in hand, she slid her free hand across his muscled shoulders until her arm draped around his neck. She wasn't sure where her sudden brazenness had come from, but she held his gaze and slowly maneuvered herself onto his lap.

He exhaled a groan.

"Is this okay?" she whispered, and bit her lip, a twist of worry tightening in her stomach.

But the way he looked at her, with his green eyes darkening, her apprehension turned to desire.

"Uh...yep...it's fine," he answered. "It's more than fine."

She swallowed. Hard.

He slid his hand over her hip and tugged her close, his stare so intense, it made her spine tingle. There was no doubt her childhood crush was now a full-fledged adult crush, no matter how much she told herself this was not real.

They were close. So close she could feel the tense muscle in his shoulders. So close she could smell his scent of musky pine cologne and it made her head dizzy. She cleared her throat and held the phone out with the forward-facing camera ready.

"Okay, now act like you're having a good time or it's not gonna be believable."

He turned to face her, holding her attention in his intense gaze. "I won't be acting, I *am* having a good time," his words came out sounding all growly.

A shiver ran down her arms and her breathing quickened. "Good. Me too." She pulled her lower lip in between her teeth for a moment before breaking eye contact. "Now look at the camera. Big smiles. Um...maybe put your other arm around me."

"Gladly," he rasped quietly against her neck.

With one hand still gripping her hip, he wrapped his free arm around her waist, squeezing a light giggle out of her and easing some of the awkwardness between them.

Time stood still at that moment, teetering at a dangerous point of no return. This guy currently holding her had been her childhood crush, had occupied her wildest fantasies, and now he was gazing into her eyes.

Norah took a few pics to ensure at least one of them would turn out and then reluctantly climbed off his lap, handing the phone back to him. "Here, now pick one and post it."

"These are great," he said, thumbing through the pictures before finally deciding on one. "Here goes nothing."

Norah picked up her wine glass and took a sip, trying to swallow the impending regret thick in her throat. She stared across the beer garden, not really seeing faces or anything particular at all.

Her phone buzzed.

MADDIE

You made your relationship Instagram official before even telling your best friend??

But whatever, you look disgustingly adorable together.

I think I might puke.

Thanks, Mads. Love you!

MADDIE

Love you!

"Hey, you wanna play cornhole?" Todd asked.

She glanced up at him and found a small, crooked smile on his lips. Exhaling a shaky breath, relief slowly slid through her. Maybe this wasn't going to be so bad after all. All the characters in the popular fake dating romcoms seemed to enjoy themselves. So why couldn't she?

"I'd love to. But I'm gonna need one more glass of wine. I think it will help improve my technique."

He quirked a brow at her. "Where's the logic in that?"

"Just trust me." She smirked. "Now, c'mon."

He continued to study her as she hooked a finger at him. He grinned, and his green eyes darkened as she caught him admiring her while she sashayed backward toward the cornhole.

The thrill that wriggled through her because of him checking her out was scorching. Sure, the alcohol was working its way through her system, too, and causing her to feel more relaxed and carefree. But she didn't think she was mistaking the attraction between them.

Smiling, she spun around and then instantly felt a light smack on her backside. She shrieked and whirled back around to face him, heat flaring across her cheeks.

The grin he gave her was the biggest she'd seen yet. "Sorry, sweet cheeks, I couldn't resist." He winked at her.

Her stomach dropped. She'd been an idiot. Of course, he was pretending. Because that's what this was. Pretend. There was no real attraction between them.

Suddenly she felt the eyes of everyone around them on her. On the two of them. They were the center of attention.

Glaring at him, she forced a smile as she fisted the front of his jacket and yanked him into her. She brought his lips a mere centimeter away from hers before she whispered through gritted teeth, "Keep your hand off my ass."

Then she kissed him hard on the mouth.

It was a quick kiss. But long enough to feel a spark as soon as their lips touched. She'd have to forget all about it though. Because the chemistry she thought she felt between them wasn't real.

After she released him, someone let out a piercing whistle. There was some clapping and cheering too. She couldn't help but shake her head and laugh.

Ready or not, she and Todd were not only Instagram official; they were Pineridge official. Which maybe held more importance.

CHAPTER 8

Todd

RYAN

Since when did you start keeping secrets from your brother?

I don't know what you're talking about.

RYAN

You have a girlfriend?

Sort of.

RYAN

Sort of? You either have a girlfriend or you don't. Which is it?

All Todd could remember about Norah was that she'd been a sweet kid. That year she'd come to New York to visit Isabella and got lost on the subway; she'd been crushed that she missed Les Misérables. How could he not sneak her in for free since he worked at Imperial Theatre?

She was so excited. And even though he'd never really been into musicals, he joined her and had a good time. But she'd only been fifteen. Way too young to have any thoughts about her other than friendly.

Now though, Norah was a woman. A beautiful, sexy, intelligent woman. And his thoughts about her weren't even toeing the border of friendly.

His gaze lingered over her backside as she bent to pick up the bean bags. He cleared his throat when she turned around. A slow smirk pulled at her lips.

Caught.

But he couldn't act on his feelings for her. They'd already made a deal that this was going to be fake. And not only that, but she'd also just had her heart ripped out and stomped on. If Norah was even looking for another guy, she was either looking for a commitment or a one-night stand.

Neither interested him.

"Okay, Mr. Langston." Norah dropped the bean bags into his hand, their fingers grazing for a brief moment. "Since you're the away team, I'll let you go first."

He smiled, gripping the bags in his hands. "Not to brag or anything, but I used to be pretty good back in the day." He tossed his first bean bag, making it on the board, but barely.

"Played a lot of cornhole in college, did you?"

"As a matter of fact, I did. How'd you know?" His next bag made it a little closer to the hole but too far to brag about.

"Oh, I don't know. You just kinda give off that nerdy college boy vibe."

He choked on a laugh. "Excuse me?"

She winced. "Sorry. But it's true."

When he threw his last bag, it slid into the hole easily. "How does being good at cornhole mean I was a nerd in college?"

She simply shrugged.

He shuffled to the board and gathered the bean bags before handing them to her.

Norah took her stance and narrowed her eyes at the board, swinging her arm back and forth a few times and concentrating. She flung it forward, releasing it and the bag landed on the ground next to the board. "Clearly, I was busy doing other things in college."

Other things?

He couldn't stop his brain from spiraling to what *other things* Norah could've been doing while in college. He remained quiet while she threw her next two bean bags—one sliding off the board completely while the other teetered on the edge of the board before ultimately falling to the ground.

She picked up the bags and spun around to face him, lifting her brows. "Best out of three?"

The corners of his lips pulled into a wide smile. "You're on."

They played two more rounds, Todd winning all three and he felt a little bad about it. But she was a good sport.

Todd finished off his beer and decided he'd better call it quits. The exhaustion from the drive was beginning to catch up to him. And he wondered how many glasses of wine Norah had and if she would be able to drive them back to the Whitley's or if they would need to call an Uber or Lyft. Did they even have car services in Pineridge?

Norah held the bean bags out for him. "Your turn."

He set out an open palm and she hesitated before handing them over.

"Remember you promised to tell me the story about your tattoo?"

He sighed. "Fine. My grandfather used to tell me that if I had my roots planted in the right soil, I'd never lose my way. I've been feeling a little lost since he died a few years ago. Then after Margo, I thought it was about time I got the tattoo as a reminder."

She lifted her eyes to meet his, her lashes fluttering, and she smiled. "That's beautiful. He must've been a special guy."

Todd's throat went dry. "He was the best."

"I wish your grandfather's analogy worked for me." Norah's eyes went glassy. "Because my roots have been planted in Pineridge, and lately, I have never felt so lost."

Something shifted near his heart. He didn't want to feel anything for this woman. Not even empathy. "Maybe Pineridge isn't the right soil?"

To his surprise, her expression softened.

"Maybe," she whispered. "Though I don't think my family would agree."

"You don't think they would support your decision to move away?"

"Who's moving away?" a voice called from behind them.

Todd and Norah both straightened and he jerked his attention up, finding Isabella standing there.

"Norah," he said.

But she was quick to answer at the same time, "No one."

"Better not be you. I just moved my whole life here to be close to you." Isabella threw an arm around Norah's shoulder.

Norah looked less enthused.

"We were just coming by to say goodbye," Isabella said finally.

Her husband, Leo, stood near her along with Norah's ex,

Landon, and his new girlfriend. All their eyes seemingly focused on them.

"We were just leaving too." Norah took hold of Todd's hand and tugged him beside her.

"We were?" he asked.

"You guys need a ride?" Leo asked.

"No, thanks. We're taking an Uber." Norah yanked Todd with her as she started across the beer garden, making her way toward the parking lot.

"Norah?" Isabella called.

"I'll text you tomorrow and we can make plans, yeah?" Todd hollered to Isabella over his shoulder.

"Yeah, okay. Chat tomorrow. But you have some explaining to do, Langston," she warned loudly.

Once they reached the parking lot, Norah let go of his hand and she tapped on her phone. Todd zipped his jacket up further while the biting wind whipped at his face.

"An Uber should be here in a few minutes," she said softly.

"Thanks," he mumbled, standing next to her but not saying anything further.

Norah stayed quiet too. She wrapped her scarf tighter around her neck and bounced from her toes to the balls of her feet. He didn't know her well enough to be able to read her. Had she been trying to get a rise out of not only her ex but Isabella as well?

In their silence, he pulled his phone from the front pocket of his pants. Tapping on the Instagram app, he checked the likes and comments on the pictures he'd posted of him and Norah. He sucked in a breath when he discovered Margo had commented. But upon reading, his mind began spiraling.

Margo: Cute!

Cute? What did that mean? He had an attractive woman

sitting on his lap and taking selfies with him and that's all Margo had to say? *Cute?*

"What the hell does this mean?" He held the phone out to Norah, interrupting their silence.

Norah furrowed her brows at him first before reluctantly glancing down at his phone. A smile slid onto her face. "It means, it worked. She's jealous."

He pursed his lips and read Margo's comment again. "That's what you get from one word? From *cute?*"

"Yep." She shrugged. "I know women. I *am* women."

"This is just one example of why I will never understand your species."

Norah looked at him, her scrutinizing eyes moving over his body and causing a tremble to course through him. She rolled her eyes at him like she was annoyed with him. "I think you're doing just fine," she muttered.

His body heated, and a satisfied smile tugged at his lips. "Yeah?"

"Don't let it go to your head," she mumbled.

The Uber pulled up to the curb and they both climbed into the back seat. He wanted to say more. He wanted to tell her that she was doing fine, too. And that she would *be* fine. Instead, he stayed quiet during their ride through the slushy parking lot and down the darkened main road. Norah kept her focus on her phone. He stared at his own absentmindedly.

When they reached the Whitleys, they climbed out of the back seat, and he followed Norah up the steps and to the front door. They stepped inside the glow of the mostly darkened house and Norah pressed her finger to her lips.

"My mom is a light sleeper."

He toed his shoes off and stepped lightly up the stairs, following all of Norah's movements. In the hallway, Norah pointed to the room he was staying in without speaking. He felt like a dog being punished, being sent to his kennel. Then he suddenly remembered about Samson. He'd probably need to go outside again before he called it a night.

"For what it's worth, I had a good time tonight," he whispered.

She smiled. "Yeah, I guess it wasn't terrible."

He rolled his eyes. "Goodnight," he said softly.

"Night."

He turned to head to his room but spun back around as she tiptoed toward her bedroom door kiddy corner from his. He followed behind her into her room, and she whirled around.

"What are you doing?" she hissed in a whisper.

"Are you okay?"

Her eyes dropped, and she sighed. "I'm fine."

"Are you sure? I know that was awkward tonight."

She barked out a quiet laugh. "Which part?"

"All of it." Todd rubbed at the back of his neck. "Except... hopefully not the parts that included me."

She tucked her chin to her chest. "The parts of the tonight that included you were surprisingly... nice. Still, partially awkward though." Lifting her gaze to him, she said, "Our history, your friendship with Izzy, Izzy's friendship with Margo, trying to make Margo jealous..." She paused and smiled flatly. "I'm not the make-someone-jealous type."

"What are you talking about?"

Norah unzipped her coat while she continued to stand nearly toe to toe with him. She was so close he could feel the heat radiating off her body causing his own to warm up. "I'm not the hot one."

"I don't understand. What does that even mean?"

She pressed her finger to her lips again in warning before she mumbled, "I'm the cute little sister, the cute best friend. You know? I'm sweet. I'm not taken seriously. I'm not threatening." She shrugged out of her jacket and tossed it on a chair before gazing back at him again.

At that moment, he wasn't picturing Norah as Isabella's kid sister. He saw her as the attractive, smart, caring woman she was. "You may be sweet... but that's not a bad thing."

"Whatever, it is what it is." She waved him off, but he took hold of her hand and pressed it against his chest.

She drew her bottom lip in between her teeth and her lashes fluttered as she peered up at him.

His desire for her skyrocketed and he wanted to feel those soft lips against his again. But for longer this time. He craved to know the taste of her mouth. He yearned to hear a moan escape her throat.

Sucking in a breath, he said, "I'm serious. Just because you're sweet doesn't mean you aren't beautiful and...sexy."

Norah's deep-brown eyes searched his.

Being this close to her suddenly made resisting her much harder than he thought it would be. He let go of her hand and took a shaky step backward. "Just don't sell yourself short. Margo and Landon will both notice if you're undervaluing yourself."

She narrowed her eyes at him. "So that's what you're worried about?"

Todd had to play off his feelings. He needed to keep them on track. He shrugged. "We want this to be believable, don't we? Your friends and family? My bosses?"

"Yeah," she muttered. "Yep, you're right."

As much as he wanted to give into the temptation and pull her into him, taste the wine from her lips, and push her the rest of the way into her bedroom, he couldn't.

"Goodnight, Buttercup."

She rolled her eyes, but he caught the mischief sparkling in them. "Goodnight, Mr. Langston." She shoved him into the hall.

After she closed her door, he stood there for a long moment like an idiot. Almost as if he hoped the door would swing open again, and she'd yank him inside. But she didn't. Which was probably just as well. He thrust both hands through his hair, tugging it, and exhaling a loud, shuttering, breath.

Entering his own room, he glanced around and found Samson passed out in his kennel snoring. The bed looked even more inviting than it had earlier. Though the only thing really tempting him tonight was the redhead on the other side of the wall.

Todd collapsed onto the bed, threading his fingers behind his head and groaning. He was too amped up. How was he going to fall asleep?

CHAPTER 9

Todd

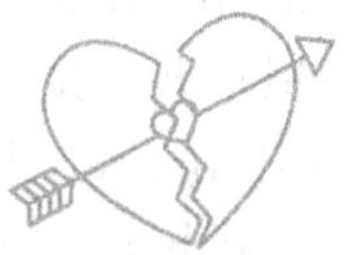

Attempting to stretch, Todd's feet pushed against the end of the daybed. He was too long for this bed. Daybeds were not intended for people who were over six feet tall. Maybe not even five feet.

After stirring in the squeaky metal framed bed for only a few seconds, Samson jerked his head up from where he lay in his kennel. Todd pinched his eyes shut. If he made eye contact with the puppy, it would be all over. He pried open one eye slowly, but it was too late, he'd been caught. Samson sat up quickly and swished his tail against the kennel walls.

Todd chuckled, wiping the sleep from his eyes. "Alright, buddy, I'm getting up." He swung his legs over the edge of the bed and picked his jeans up from where they were draped on top of his duffel bag. He stood and wrestled them on before finding a sweatshirt in his bag and throwing that on too. By this time, Samson was standing in his kennel, impatient, and whining to get out.

"I know, I know, I'm hurrying. You're not the only one who needs to pee, ya know?"

Todd opened the kennel and Samson barreled out. He quickly gave the dog some attention before attaching the leash to his collar and scooping him into his arms. It was a long way back down to the Whitley's front door and he couldn't risk Samson having an accident before they made it out of the house.

He stuffed his feet into his boots that rested by the front door, and he hurried outside, the air chilling his face instantly. While the dog yanked Todd through the front yard, sniffing the snowy ground, Todd hugged his body with his free arm. He wished he had put on his jacket. It was freezing.

He breathed hot air from his lungs into a closed fist. "You about done, buddy?"

Samson ignored him.

"C'mon." Todd tugged the leash. "You've already done your business. Time to go."

The dog wasn't a fan of the leash and was still learning to go on walks with it. Reluctantly, Samson gave in and jaunted back toward the Whitley's front door when Todd began heading in that direction.

In the front entryway, Todd toed off his snow-covered boots and unhooked the leash from Samson's collar. The puppy trotted off in search of breakfast. Todd had left Samson's food and water dish by the backdoor in the kitchen.

"Good morning," Mrs. Whitley greeted him after he entered the kitchen, while she stood in front of a sizzling pan of bacon on the stove.

Todd cleared his throat. "Good morning."

He wasn't *not* a morning person, but he wasn't used to having people around to talk to either. While living with Margo, she awoke before him, going for a run and then she'd already be showered and practically out the door heading to the closest Starbucks by the time he was sipping his mug of coffee.

Since he'd moved back in with his folks, it was the opposite, he was the first one out of the house.

"You sleep okay?"

"Yeah, I slept great. Thanks again."

"Psh," Mrs. Whitley waved him off. "It's nothing. You hungry? I'll fix you a plate."

Typically, his morning routine involved coffee, a few games on his phone, a shower, more coffee, and followed by a smoothie. Definitely never bacon.

But Todd didn't want to be rude to his hosts. "That sounds great, thanks."

Samson finally found his bowl and dug into his food. At least one of them was hungry.

Todd couldn't help but wonder where Norah was. Maybe she was less of a morning person than him and was still sleeping. Or maybe she'd drunk more than he thought the night before and was hungover.

"Here ya go." Mrs. Whitley set a plate down in front of him. Bacon, eggs, and a giant cinnamon roll nearly the size of Todd's head.

He forced enthusiasm into his voice. "Thank you."

"You're so welcome. Coffee?"

"Yes, please." He hoped he didn't sound desperate. But thank God they had coffee. Now he only hoped it was good coffee.

She set an extra-large mug filled with the glorious brew in front of him. "Cream? Sugar?"

"No, thank you. This is perfect." And it was. The first sip was like heaven to his taste buds and set fuel running through his veins nearly instantly. "So...Norah still sleeping?"

Mrs. Whitley exhaled a laugh. "That girl? Still sleeping?" She shook her head, amused. "She's been awake for hours. She's never been one for sleeping in."

Todd glanced around. If she was up, where was she?

Mrs. Whitley checked the time on her watch. "She's probably been at the rink for an hour or two by now."

Todd scratched at the scruff on his chin. "The rink?"

"The ice rink. She goes every morning. Skates for about two hours and then she teaches a few classes." Mrs. Whitley busied herself at the sink, filling dirty pans with soapy water.

"Ah, that's right. Guess I forgot."

He slid his phone from the front pocket of his jeans and sent a text to Isabella.

> What are you up to today?

ISABELLA
I'm on deadline.

> When are you free to hang out?

ISABELLA
Gotta get this article in by six p.m.

He checked the time on his phone. It was only almost 8 a.m.

ISABELLA
Come over at 6 for dinner.

> Sounds good.

ISABELLA
I'm sorry. Are you sure you can find something to do until then?

> I told Norah I'd help her with party stuff.

ISABELLA
Great idea. See you tonight!

Oh and Langston, you've got some explaining to do.

Todd didn't even need to ask what Isabella's text was about. She'd either heard the rumors about him and Norah dating or she'd seen the kiss at Tapp's last night. Maybe both. He'd wait to respond until after he and Norah talked and made a plan.

He tapped on the Instagram app, searching for Margo's profile after it loaded the feed. He really was a glutton for punishment. Why was he doing this to himself? And why did he care?

The picture she'd posted the night before sat there, front and center as if mocking him. Aaron Brown had his sleazy arm draped over Margo's bare shoulders. And she had a wide, bright smile stretched across her face, not seeming to mind one bit. Aaron was a partner at Santos and Cho. He was older than Todd, and made more money, but Todd wouldn't admit he was more handsome than him. Who was he kidding, of course, Aaron was more handsome. If Aaron was Superman, Todd was Clark Kent.

"Pft," he said on an exhaled breath.

"What was that, hun?" Mrs. Whitley asked over her shoulder, her hands dunked in a sink full of soapy water.

Todd cleared his throat. "Um, nothing."

Samson stood in front of the sliding glass door looking out at the backyard and started to whine.

"Hold on, let me get your leash, buddy."

"The backyard is fully fenced. He should be fine on his own back there."

"Good to know, thanks." Todd slid the door open, and Samson ran out.

This was one benefit of not living in the city with a dog. No putting his shoes and jacket on and attaching the leash to Samson's collar. It had been convenient since living at his folks' house to let Samson run around in their fenced yard.

The puppy ran around in the leftover snow, shoving his

nose into the wet stuff while barking a tiny bark. After Samson did his business, Todd called him back inside.

"Thanks again for breakfast." He took his empty plate and mug to the kitchen sink.

"No problem at all. As if I'd let you go hungry." Sue grinned.

"Well, I think Samson and I are gonna go sightseeing around town."

"That sounds lovely. Then be sure to be back here at six o'clock for dinner."

"Oh, uh..." Todd scratched the back of his neck, watching as Samson found one of his toys on the floor and pounced on it. "Actually, Isabella has already invited me to join her and Leo tonight. But thank you."

She frowned. "Oh. Okay. Well, tomorrow is family dinner night so hopefully you can join us then. Isabella's brother, Finn, and his family will be driving over from Denver."

"That sounds great, thank you."

Todd backed up a few steps before spinning around and hauling ass toward the front entryway. He was beginning to worry he'd never get out of this house. He packed a few things for Samson, grabbed his leash, and scooped up the puppy before rushing out the front door.

In town, he drove past the brewery from the night before, an outdoor shopping center, a coffee shop, a bakery, and Leo's photography studio. But no ice rink. He pulled his car off to the side of the road and put Google to the test. It brought up three ice skating rinks.

Three? That was a lot in a small town. Hell, that would be a lot in a large town.

Two were outdoor, and one stated it was public and currently closed. The other showed as private and always open; whatever that meant. The third was an indoor rink. He took his chances with the third one, pulling his car back onto the main road and heading in the direction of it.

After parking in the lot, he climbed out of his car and told Samson to stay put. As he walked through the lot, he shivered against the cold and zipped his jacket up his neck further. The sky overhead rolled in a thick gray, giving the impression of impending snow.

The indoor ice rink was large. Much bigger inside than it looked from the outside. With a few rows of bleacher-style seating all around, a small concession stand that was currently closed, and penalty boxes set up for ice hockey. It even had plexiglass walls like he'd seen on TV. He'd never been to an actual hockey game or even been ice skating, despite living close to one of the most popular rinks in the country.

Other than a few young girls who gathered in a section of the bleachers chatting, a janitor cleaning the plexiglass, and soft music playing through the speakers, it was quiet inside. Todd shoved his hands into his coat pockets and turned around.

But he instantly froze in place—mid-spin. He caught sight of Norah out on the rink. Gliding across the ice, her hands moved with a kind of grace and agility, unlike anything he'd ever seen before. His feet seemed to have a mind of their own and they moved him toward the rink so he could get a closer look.

Todd's eyes skidded up the length of her, taking in the way the fitted pants and shirt hugged her body like a second skin. Heat clawed up his neck and he tugged the zipper of his jacket down. The way she drifted over the ice, it was as if the song playing through the speakers had been choreographed for her. Like it was following *her* routine, not the other way around.

She spun, twisted and bent, and reached, and he couldn't help but feel guilty for watching her in this intimate moment between her, the ice, and the music. But he also couldn't look away. He was completely captivated by her. His fingers tingled, itching to touch her.

His throat went dry.

Todd didn't know how long he'd been staring at her after the song finished and she had skated to the side of the rink, chugging a bottle of water. But when she twirled around, she caught him watching her. An adorable, abashed smile appeared on her lips as she dipped her chin to a shoulder. His chest expanded and his feet started to move, picking up momentum the closer he got to the entrance of the rink.

She skated slowly toward him.

"Hey," she greeted, tossing a small towel over her shoulder, and taking another swig from her water batter.

"Hey, yourself."

Hey yourself?

Dumbass.

He cleared his throat. "What are you doing?"

Her brows pinched together as she gave him a confused smile. "Um, skating," she said. "Why? Have you seen other people do it differently? Was I doing it wrong?" She teased.

"Ha, ha. Very funny," he muttered. "It's just...I don't think I've ever seen anyone skate quite the way you did just now."

"Yeah?" Her brows lifted.

"You were," he paused, *fascinating, magnificent, striking, sexy...*"incredible," he finally said.

She waved him off, her cheeks blushing. "That was nothing. You should see me on a good day." She slipped something over her skate blades and stepped off the ice, joining him on the floor.

"That was a bad day?"

She shrugged a shoulder. "Not a bad day...just an off day."

"I'd love to see you on an *on* day." He couldn't hide the grin spreading on his lips.

"That would most likely be a day when I didn't drink the night before. Or...you know?" She looked pointedly at him, a hand drawing to her hip.

"Wait. Are you trying to blame me for your off day?" He mocked innocence, pressing his finger to his chest.

She rolled her eyes playfully before walking past him.

He jogged to catch up to her. "What did I do?"

"This whole fake dating thing, I don't know if I can do it," she whispered and shook her head. "They make it look so easy in the movies."

He scratched his chin, his mouth going dry. The last thing he wanted was Norah second-guessing her decision to help him.

"I'm sorry." He didn't know what he was apologizing for but for some reason, it felt like it was necessary. "It's not too late to back out," his words rushed out.

What was he saying? He needed her. He needed this to work. Losing the promotion would be devastating. But losing it to Margo would be unbearable.

She furrowed her brow. "There's something you should know about me, Mr. Langston. When I agree to something, I don't change my mind."

The way she said *Mr. Langston* had his skin buzzing.

She gave him a reassuring smile before she picked up a sweater off the bleachers and pulled it over her head. "So, now that we got that settled, what are you doing here? I figured you'd be hanging out with Izzy this morning."

"I guess she's on some kind of a deadline and she's busy until tonight."

"Oh, so I was runner-up. I see how it is."

"Huh? Oh, no...that's not what I meant." He rubbed the back of his neck while she headed in the direction of the girls he'd seen on the bleachers.

"I'm kidding. It's fine." She waved a hand nonchalantly over her shoulder. "Izzy stays pretty busy." She finally stopped walking, planting her fists on her hips. "And I'm sorry, but I'm actually busy too. About to start lessons."

"Oh, right. Your mom told me."

She dropped her chin to her chest. "Of course she did," she mumbled.

"It's cute."

"What's cute?"

"The way your mom talks about you. She's proud of you. And I can see why. You're amazing out there. Why aren't you competing yourself?"

Lifting her gaze to him, she said, "First, class." She pointed to the girls who were heading out to the rink. "Then, discussions on where I went wrong in life."

"Yeah, okay."

"You wanna meet me back here in two hours?"

He cocked his head. "Back here?"

She gave him a mischievous grin. "Yeah, something tells me you've never skated before."

"Then you'd be right." He had considered trying to ice skate a few times before—to please Margo, to impress a date— but when he was younger, he couldn't even stay up on a skateboard. His brother Ryan had apparently gotten all the coordination genes.

"Good. Because we're gonna skate," she said.

His eyes widened. "Uh...I'm not so sure that's a good idea."

"Don't worry. I'm gonna teach you."

"You sure there's time for that? You said there's lots left to do for the party."

She waggled her brows suggestively while backing up, and he could feel himself relenting.

"You mean, do I have time to watch you fall on your butt?

Yeah, I think I can make time for that." She threw a wink over her shoulder, before spinning around.

"See, you're wrong about people thinking you're sweet. You're a cruel woman." He watched her walk away, unable to resist his vision from drifting over her backside. "And trouble with a capital T," he muttered to himself.

In more ways than she probably even knew.

CHAPTER 10

Norah

Norah had a feeling Todd would be inexperienced at ice skating even before he told her he'd never been, what with those lanky arms and legs. And it had absolutely nothing to do with the fact that she couldn't wait to teach him something. He'd schooled her in cornhole the night before.

But this—ice skating—was her thing.

Landon hadn't taken to ice skating like she hoped he would. He was decent but he didn't enjoy it. Which meant not only did he not share in her passion, but he also never came to any of her class events. Most of the time when she tried to even talk to him about ice skating he zoned out or didn't bother glancing up from his phone.

Norah finished lessons for the young teens class followed by the toddler class. There was an hour until her next two classes. She hoped that would give her plenty of time to teach Todd the basics.

She waved goodbye to the last two toddlers and their

mothers when she spotted Todd on the edge of the rink. He'd stripped off his jacket and stood there, on wobbly long legs and she couldn't help herself, she snorted a laugh into her hand.

She skated toward him, stopping when she reached him. "Ready?"

He glanced down at his skates. "I can hardly stand up straight and I haven't even made it out to the ice."

Smiling, she said, "You'll be fine. Trust me." She raised her brows and held out her hands to him. "C'mon."

"I really don't know if this is a good idea."

"Look, do you want to make this relationship look real, or not?" she asked, brows raised.

Reluctantly, he placed his hands into hers. "I'm not sure how this will help our..." he paused, "relationship."

"Well, ice skating is practically my life. I think it's kind of important for you to know at least a little about it, don't you?" She tugged him gently toward her while she skated backward at a snail's pace.

Todd yelped and Norah found it sort of cute.

"Whoa, whoa. Slowww," he warned.

She fought back a laugh. "Calm down, you're fine."

"I'm going to be zero help to anyone this week if I'm in a full-body cast."

"Quit being so dramatic, you baby, I've got you," she said. And she did. She held his hands tightly and he squeezed hers with a death grip while she continued to lead him slowly.

"You better," he answered.

There was a moment, a flicker when their eyes locked and she hated how it sent desire rushing through her. And maybe the worst part; she didn't think this feeling was one-sided.

Todd cleared his throat. "So, I got a text from Isabella. I think she wants to know what's going on between us."

She stopped them both on the ice. "Yeah?"

"What's the plan? I mean, what do you want to tell her?"

It's not as if she didn't know this issue was going to arise, but dealing with it was different. Though she knew they had to keep the charade going for everyone. Even Isabella.

"I guess we need to tell her the same thing we're telling everyone else."

He lifted his brows. "You sure?"

"We can't tell anyone this is pretend. We can't risk the truth getting out. I don't think either of us will end up getting what we want if it does."

She could feel him trying to draw her in with his gaze, but she resisted. If she overthought all of this, she would change her mind and put a stop to it right now. Moving on was the best idea.

"Okay," she said, beginning to skate backward again and pulling him with her. "The first thing you need to learn is how to fall down,"

He gave her an unimpressed glance, before focusing on his feet again. "I'm sorry, but wasn't the whole point of having you teach me, so I don't fall down?"

"No, the point of me teaching you is so you can learn to do it on your own, without holding onto me."

"You don't see me complaining," he mumbled under his breath.

Her cheeks burned, but she pretended she hadn't heard his comment. "Landon couldn't skate without my help. I want you to learn."

"Okay fine," he relented.

She eased her grip around his hands, slowly letting go when she knew he had his footing. "First, bend your knees. You want to bend them enough that your butt feels heavy. The goal is to land on one of your butt cheeks and thigh to avoid landing on your tailbone."

Raising his brows at her in a, *you serious* look, he eventually forced himself to fall gracefully, but not without flailing his arms at the last second and pulling her down with him. She'd fallen numerous times on the ice before and lucky for her, she had the falling down correctly technique perfected. Except being yanked down by someone made it extra difficult to presume the position. Fearful she'd land on her knee—or worse—on top of him, she turned her body and her thigh touched down hard against the solid surface.

Norah squeezed her eyes shut and groaned on impact. Todd instantly cracked up from where he lay with his back flat against the ice. She couldn't help herself from laughing along with him. She propped herself up on her elbows, her thigh already throbbing and warning her that instead of that hot bath ritual she usually looked forward to, she'd be icing instead.

"Maybe we should get a picture?" Todd suggested while he remained on his back.

Somehow, she'd forgotten in the last few minutes that Todd could be putting in effort strictly for show. It would be something he could tell his boss or the other partners at his law firm. It would make a cute story: *his girlfriend tried teaching him how to skate and he fell on his butt, accidentally taking her down with him and they laughed and kissed right there on the ice because they're so incredibly in love with each other.*

That was what she had agreed to though, wasn't it? Pretending to be his girlfriend so he could get a promotion at work. She supposed she had to play along and make it believable, but that didn't mean she had to kiss him.

"Sure. A picture is a good idea."

Todd had already tugged his phone from his pocket. He

positioned it so he'd get a shot of their bodies pressed closely. They both attempted to reenact the moment after their fall, including stupid smiles spread wide on their faces, and eyes gazing longingly at one another.

But when he leaned in for what Norah assumed would be a kiss, she panicked and smacked him in the gut playfully. "C'mon, we still have lots of work to do." She rolled to the opposite thigh and hauled herself up onto one knee. "Now that you've mastered the correct way to fall down, you should practice getting back up."

"Look at that, I'm an honor student already," he teased.

"I don't think I'd go that far." She rolled her eyes, setting her hands on her hips so she wouldn't be tempted to help him up. "Now twist your body to the side and put both knees on the ice. Lift one leg up to a kneeling position and then you can use one or both hands to push yourself up."

Norah waited as Todd hoisted himself up with ease. It surprised her how effortlessly he was back up on his skates. And he didn't even complain about the rough fall. At this point in her lesson with Landon, he'd already be whining and asking to go sit on the bleachers.

"What's next?" he asked, eagerly.

"Forward marches."

He rolled his eyes but besides that, he was a good sport as she took him through the next several steps, performing them herself while he watched closely and emulated her. It wasn't lost on her how intensely he kept his focus on her.

The way he studied her movements, and not just her hands and skates, but her physique, with such precision was intense. Heat flooded through her, and yet she couldn't allow herself to react.

She wouldn't.

Before long, Todd was not only gliding on his own, but he'd

also learned how to stop himself too. His quick learning and graceful movement on the ice had Norah not only impressed but completely captivated.

Maybe his effort wasn't strictly for show. Maybe he genuinely wanted to learn. They made eye contact across the ice, and she felt a fluttering sensation in her chest.

When Norah caught sight of one of her students for her next class on the bleachers lacing her skates, relief filled her. Being this close to him, teaching him something she loved, it was too much. Too dangerous. She couldn't get her feelings involved.

"Do you want to meet me at Sweet Cakes Bakery in about two hours?"

"A bakery?" He scratched his chin. "I guess. But I don't typically eat sweets."

She arched a brow. "You said you wanted to help with the party? And I need help picking out treats for the party. I guess if you don't want to try any, more for me." She shrugged and turned, skating toward the edge of the rink where more of her students gathered.

"I'll be there," he finally called.

After all her pre-teen students were out on the ice, she glanced over her shoulder and Todd was gone. *I don't typically eat sweets.* She shook her head and chewed her bottom lip. Who didn't like sweets? Honestly, it was a good thing because it was a reminder that she and Todd would never work out for real. Lemon bars from Sweet Cakes Bakery were life.

AFTER NORAH'S SECOND CLASS ENDED, SHE TOWELED OFF in the locker room and changed back into her jeans and sweater. Outside, the temperature had risen slightly from when she'd first arrived at the rink, so she tossed her scarf onto the passenger seat after climbing into her car. She drove to Sweet Cakes. It was the best bakery in Pineridge, okay, so it was the *only* bakery in Pineridge. But still, Rita Sanders was a genius when it came to all things confections.

Norah pulled into a parking spot on the street near Sweet Cakes Bakery. She snatched her lip gloss from her purse and ran it over her lips. She slid out of her car and ran her fingers through her long hair that had gotten tangled after all the hours at the rink. Spotting Todd rounding the front of his car, she waved and waited for him to catch up to her before going inside the bakery.

"Will Samson be okay in the car?" she asked.

"I cracked the windows. He'll be okay for a little while at least. Don't want to leave him too long or he'll probably eat something—like my seat."

She snorted a laugh while he held the door open for her and she shuffled past him.

Marissa, a local high schooler and what Norah would label as a Pineridge "lifer" stood behind the counter.

"Hi, Norah. How are you doing?" Her voice sounded too sweet, too practiced.

Norah wished everyone around town would stop treating her like she was fine china. Sure, she'd been fragile at first, but the divorce had been finalized months ago. She was fine.

Okay, today she was fine. Tomorrow might be a different story.

"Hey, Marissa. I'm great. Just here to meet with Rita."

"Damn, Norah, you're one of the strongest women I know. You're like, my idol." Marissa handed a box of cupcakes to a tall, graying man. "Here you go, sir. And happy birthday to your daughter."

The man nodded, then tipped his imaginary hat at Norah and Todd while he passed. Norah recognized him. He was the father of one of her prior figure skating students.

"Is Rita ready for us?"

"Um...us?" Marissa glanced between Norah and Todd.

"Yep, I brought a friend with me."

"Ohhh, a *friend*." Marissa winked at Norah.

"Is she in the back?" Norah ignored her, standing on her tippy toes while attempting a glance in the back of the shop. "Should we just head back there?"

"Oh, no, I'll go grab her." Marissa walked toward the back but didn't take her eyes off Todd.

"Sweet girl," Todd mumbled. "I had no idea I was in the presence of an idol."

"Shut up," Norah muttered, shooting a glare at him.

Rita came around the corner, a wide smile on her face and looking at her watch. "Norah, right on time, as always."

"I'm nothing if not predictable." Norah winced before the words had even slipped out of her mouth.

Was that her thing? Was that her brand? Because oh, heck she really hoped not. What guy wanted predictable? Not that she wanted a guy.

She absolutely did not.

This thing between her and Todd was pretend and that was totally fine with her.

"That you are." Rita smiled and Norah couldn't help but see it as condescending. "Okay, c'mon over. I have everything you requested." She waved at Norah to follow her. "Who's your friend?" she asked over her shoulder.

See, *friend*. Rita got it.

"This is Todd Langston. He's visiting from New York."

Rita took him in, head to toe. "What brings you to Pineridge?"

Todd looked to Norah as if waiting for her to answer but she found herself tongue-tied. Was she ready to do this? To lie? To her friends and family?

"I came for the Galentine's party," he finally said.

Rita's brows raised. "That's sure a long way to travel just to attend a party."

"It's worth it when your date is as beautiful as mine."

His gaze held Norah's and it felt as if flames licked her cheeks.

Ready or not, the floodgates of lies were about to gush open.

"I guess not so predictable after all?" she mumbled.

"I guess not," Rita teased with a hip bump into her own.

Norah couldn't deny the bit of satisfaction Rita's statement brought her. It also did something to her confidence. To have someone she loved, and trusted, not pity her but look genuinely happy for her. It had been too long since she'd seen these looks from her friends.

"And little did he know when he agreed to be my date, he was also agreeing to be a co-party planner."

"Isabella's still swamped with work, huh?" Rita asked.

Norah nodded.

It was depressing that the assumption of Izzy's busyness was a fact and one that even Rita knew. Sometimes it had Norah worried about how hectic work was for Izzy when she was home. She seemed to have a better handle on things when she and Leo were in New York. Juggling tasks from Pineridge took a skill Izzy hadn't mastered yet but Norah hoped she would soon.

"Well, then let's hope you like cake." Rita grinned at Todd while she displayed the spread of treats on the table with a sweep of her arm.

Norah eyed all the delicious goodies on the table. Pink heart-shaped cookies, red iced heart-shaped cookies, mini cupcakes, macarons, cake pops. Everything looked so pretty and delicious. The scent of fluffy icing and sweet sugar filled her nose, making her head feel dizzy.

"Everything looks fantastic. I think Izzy is gonna love all of it."

Todd picked up a red heart-shaped cookie and held it out to Norah, reading the piped icing aloud with a quirked brow. "Love Stinks?"

Norah snorted. "Rita, it's so perfect."

"I thought you'd approve." She smirked. "That good-for-nothing cheater," Rita muttered before composing herself and smoothing her hands over the front of her dress. "Anyway, I'll let you two at it. I gotta go prep some orders. Let me know when you're done and then we'll finalize your order."

"Sounds great, thank you," Norah called over her shoulder.

Todd held out another cookie to her. This one said *Bite Me*, and heat filled her cheeks. Was he simply questioning the phrase on the cookie or was he insinuating something?

Probably the former, but it didn't stop her mind from wandering to places it shouldn't go when they were only pretending.

She swallowed. "Guess you should probably take a bite then."

"I already told you; this really isn't my thing. You try it." He held it out to her as he stepped closer, and she inhaled a sharp breath. "Okay, fine. I'll take a bite if you do."

The challenge tempted her with not only the delicious-smelling cookie but also the lustful look in his darkening green eyes. She wanted not only a bite of the cookie but maybe a bite of that luscious lower lip of his. Holding the cookie so close to her mouth, that she barely had to open it to take a bite. She bit off a bite before taking a small step backward. The cookie tasted amazing. But she couldn't lie, she was a little disappointed. Biting that luscious lip of his had to taste a thousand times better.

Pushing the bite to the side of her cheek, she attempted to talk around it while she shoved the cookie in his face. "Okay, your turn."

He hesitated at first, studying it before finally taking a small bite. As she watched him chew, a thrill wriggled through her at the sight of his expression while the flavors exploded on his tongue.

She raised her brows. "Well?"

He nodded and swallowed. "That was pretty good."

"*Pretty* good?"

"Okay, it was pretty delicious. Is that better?"

"A little." She picked up a pink cookie and held it out to him. "Now try this one."

He wrinkled his nose. "That one looks really sweet."

"It's no sweeter than the last one," she urged.

Ever so slowly, he opened his mouth and leaned forward, taking the cookie between his teeth without taking his eyes off her. Heat crawled up her neck, pooling into her cheeks and burning the tips of her ears. Her throat went dry. An intense desire swooped low in her belly. She wished he didn't look so tempting. All he was doing was eating a cookie, but she found herself stuck in a fantasy of wishing she was that cookie; his teeth on her skin, his mouth on hers.

Todd's eyes widened while he chewed, and he nodded approvingly.

She smiled. "See, told you." She was about to pop what was left of the cookie into her mouth, but he snatched it out of her hand. "Hey," she protested.

But he'd already tossed the entire thing into his mouth. She swatted him in the chest and there was that firm, hard, delicious muscle again.

"I'm sorry, I couldn't help myself. That was really good."

"What happened to, *I don't usually eat sweets?*"

"I don't. I haven't had a cookie in months. Maybe longer."

Norah loved watching his pleasure as he tried the different desserts. She hoped he liked chocolate and couldn't wait for him to try the mini cupcakes. A chocolate cupcake with real chocolate chunks baked right in and salted caramel frosting with a caramel drizzle and sea salt topping. To match the theme, Rita had topped them with pink heart sprinkles.

Norah picked up one of the mini cupcakes from the tiered tray and pinched it between her fingers as she spun around, a wide smile pulling at her lips. "Okay, now try this."

He rested his hands on his hips and dropped his chin to his chest, exhaling a moan. "I can't do it."

"What? Why not? This is the best one. Promise."

"Well, if you promise," he said in a teasing tone, lifting his chin while his green eyes sparkled.

She wanted to feed it to him, insisting he'd have to suck the frosting from her fingers.

But she wouldn't. Because they were alone. They didn't need to pretend if no one was around.

When she held the cupcake out for him to take, a subtle expression of what looked like disappointment ghosted his face. *Had he wanted her to feed him?* He took it from her and peeled off the wrapper before popping the entire thing into his mouth. He chewed slowly and his eyes rolled back in his head while a throaty groan escaped his mouth.

Her knees went wobbly.

"Good?" she forced out.

"So good."

Satisfaction snaked through her. "Told ya."

"You do realize that now I'm probably gonna overdose on sugar or something."

She snorted. "Has anyone ever told you that you're dramatic?"

"Me?" he mocked, pressing a finger to his chest.

And she laughed softly.

He snatched another mini cupcake off the tier of goodies.

"Hey, you were just whining about your sugar intake."

"Oh, this isn't for eating." He waggled his brows while a mischievous grin appeared on his lips.

But when he pounced, her reflexes weren't quick enough, and he squished the cupcake onto the tip of her nose. She squealed, pushing him away and lurching backward out of his reach.

"I'm sorry," he said through laughter, handing her a napkin. "I just couldn't help myself."

"Suuuure, you just couldn't help yourself, huh?"

"What? You have an adorable nose."

Heat flared across her cheeks, but she tried to play it cool. She could be cool. She could handle a little harmless flirting. They were flirting, weren't they?

He held up his phone and took a selfie of the two of them before Norah cleaned her face.

"And here I thought I had a regular old plain nose." She wiped the frosting from her nose.

Todd gave her an impish grin and her stomach flipped. And that was it. That was the moment she knew she was wrong. She *couldn't* handle harmless flirting. Because this didn't feel harmless.

If he didn't stop flirting with her, she was going to come undone. All those feelings she had for him and stuffed down years ago were going to rise. And she was afraid she wouldn't be able to force them down again.

Todd's phone rang.

The color practically drained from his face when he glanced at the screen. "It's my boss, Jack. I wonder what he wants?"

She winced and shrugged her shoulders.

"Hey, Jack, everything okay?"

But Jack wasn't alone. Another man, she could only assume was Todd's other boss, Dan, leaned against Jack's desk gazing into the camera. He lifted his hand in a wave, giving him a curt smile.

"Everything's great, son. Dan and I just met with the partners, and we wanted to let you know, the discussion was tremendously positive in your favor. We're all loving the content you've been sharing on your socials," Jack explained.

Todd passed Norah an uneasy look.

"And we were hoping you'd introduce us to your lovely girlfriend," Dan chimed in.

Showtime.

Norah tilted Todd's phone in her direction as she draped her arm around his neck, giving the camera a big, cheesy grin. "Hi, I'm Norah. I can't wait to meet you both when I'm in New York visiting Todd next month."

They hadn't discussed when she would come to New York. But this promise of an early introduction seemed to please his bosses based on the way they grinned back at her. She felt a small pinch in her gut from lying to them.

"That sounds wonderful, dear."

"We're looking forward to it," Jack seconded. "And Todd, enjoy the rest of your vacation. You'll be hearing from my secretary regarding the date of our meeting to make our announcement."

"Thank you," Todd barely got in the words before Jack ended their Facetime. "And thank you," he said to her. "But if you really wanted to make it believable, you should've kissed me."

Norah glared at him and gave him a soft punch in the shoulder. "Don't push it."

She'd never admit that kissing him was just about the only thing on her mind.

CHAPTER 11

Todd

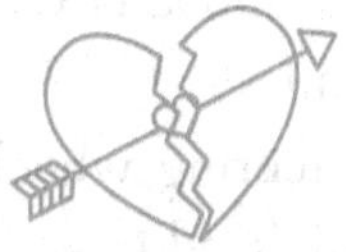

Todd didn't want to be late to Isabella's for dinner that night, so he took a quick shower and then dressed in something simple—jeans and a long-sleeved t-shirt. He wasn't used to so many days in casual clothing. Typically, his wardrobe consisted of suits and ties.

He was glad Norah wasn't at the Whitley house as he was preparing to leave for the evening. Not that he didn't want to see her—because he did. And that was the problem. He had this intense craving to see her and be with her, and worse—to touch her and kiss her.

And that was stupid.

Stepping out of the house, he pulled Samson along on his leash and he allowed the dog to sniff around and do his business before they got into the car. The sky was clear tonight, inky and stretching with an expanse of bright stars. But it was still cold. Todd hadn't packed enough warm clothing on this trip. He'd hoped since it was February, the temps would've been at least a tad bit warmer.

"Alright, little buddy. Time to get into the car." Todd tugged on the leash and the dog resisted. "C'mon. Samson?"

Finally, the dog relented and pranced along with him toward the car. Todd picked him up and tossed him onto the passenger seat covered with a towel. The puppy shook before sitting like he was Todd's co-pilot.

Todd patted his head. "Good boy."

Samson wagged his tail.

Sliding behind the steering wheel, Todd closed the door and then entered Isabella's address into his maps app. Her home was only about twenty minutes from her parents, but it felt far as he left the Whitley's neighborhood, drove through the town, and past the indoor ice rink. The map took him down a road that he continued straight on for at least ten miles before he was winding around curves.

Finally, he reached his destination and pulled into the long driveway ending with a beautiful log home. Todd put the car in park, and he peered out the windshield. He let out a whistle. "Samson, you better not piss in their house. I bet the floors are expensive."

But the dog just wagged his tail from where he still sat on the passenger seat.

Todd picked him up, tucking him underneath his arm, and trudged up the recently shoveled walk. He knocked on the solid wood door and waited, glancing over his shoulders, and spotting a body of water wrapping around part of the yard.

The door opened and Isabella smiled wide. "Come in, come in." She waved him inside. "Aww, is this Samson?"

"The one and only." Todd held out the puppy.

Isabella snatched him, cuddling him close to her chest. "Oh my goodness, he's so soft. Aren't you boy? You are the sweetest thing ever," she cooed.

"You sure you don't mind me bringing him?"

"Do we mind you bringing this adorable baby? Of course not."

Leo strolled into the entryway and shook his hand. "You better keep a close eye on him or this one might try to keep him." He chuckled, eyeing Isabella accusingly.

"Hey, thanks for the invitation," Todd said.

"No problem. Izzy is thrilled you're here. She's been talking about you and Margo coming for a visit for the past year." Leo winced. "Oooo sorry, man."

Todd ignored the mention of Margo. "Well, I'm sorry it wasn't sooner. This town is incredible. And your house, it's impressive." Todd glanced around the space inside the living room, practically drooling over the vaulted, wood-planked ceiling and exposed beams.

"Thanks. C'mon in and I'll give you the tour. But honestly, there's not much to it."

Todd followed Leo further into the house, taking in the beauty of the fireplace in the corner and large windows. He grazed his hand along the smooth logs that ran the length of the walls. The artwork displayed had to be Leo's. Fascinating prints of a frozen lake with the mountain behind. A smaller one of two kids making snow angels hung at the end of the hallway before turning into the kitchen.

"Want a beer?" Leo opened the fridge, poking his head inside.

"Uh, sure."

He cracked a bottle open before handing it to Todd.

"Thanks."

"Upstairs is just an office and the primary bedroom. Not too exciting." Leo shrugged.

"Though the views are amazing. I'll have to show you during the day so you can fully appreciate it."

Isabella set Samson on the floor, and he teetered around

inside the kitchen, sniffing the hardwood floors, and holding Todd's attention. He kept a close eye on the dog, watching for signs he might need to go to the bathroom yet again.

"Dinner is almost ready," Isabella said.

"It smells great."

Isabella washed her hands before pulling a pan out of the oven, golden cheese bubbling. "Hope lasagna's, ok?"

"It's perfect."

Todd wasn't a complete jerk. Sure, most of the time, he tried to eat healthy but that didn't mean he wouldn't splurge occasionally. Margo was the one who'd made him health-conscious. In college, he never cared. He liked how he felt now, but his mind traveled back to earlier today when he and Norah had been at the bakery. Eating all that sugar probably wasn't good for him but he hadn't had that much fun eating in a long time.

"Todd?"

He whipped his head in Isabella's direction and found her staring at him, brows raised with the bread knife mid-cut.

"Huh?"

"I asked how it went with Norah today?"

"Oh, great. Fantastic. Perfect." *What was he saying?* His chest burned and he tugged at the collar of his shirt.

She pursed her lips, brows furrowed. "Perfect?"

"Yeah, you know? As perfect as taste testing baked goods can go."

"Oh was that today?" She winced. "Sorry. I know you don't eat sweets."

"It was fine. I pushed through. Norah is fun."

He didn't miss the look Isabella shared with Leo.

"What?"

Isabella lowered her chin, arranging her facial features into serious. "Langston. I've been hearing the rumors. What is going on? Are you starting to have feelings for my little sister?"

Starting to put it mildly. No, he was waist-deep in quicksand and sinking fast in his feelings. "What?" His tone came out too high-pitched.

"Langston," she said sternly.

"That's crazy. Of course not. She's your sister."

Her jaw dropped. "What's so crazy about it? You can't like her because she's my sister?"

"No. I didn't say that."

"So you *do* like her?"

Todd pushed his glasses up the bridge of his nose, his fingers trembling. "What?"

Leo smacked him on the back. "Just quit now. You're not gonna win this."

Todd attempted to resist an eye roll. "Norah is great. We've hit it off. She's easy to be around. And she's cute." Oh no, did he just say that? He actually called Norah *cute*? If that got back to her, she'd be pissed. "I mean, she's cool. And it sounds like she could really use some help with this party. Since I've got nothing to do all week, I'm happy to help."

"You think she's cute?"

Of course that was the only word Isabella heard and clung to?

"Any guy would find your sister attractive—"

"For the record," Leo interrupted, "not *any* guy." He raised his hand.

Isabella rolled her eyes playfully at him.

"But...it doesn't mean anything," Todd continued.

"Good," she said, cutting the lasagna as the steam swirled into the air.

He rubbed at the back of his neck. "Good?"

"Yeah, I mean she's going through a lot right now. What

with the being cheated on and the divorce, and Landon moving on. The last thing she needs right now is a guy pouncing on her."

Todd fake laughed. "Ha, ha, pounce? I'd hardly think I'm the kind of guy to pounce. You know it took me four years to even ask Margo out on a date."

Isabella snorted. "Yeah, I remember." She exhaled, as she scooped a square of the lasagna and set it onto a plate. "You're right, I don't have anything to worry about with you."

Wait. What was that supposed to mean? Should he be offended?

Sure, Todd was no Casanova, but he'd done okay in the lady department. He landed Margo and she was not only hot but was smart and driven too. And since their breakup, he'd gone out with plenty of women and had a handful of one-night stands.

Isabella handed Todd a plate with a generous portion of lasagna, garlic bread, and Caesar salad. "We aren't too formal here. We just fill our plates, and some nights we don't even sit at the table. But tonight, we will. Wine?"

"Nah, I'll stick to the beer. But thanks." He sat at the four-person table in the dining room and laid a napkin in his lap. The house was quiet, and he hated the stifling awkwardness that filled the space.

"So," Leo finally interrupted the silence, "How's work been?"

"Busy. Fast-paced. But mostly boring."

"Hmm." Leo chewed a bite of lasagna.

"What about you? How's the photography business going?"

"It's good. Can't complain." He pressed his beer bottle to his lips, taking a long swig.

"Oh stop." Isabella waved her bread at Leo. "He's just being modest. He's doing better than good. Word is spreading about his prints. That's why we could afford to open the studio."

"Right. I went by there yesterday. It's a beautiful studio. Did you design it?" Todd asked.

"I wish I could take the credit. But it was the Renovation Dudes. Have you heard of them?"

"I don't think so. Should I have?"

Isabella shrugged. "Makes sense, you're busy and don't have much time for TV. These two brothers in town have a business together and they have a show on HGTV. The first season just premiered last year. So, our little town has another thing besides the Love Lock Bridge to put us on the map."

"That's cool."

"They do great work." Leo pushed his salad around his plate with his fork. "But if you ask me, I think our town was popular enough without the Renovation Dudes. I personally find all the hype and increase in tourism annoying."

"Well, it's a good thing no one asked you." Isabella grinned and he reached for her hand across the tabletop.

Todd smiled, but his gaze flicked down to his plate. Don't get him wrong, he was thrilled to see his friend happy, but that didn't mean he wanted a front-row seat to their intimate moments. And he was notorious for becoming uncomfortable around others' PDAs. He usually got fidgety and awkward himself.

"So, Norah's ex is your brother, right?" *Yep, he was awkward.* Like asking questions from left field during inappropriate moments.

Leo cleared his throat. "Yeah, that's right," he answered, sighing, and sounding exhausted.

"How does that work? Isn't that uncomfortable?"

Just like this conversation was.

"A little," Isabella answered for Leo. "It's hard not to choose sides, so we try not to. But Landon knows he was at fault for their split."

"And yet, you're all buddy-buddy with him and his new girlfriend?"

"It's not like that," Isabella said, pain in her stilted voice.

"No?" *What was he doing? Just stop, Todd. This is none of your business.* "Because it looked like you were all pretty cozy last night."

"We do what we have to, to keep the peace." Leo shoveled another bite of lasagna into his mouth.

"Even if it hurts Norah?" *Okay, he was officially the worst dinner guest in the history of dinner guests, and he wouldn't blame them if they kicked him out right now.*

Isabella bit her lower lip, her eyes downcast. "Did she tell you that?"

He hunched a shoulder. "Not in so many words. But if she was willing to go along with him believing she and I are dating, she's not okay."

"You're right." Isabella wiped her mouth with her napkin.

She looked like she might cry. What had he been thinking? Why couldn't he just eat and shut the hell up?

"I wanted him to think she'd moved on, too. Partly so he wouldn't think she was just sitting at home pining after him and partly so she would think moving on was a possibility. And honestly, I planned this whole Galentine's Day party for her."

"If it's any consolation, I think the party planning *is* helping her. She's staying busy. It's giving her purpose. And she seems to be really good at it."

"See." Isabella pointed a finger at him. "That's what I've been telling her. She has a knack for party planning. She should start a business."

"And give up the figure skating lessons?" he asked, tearing a big bite off the bread.

"You know about her figure skating?" Leo arched a brow.

Todd's chewing slowed and his eyes danced back and forth between both Isabella and Leo. "I watched her skate today. She's pretty good."

He lied. She was better than good. She was amazing. She was angelic. She was sexy as hell.

Isabella and Leo shared a look before she turned back to Todd, giving him a knowing smile, and nodding her head slowly. "And I have nothing to worry about with you? Yeah right," she muttered, smirking at him.

"What?" His temperature spiked and he pushed up the sleeves of his shirt. "Okay, fine. We've got passed all that BS from years ago and we've really hit it off. I really like her. We've talked and maybe we could try long-distance. Who knows?"

"Just promise me, you won't hurt her." Isabella gazed at him warily. "Her heart has been through enough."

A lump materialized in his throat. Could he promise that? If Norah didn't have any feelings for him, she would come out of this thing unscathed. But could he say the same thing about himself?

What about his heart?

He swallowed and answered the only way he could. "Promise."

CHAPTER 12

Norah

Maddie had nagged Norah for the past two weeks to go dress shopping with her for the Galentine's party. After spending the day with Todd, pressed up against his solid body at the skating rink, and then feeding him desserts at Sweet Cakes, she felt sexy for the first time in a long time, so she finally agreed.

Todd didn't treat her like she was young, or immature. After just one day, he'd already boosted her confidence by listening to her ideas and her feelings.

In the dressing room at a local women's clothing store, Norah pulled a slinky, sparkly, rose gold-colored dress over her head, stretching it over her hips. She adjusted the spaghetti straps, putting them in place before stuffing her boobs inside the v-neckline of the dress. Swaying back and forth in front of the full-length mirror, she pursed her lips.

The dress looked sexy on the hanger and that was the exact look she was going for. She liked how it fit her body shape. But it was a bit fancy for a Pineridge party.

"Are you dressed yet?" Maddie called from the other side of the door of the dressing room.

"Yeah." She bit her lip, still analyzing her reflection.

"Finally. Well, come out already and show me."

Norah unlocked the door and stepped out in her stocking feet.

Maddie gasped. "Oh, Nor, it's so pretty. And dang, where did those boobs come from?"

"I know, right?" Norah smiled, tilting her chin upwards as a bit of pride wriggled through her.

"You look amazing."

Norah took in her friend wearing a red strapless, floor-length dress that was fitted on top and flowed out at the waist. "Maddie, you look gorgeous in that dress."

"You think so? Because I feel a little silly in it. It feels a little over the top."

"But that's why we're dressing up. We're not dressing up for men. We're dressing up for ourselves," Norah said.

Poor Maddie. She'd made plans to go to the party with Garrett Vance as her date. But the guy canceled on her with the excuse he had to go to Denver to look at a house for a possible reno for the show. If Norah found out he lied to Maddie, she'd kick his ass.

"That's true." Maddie smoothed the dress over her hips. "I have to admit though, as a single woman who's on three different dating apps, and actively looking for a boyfriend, I'm not really feeling the whole *girl power*." Maddie pouted.

Norah hated seeing her friend sad. Maddie was not only gorgeous, but she was intelligent, and successful too. When she was only twenty-one and fresh out of college with a business degree, she rented space from Pineridge's only fitness gym and she started her own smoothie shop.

"You know you don't have to go to this party, right? Izzy

planned it mostly for me. To help me not feel lonely or depressed on such a romantic holiday."

"Don't be silly. I want to help with that too. And besides, it's not like I have other options." She headed back inside her dressing room. "Let's try on another dress."

Norah stared after the closed door for a beat before slipping back into her own dressing room. "What about Rowan? He's still single right?"

"No," Maddie groaned. "He and Scarlet are dating."

Norah yanked the dress over her head, her mind buzzing with possibilities. But she hated to admit, that their hometown wasn't necessarily crawling with available men.

"Jason Pitts?"

"Married."

"Seriously?" There weren't many guys left in Pineridge since they graduated high school. Most had gone to college out of state and never returned.

"Just give it up. Believe me, whoever you think of, I've already considered."

The door next to Norah's unlocked just as she stepped out of her own dressing room, her hand pressed to the top of the red rayon one-piece jumpsuit.

"Can you zip me please?"

"That looks fabulous on you. Dang girl, I'm drooling over those long legs."

"And I love that dress on you. It's really flattering, with that red lace popping over the top of the cream and that high slit.

"You sure it's not too slutty?"

"Absolutely not. If you've got it, flaunt it. Isn't that your motto?" Norah teased.

"Usually, yeah." Maddie bit her lip.

"You've got to get that one."

Maddie's face slowly brightened while she glanced at her

reflection in the full-length mirror. She smiled wide. "Okay, I think I will."

Norah wanted to tell Maddie about the deal she and Todd had made. She never kept secrets from her best friend, even though she and Todd promised they wouldn't tell anyone the truth about their arrangement. "So...Mads, about Todd..."

Maddie gave her a knowing smile. "You mean, Mr. New York?" She waggled her brows suggestively. "You two have been spending a lot of time together since he rolled into town."

Norah's cheeks burned and she tried to distract herself by swaying side to side in front of the mirror. "I already told you; he's helping me with party stuff. Plus, I can't resist his adorable puppy."

Norah arched her thick brows at Norah's reflection in the mirror. "So you're spending time with this guy because of his puppy?"

"It's a sacrifice I'm willing to make, yes." Norah grinned.

"That's funny because I didn't see his puppy in that pic you posted on Instagram," she teased.

"Ohhh right." Norah's face heated.

After Todd posted the pic on his Instagram, an attempt to make their relationship official, and after two glasses of wine, Norah thought it might be kind of fun to share it. She wanted Landon to know he wasn't the only one back out there finding someone new. Besides, now that she and Todd had made that deal, they needed to make their relationship look believable.

Maddie moved closer to her, lowering her voice conspiratorially. "Was that a tattoo I saw on his arm?" She waggled her brows. "So sexy."

"Yeah. A pine tree."

"Oooooo smart and tats? He could be the entire package."

"He might be."

"You're not fooling anyone, ya know?"

A lump lodged in Norah's throat.

"Okay, you might be fooling everyone else. But not me. I can tell you've got it bad for him."

"What? Oh." Norah laughed nervously. "I...um no. I can't."

"You can't what?" Maddie raised her brows. "Nor, you're single. So unless he's not, you can." She spun around, turning her back to Norah. "Unzip me, will you?"

Norah's fingers trembled while she pulled down the zipper of Maddie's dress.

"What's his situation anyway?"

This felt like a trap. If she told Maddie that Todd was single, she'd tell Norah to go for him. But she couldn't lie to Maddie.

"He just broke up with his girlfriend."

Maddie whipped around, giving her a devilish grin. "Perfect."

"What's perfect?"

"He's not only available, he's on the rebound."

"Well he might be, but I'm not. I've never been good at the whole one-night stand or rebound sex thing." She fidgeted with the strap of the dress that kept sliding off her shoulder.

"What better time than now to practice?"

Norah groaned, traipsing back into her dressing room, and pushing the door closed with a little more force than necessary.

"C'mon, you're young. And it's not your fault you married a complete jackass. It's time to live a little," Maddie coaxed from the other side of the door.

Norah pinched her eyes shut. She wanted to do exactly what Maddie was suggesting. She wanted to go out and hook up with a total stranger, have meaningless sex, and feel justified about it the next day. But she wasn't sure she was wired that way. Her heart was always too big, dangling on the edge of her sleeve, weighing it down.

"You know I push you because I love you?" Maddie's words vibrated through the door, muffled but clear enough to hear.

"I know," Norah's words croaked out.

She decided to wait to tell Maddie about the deal she and Todd made. Partly because they hadn't discussed the terms beyond the most crucial ones. Like, were they allowed to tell anyone the truth—that this relationship was all a big sham? But Norah also didn't want to tell her because having Maddie harass her about sex and one-night stands was the last thing she wanted to talk about right now.

Because being intimate with Todd was already about the only thing on her mind since he rolled into town.

Norah took one last glance at herself in the mirror before slipping out of the dress. She had a busy day. After dress shopping, she had two figure skating classes that afternoon. Followed by working on a playlist for the Galentine's Day party.

Music had never been her forte, at least as far as musicians, genres, and bands were concerned. She knew what she liked. But she couldn't be bothered with knowing who the artists of her favorite songs were. Or the titles of the songs, for that matter. But she knew how important music was for a party. The genre or song choices could literally make or break a party.

So, for this, she was calling in the big guns.

She pulled her phone out of her purse and sent a quick text to Todd.

> You available this afternoon?

Todd's replay came almost automatically.

> TODD
>
> What did you have in mind?

> I need help picking out songs for a playlist for the party. Do you know anything about music?

TODD

> I'm definitely your man.

Heat flared across her cheeks.

TODD

> Music is my thing.

> Can you meet me back at the house in about two hours?

TODD

> I'll be there.

Norah slid her phone back into her purse before tugging on her favorite black leggings. She couldn't stop thinking about her conversation with Maddie. Could she have a fling with Todd? Would he even want to have a fling with her? Sure, they'd kissed once. But that had been strictly for the camera.

Thinking about the kiss they'd shared got her mind spiraling. And her body humming. She wondered what it would feel like to kiss him again and mean it. What would it feel like to have those large hands touch her body? She'd already seen him practically naked, and she couldn't get the image of his bare skin, muscles, tattooed arm, and firm chest with hair trailing south out of her memory. It was like it had been permanently branded into her mind.

Maybe this idea of Maddie's wasn't the worst one she'd ever had. But how did someone go about having a fling? And was it a fling if you planned it out first?

She supposed not. Clearly, she was overthinking this, like always.

CHAPTER 13

Todd

Taking Samson for a walk in the freezing cold park should've been a brilliant idea. Todd assumed it would help get out the puppy's energy and he'd sleep so Todd and Norah could focus on creating the playlist for the party. The jaunt in the frigid late afternoon air had at least succeeded in zapping Samson's typical puppy energy, but Todd had given Samson so many treats, that he now had the worst gas.

As Norah stretched out on her stomach on the rug in her bedroom, Samson lay pressed against her leg sleeping. Todd had to admit, he was a little jealous of the gassy pup. He wouldn't mind being pressed up against Norah. Instead, he sat on the floor with his back leaned against her bed, his legs stretched out and ankles crossed.

The two of them hovered over her iPad, as she scrolled through music on Spotify and added to a playlist they had titled *Cupid is Stupid*. Seemed fitting for the type of party they were hosting and for how the two of them felt about love right about now. So far, the playlist consisted of a few love ballads from the

80's which Todd absolutely found the irony in, a few feminist songs from the 90's, and some love/hate songs from the 00's. But the playlist was minuscule. The party would last at least three hours and so far, they had about forty-five minutes of music.

Either this playlist would play on repeat, making the guests suffer through Michael Bolton's *When a Man Loves a Woman* at least four times, or there would be a lot of dead air.

For someone who claimed to be uneducated about music, Norah sure was picky about the selection. But if they had to stay there all night together until they finally created a decent playlist, he'd be willing to put in the sacrifice. He didn't mind sitting on the hard floor, missing dinner, and choosing music with this woman.

He was captivated by Norah and the way her laugh sounded when it bubbled out of her, the way her face lit up when a song interested her, the way her neck reddened and became blotchy when an intimate song came on. The few inches of bare, smooth skin showing as her shirt rose up further wasn't a terrible view either.

Nope, he didn't mind this one bit.

They listened in mostly silence while Foreigner's *I Want to Know What Love Is* sounded out. Norah pretended she was distracted by something on her phone, but he caught the redness crawling up her neck and working into her cheeks. He wouldn't admit to her that he found her embarrassment over these sexy songs completely adorable.

He could see how being referred to as cute would be infuriating to an accomplished woman like herself. But he couldn't help but think it about her at that moment. There was something about the innocent way she saw the world. Her positivity. It was magnetic.

And he wanted to relish in it.

Todd had never known a woman like Norah. Margo was a skeptic—not unusual for a lawyer. But with her, a person had to prove their value before she'd let them in or even attempt to trust them.

Being with Norah was refreshing.

The song ended and Norah cleared her throat, tapping a pen on a notebook where she'd been taking notes about the music. "So what do we think? Yay or nay?"

Todd threaded his fingers together and leaned back, resting them behind his head. "It's my professional opinion that a Valentine's Day playlist must include that song."

Her brows raised. "Your professional opinion?"

He shrugged one shoulder. "You did ask me to help you out today because I'm a music expert, right?"

She snorted. "I think you were the one who called yourself that."

"Fine. Do what you want. But you'll be doing a disservice to your guests if you don't include that song."

"Fine. You're probably right. It's a good song." She added it to the playlist, going from the rough draft in the notebook to the final on Spotify.

"Okay, what song is next?"

Samson sprawled out further on his side, reaching his paws out and Norah petted him.

"Looks like, *Here I Go Again* by Whitesnake." Norah frowned. "I'm not sure if I know this one."

"What?" he asked, bewildered. "Everyone knows this song. It's a classic."

"Well then clearly it's before my time."

He gasped. "I'm not that much older than you." He toed her in the rib causing her to yelp and jerk on the floor.

She giggled and hit *play* on the song. It started and she

glanced up at him, her mouth in an O shape before she finally said, "I love this song."

"See, told you everyone knows this song."

She moved her body on the floor to the beat of the song, looking like she was convulsing.

"Turn it up," he said.

She did and then she jumped to her feet. "This is a song you have to move to."

He chuckled, watching her.

When it got to the guitar portion during the chorus, she pretended to strum her fake guitar and headbang while jumping around the room like she was in her own personal mosh pit. It was simultaneously the most hilarious thing he'd ever seen while also being the cutest thing. He had to capture it on video. If not for Instagram, for himself.

She waved her arms encouragingly at him to get up. "C'mon, dance with me."

Todd didn't know how to dance, and he didn't want to look like an idiot in front of this girl. But her infectious personality did something inside of him, making him feel alive and prompting him to stand and wave his limbs around while shaking his hips to the music.

Samson sat up, stared at them for a moment, and then stretched before he climbed to his feet and grew excited. Todd and Norah danced together, the two of them with zero rhythm or expertise but he hadn't let loose like this in so long. He felt like a caged animal who'd just been set free.

When Samson jumped up, landing his paws on Norah's legs, and throwing her off-kilter, she slammed into Todd's chest. He gripped her forearms, holding her close. Samson let out a few barks and both Todd and Norah laughed.

"You, okay?" Todd asked, still clinging to her.

She exhaled a laugh. "Yeah, fine."

When her lips pulled into a smile, and with her body pressed against his, it did something fluttery in his chest and worked its way down the rest of his body. It quickly created a problem that was going to be obvious to her any second. There would be no hiding the fact that he was turned on.

With her face only a few inches from his, she was so close he wouldn't have to maneuver much to kiss her. But he wanted to do more than kiss her, he wanted to press his lips to her bare collarbone, to the smooth skin at her navel that she'd been showing off all night. He wanted to—

The bedroom door swung open, drawing both of their attention to the person standing in the open doorway. Todd felt his chest fall in relief when he realized it wasn't her parents. And even though he didn't know the man who stood there, he recognized him from the pictures displayed all around the Whitley's home.

The brother.

"Uhhhh...hey," he greeted. "Am I interrupting something?"

Norah stepped backward and adjusted her shirt.

Samson ran to greet the new stranger. Some watchdog he was shaping up to be, he hadn't even barked.

"Hey, Finn." Norah hurried to pick up Samson so he wouldn't escape out of the room. "You ever heard of knocking?"

"Who is this little guy?" Finn scratched Samson behind the ear.

"This is Samson. And this is Todd Langston."

"Nice to meet you." Todd went in for a handshake.

"Yeah, likewise." Finn shook his hand. "Mom mentioned she had extra company this week." He bent closer to Samson. "Man, Ava is gonna flip when she sees this guy."

"Nice change of subject." Norah narrowed her eyes at him. "Since when is it okay to just barge into my room?"

Todd didn't miss the look Finn gave him, narrowed eyes and tight jawline—accusing.

"Well, technically it isn't *your* room."

Norah shoved a finger into Finn's chest. "The hell it isn't. I live here, don't I?"

"Yeah, but it's temporary." He rubbed at the spot on his chest absentmindedly. "You're gonna get back on your feet and be on your own again soon."

Norah pulled the puppy closer to her chest, nuzzling her chin to the top of his head. "Yeah, sure."

Samson struggled to get out of her arms.

Besides the uncomfortable conversation causing Todd's fingers to twitch, Finn continued to give him an unpleasant look.

"I think Samson may need to go out." Todd took the puppy from Norah, relieved he had an excuse to get out of there, and he scooted past Finn out of the room in search of Samson's leash.

DINNER WITH THE WHITLEY FAMILY WAS...EVENTFUL, TO put it mildly. It was definitely more than Todd had been prepared for. The Whitley's were loud. They were comfortable with one another. And he felt like the odd man out, either being easily left out of the conversation or being the topic of it since he was technically the guest.

Not only were Finn and his wife, Nina, and their two kids visiting for the rest of the week, but Isabella and Leo were there for dinner too, as well as their neighbor, Howard—who Todd discovered much too late was Norah's ex-father-in-law.

"What kind of lawyer are you, son?" Mr. Whitley asked Todd.

"Corporate," he answered.

"So, what's it like being a lawyer?" Howard asked him right after Todd had just taken a big bite of chili.

After he chewed and swallowed quickly, he wiped his mouth with a napkin before answering. "To be honest, it's pretty boring. There's lots of time being holed up in an office, alone, reviewing cases, and writing briefs and contracts."

Howard screwed up his face. "I thought lawyers were always in a courtroom, delivering powerful speeches in front of juries?"

Todd chuckled. "I think the movies have given most people a jaded view of what it's like being a lawyer."

"But I bet the money is good," Mr. Whitley chimed in.

"Dad," Norah and Isabella hissed in unison.

"It's fine," Todd assured them. "My salary is pretty good. I'm lucky enough to work for one of the best firms in Manhattan."

Mrs. Whitley hovered over him with a pitcher of ice water, refilling his glass. "That's impressive."

"Actually," Isabella said, "Todd is up for a big promotion. He's being considered as partner."

Todd whipped his head in Isabella's direction. He hadn't told her. Fear prickled his skin. Had Margo told Isabella about the stipulations of the promotion? Did she know that he and Margo were in a weird combat to the death for the one position as partner at the firm?

When he swung his attention back, he found all eyes around the table focused on him, including Norah's. Guilt smeared her expression. She was not a very good liar. Which meant she wouldn't make a very good lawyer either. What if she cracked under the pressure and told someone? He couldn't risk it. If Isabella found out, Margo would be soon to follow? And if Margo found out—well, he could forget about not only the promotion but a job at Santos and Cho period.

"That sounds promising," Mr. Whitley said.

Todd repeatedly folded and unfolded the napkin resting on his lap. "Yeah, I'm excited about it. But I'm up against some tough contenders."

Isabella cleared her throat. "Like his ex-girlfriend."

Todd's jaw dropped. Shit.

"Oh?" Mrs. Whitley questioned as she joined the rest of them at the table once again. "That ought to keep things interesting."

"Nothing like a little competition." Mr. Whitley jutted out his chin.

"I'm sure the best person for the job will get it," Isabella said, giving him a reassuring smile.

Or was it a knowing smile? As in—she knew exactly what he was up to with Norah. If she didn't know about the stipulations, Todd wasn't so sure who Isabella thought the best person was. Him or Margo? The three of them had been an inseparable trio all through college and practically since. Who was she rooting for?

"Grandma, guess what?" Finn's daughter, Ava called. "I got thirty-two Valentine's cards in my mailbox at school today."

"Wow. Aren't you special, sweets? That's a lot of friends."

Sneaking a glance at Norah across the table, her focus remained on her plate. He stretched out his leg until it reached what he hoped was her foot. Then he proceeded to glide his own foot up the back of her calf. Her eyes flashed up at him, sending his heart skidding. A smile snuck onto her lips. A bit of relief filled him.

As soon as Norah finished eating and stood, carrying her dishes into the kitchen, Todd sprang to his feet and followed her. No way was he about to be left alone with the wolves. Okay, maybe he was exaggerating. They were plenty nice. Even Howard, especially Howard. He had brought over a crockpot of chili and he and Mrs. Whitley appeared to have some kind of ongoing chili feud going on. It was comical to witness.

But after nearly two hours of feeling like he was in the hot seat—he was done.

"Hey," he whispered into Norah's back, waiting to rinse his plate in the sink. "You wanna get out of here?"

She shot a mischievous grin over her shoulder. The kind that caused him to suck in a breath.

He gave a nonchalant shrug. "Samson could probably use a walk. And I don't really want to go alone. It's dark out there and I don't know my way around this neighborhood."

She stepped aside, allowing him access to the sink, but didn't move too far. "Are you scared, Mr. Langston?"

He grinned. "Maybe a little."

"Hey, what are you two being so secretive about in here?" Isabella asked from behind them.

"Just talking about taking Samson for a walk."

"Oh yeah?" Isabella's accusatory eyes flicked back and forth between them. "Want some company?"

Todd loaded his bowl into the dishwasher, hoping Isabella couldn't see the disappointment on his face. He shouldn't be opposed to the idea. He hadn't come all the way from New York to only be Norah's date to a party, he wanted to spend time with Isabella too.

But he had the increasing urge to spend the rest of the evening with Norah, alone. Heck, maybe the rest of the week alone with her. When she'd fallen on top of him earlier and he'd caught a whiff of her cherry blossom-scented hair, he hadn't been able to think about anything else except kissing her.

"Sure," Norah finally said.

Isabella turned the faucet on, spraying the water over her dishes. "I have an idea. Why don't we walk up to the school and skate for a while?"

"Seriously?" Norah asked, eyes wide. "But you hate skating."

"I don't hate skating. I'm not very good at it, but I've never hated it."

Norah's fingers fidgeted with the hem of her sweater, drawing Todd's attention there, to the soft, bare skin of her torso.

"Todd doesn't have skates," she said.

"Between all the extras we've got around this house and the Hoffmans, I'm sure we have a pair that will fit him." Isabella raised her brows, looking at him expectantly. "What do you say?"

What could he say? *No, I'd rather spend the evening alone with your sister.*

"Sounds great."

"Yay!" Isabella clapped once.

"What's going on?" Finn entered the kitchen, hands propped on his hips.

Despite the open floor plan, the room felt stagnant and overcrowded. And Todd began planning his exit strategy.

"Skating at the school. You and Nina in?"

"Heck yes, we're in. Let me double-check if Mom and Dad can watch the kids."

Isabella left the kitchen looking rather pleased and following behind Finn.

Once alone, Norah stepped closer to Todd. So close, her breathy words heated his neck. "You have no idea what you just agreed to."

The warning was followed up with a defeated look shining

in Norah's eyes that had him clutching his twisted stomach. "That bad, huh?"

"Let me just say, if you were hoping for a quiet evening; you're going to be wildly disappointed." She shuffled out of the kitchen.

Didn't he know it.

Todd already felt the dread, like a massive weight sitting at the pit of his stomach. But how would he get out of it now? And skating? He'd already proven he wasn't a pro in that activity.

He dashed out of the kitchen, tugging on Norah's sweater in the hallway. "Is it too late to get out of this?"

She spun around and stepped in close, nearly pressing her chest against him. "Nope. Sorry. Gonna have to ride it out now."

He nearly lost his train of thought because of her proximity. Unable to resist, he wrapped an arm around her, a hand against her low back and drawing her even closer. "Any tips?" he asked, low and husky.

Norah blinked up at him. She pushed her lips into a thought before finally saying, "If you wanna stay on Finn's good side, no cursing. He hates it. Nina is sweet and the easiest to please. And Isabella is simple, you know you just have to let her win. Leo? Just keep Izzy happy."

"Good to know. Thanks." Reluctantly, he released the pressure on her back.

But she didn't relent and remained pressed against him. "What about me?" Her words came out breathy.

"What about you?"

"Need tips for surviving a night with me?"

His brows shot up. *Surviving a night with her?* Man, what he wouldn't give to experience that.

He swallowed. "I don't think I need any pointers in that department."

She snorted, glancing over her shoulder. She trailed her finger down his chest and torso, slow and sensual. There was no mistaking the flirting here.

At least he hoped not.

Her finger stopped at the top of his belt, and he sucked in a breath.

"We'll just see about that," she whispered before taking a few steps backward and turning around.

Todd released a shaky breath as he watched her disappear down the hall. He stood there for a moment trying to compose himself and shoved a frustrated hand through his hair.

This woman was turning him inside out.

He had no off switch. Nope. He was completely and fully turned on. He wanted her. And if the two of them didn't do something about it soon, and act on this attraction, he was going to burst.

CHAPTER 14

Norah

MADDIE

Did you talk to Mr. New York?

What's the verdict?

One night stand or long distance?

The jury is still out.

MADDIE

Better figure it out soon, girl. Before your
heart gets involved.

I t was probably already too late for that.

APPARENTLY, NORAH HAD MISTAKEN THE FLIRTATIOUS
banter between her and Todd. Because once at the old school,

ice skates laced around his feet, Todd had barely left Izzy's side. Norah wasn't jealous.

She wasn't.

It took a lot for her to get jealous. And she wasn't stupid, she knew nothing was going on between Izzy and Todd. They were only friends. And Izzy was crazy about Leo. The two could hardly keep their hands off each other—something she used to find irritating but now found really sweet.

But maybe Norah was jealous of the history Izzy and Todd shared. They'd been friends for years. Izzy knew things about him that maybe she'd never know.

While Leo, Isabella, Finn, Nina, and Todd skated around the frozen rink together, Norah kept mostly to herself. Once you were professionally trained, skating for fun felt unnatural to her. It was sometimes difficult for her to shed the structure and just let go.

"We're gonna head back to the house, I'm freezing," Nina called from the bleachers, slipping her skates off.

"Hopefully Mom has some hot cocoa waiting." Finn shoved his ice skates underneath his arm and held a hand out for his wife.

Nina rolled her eyes fondly at him while Finn hoisted her off the bleachers. "You're such a kid."

"Hopefully she has some peppermint vodka." Norah waggled her brows.

Nina pointed at her. "Now you're talking."

"Leo and I should probably head home. He's going to Denver in the morning for a shoot and I have another deadline."

"Still leading a busy life even in Pineridge, I see," Todd mused.

Isabella winced. "Guilty."

Norah noticed Todd didn't seem to be in a hurry like the rest of them as he stayed on the ice near her, skates still intact.

"Well, you two have a good night." Todd gave them a chin nod.

"You guys aren't heading back to the house yet?" Isabella pinned both Norah and Todd with a look, chewing her bottom lip.

Norah knew exactly what that habit meant; Izzy was anxious. If Izzy only knew about the deal she'd agreed to.

When she glanced at Todd, he held her gaze, and all her previously frozen body parts warmed in an instant.

"I think we'll stay out a little longer. Todd is just getting the hang of it."

"You think so?" Todd lifted his brows.

"C'mon." Leo tugged on Isabella's hand, and she seemed to hesitate for a moment longer before eventually giving in.

"Okay, fine. Have fun. And Langston, let's try to meet for lunch tomorrow."

"Sounds great."

"Oh, and Norah, you're supposed to pick up the cotton candy machine from the elementary school tomorrow."

Norah suppressed a groan. "I remember."

"Okay, night," Leo called as he continued to drag Izzy away.

As her siblings turned into dark shadowy specks against the brightly lit snow, Norah skated backward, releasing a pent-up sigh. Finn and Isabella were acting so strange, both treating her like she was a child. She hadn't minded when they looked out for her when she was young, but she was a grown adult. And she wasn't that naïve, soft girl anymore.

Suddenly she smacked against something hard—Todd's chest. She twirled around in his arms that gripped her waist and found herself staring directly into his green eyes. Instantly her body went limp, her legs turning into wet noodles, and it was a good thing he was still holding her.

"You okay?" His voice seemed to come out in a growl, rough and scratchy.

"What? Yeah," she stumbled over her words. "Why?"

He released her then, pushing a hand through his messy hair. "You just haven't seemed like yourself tonight."

Pushing against his chest, she skated backward and away from him. "Sometimes my siblings have that effect on me."

He stood there, unmoving, watching her with an intense gaze. Maybe she should've felt self-conscious or exposed, but she didn't. The streetlamps illuminated the ice, causing it to gleam and sparkle. The look of the ice, and the smell of it, had always been two of her favorite things. They calmed her, making her feel at home.

It was serene being out on the ice. Here, she could forget about her current situation. About Landon, and their failed marriage, about living back at her parent's home, about the unsettled feeling she'd had since. Here, she could push away the negative thoughts that tried to consume her, tried to make her feel less than, and as if she wasn't enough.

Here, she was whole.

Skating up next to him, Norah slowed and reached out for his hand. A grin tugged at one side of his mouth, and he slipped his cold hand into hers, her body shuttering at the contact. She yanked him along with her and he jerkily followed.

She stifled a laugh but tried to recover. "You're doing great."

"You're lying. But thank you. I told you; I've only been skating a handful of times."

Norah maneuvered herself in front of Todd, taking hold of his other hand and she skated backward. "This is how I teach my toddlers."

"Gee, thanks," he muttered.

She snickered. "But don't worry, you're doing way better than them. They have bumpers on their skates."

"Maybe I should've opted for a pair like that. Would probably help combat the number of times I've fallen."

"At least you've mastered the correct way to fall now."

"Silver lining."

She smiled, watching him, and finding the determination in his green eyes an anomaly. Todd came across as a person who was driven and goal-oriented. Being around him was inspiring.

Landon only ever skated with her during her family's tradition of Eight days of Christmas and most of the time he'd end up on the bleachers sipping hot cocoa.

But Todd was actually trying.

"So, tell me some things a girlfriend should know," she began.

"Okay, like what?"

"Like, where'd you grow up?" she asked.

"New Jersey." He didn't take his attention off his feet, studying them as they shuffled along the ice. "Then when I was going to college in New York, I fell in love, so I stayed."

Her stomach clenched and she lowered her head. "Right. Margo."

"No. New York. I fell in love with New York."

There was a flutter in her chest as she lifted her gaze to meet his. This was dangerous territory, talking about love and Margo. She needed to change the subject.

"And you never went skating there?"

"Not never. I said I went a handful of times. You can't live in New York and not go skating at The Rink at Rockefeller Center. And you can't live there without going on at least one first date there either."

She laughed. "You went skating on a first date?"

"A couple first dates, yep."

"And was there ever a second date?" She held in a laugh.

"Ha, smart ass. But no."

She couldn't help herself; she barked out a laugh, still skating backward while his eyes darted from her to his feet.

"What about you?" he asked.

"What about me, what? The date thing?"

"No." He smiled. "Did you grow up here?"

"Yep. Pineridge, born and raised."

"Do you ever think about leaving?"

Norah looked at him, and studied his face, the pronounced cheekbones, the messy hair flopping onto his forehead, and the light scruff on his jawline. She'd never wanted to leave Pineridge. Sure, she joked about it, especially lately. But she loved it here. And yet, for the first time in her life, her mind wondered what it would be like to leave.

If other places in the world had men like Todd—attractive, sweet, intelligent—tucked away in caveats, maybe she should explore and discover who else was out there.

But Pineridge was her home. And she wasn't adventurous. She was what people from small towns called a *lifer*.

"Pineridge is my home. I love it here."

"Okay, I'm sorry, but, besides your family, what do you love about this place so much?"

The question threw her a bit. Her throat thickened, and she opened her mouth to speak but clamped it shut again. Saying she loved living in Pineridge had always been her go-to response. What *did* she love about living here?

He continued. "Not that I can't tell this place is great already. But I'm genuinely curious what you love about it."

She shrugged her shoulders. "What isn't to love? The town is small. You get to know your neighbors. People care about one another. The best brewery in the world is just down the road. And there are three, *three*," she emphasized, "ice rinks."

He laughed. "Okay, okay, I get it."

"Did I forget to tell you about the Daily Grind and how the best barista works there? She makes the perfect caramel macchiato." Norah gripped his hands a bit tighter, trying not to be distracted while his thumbs rubbed across the tops of her knuckles sending goosebumps shooting down her arms.

"It sounds nice. It does. I just don't know if it would be enough to keep me in the same town."

"Pineridge is awesome. We're not this little ho-dunk town. I'll have you know; we're very well known all over the US."

"Yeah?" His brows lifted. "Okay, then tell me, what is it that puts Pineridge, Colorado on the map?"

She finally let go of his hands and they slowed to nearly a stop.

"For starters, have you heard about The Renovation Dudes?"

"Actually, I have."

"See. Map." She pointed at him, sounding overly confident for such a small thing. So what if a popular show was filmed in town and aired on the well-known HGTV station. She needed to give him more. Something on a personal level. "And we have a love lock bridge."

"Oh, right. What even is a love lock bridge?" He stopped skating and rested his hands on his thighs, breathing in an accelerated rhythm.

"You've never heard of a love lock bridge?" She skated circles around him, and then back and forth. "They're starting to pop up all over. I think maybe the most popular is in Paris. Ours has been around forever. My parents even have a lock on it. People travel from the East Coast just to see it and take pictures."

"Okay, if people are traveling that far just to get a picture of this bridge, then I guess it's something I need to see while I'm here."

"Just Google it. You'll find it." She skated to a stop in front of him, spraying ice in his direction.

"I was hoping you'd take me there." He wrestled his fingers through his hair. "How about tomorrow? I mean, what better way for a tourist to see the famous Pineridge Love Lock Bridge than with a local tour guide?" He wiggled his brows, and her insides did a weird wiggle of their own.

"Okay. How about you help me pick up the cotton candy machine and then I'll take you to the love lock bridge?"

"A picture of us on this famous bridge...kissing...will be perfect for Instagram."

"Right," she mumbled.

Her heart sank in her chest like it was attached to an anchor. Of course, it would be perfect. That's what they were doing anyway. Creating a fake relationship to make Landon jealous and make Todd's bosses think they were a real couple.

So he caught her off guard when he gripped her hips and tugged her toward him. She inhaled a sharp breath. "Maybe we should practice now?"

She swallowed. "Now?"

He had her so close, her chest thrust against him with each deep inhale and elongated exhale.

But just as she lifted her chin to gaze hopefully into his eyes, her stomach tight with anticipation, his feet slipped from underneath him and his body tumbled to the ice in one swoop, yanking her right along with him.

Norah held her breath and pinched her eyes shut, bracing herself for the blow. But as she landed against the sturdiness of Todd's chest, his hands clutching her waist, she wasn't in pain.

Instead, her senses were heightened, overloaded. An intense yearning wriggled through her.

She wouldn't mind practicing if it meant being in this position.

He moaned but didn't loosen his grip on her.

"You okay?" she asked, peering down at him.

"Uh, yeah, I think so," he whispered into her neck.

This was dangerous. Their relationship was supposed to be fake. Teetering on the edge of fake and reality was like walking a tightrope. Getting attached to this man wasn't an option.

She pressed a hand to his chest, preparing to climb off him, but Todd grasped her snuggly against him. She tilted her chin, lifting her brows in question.

"I think I just need to lay here for a minute." His eyes held hers, dark and smoldering. A slow smile spread on his lips, growing wider with each second.

She nudged him in the chest. "You're sure enjoying this, aren't you?"

"Maybe a little," his voice rumbled against her skin.

Norah narrowed her eyes and smirked at him. But as dangerous as it was, she was in no hurry to climb off him. With his hard, warm body pressed against hers, she wanted to curl into him and stay there all night. She wanted to live there—in the safe comfort.

As the craving for him deepened, suddenly feeling his rock-hard arousal beneath her, heat pooled between her thighs. Her breathing quickened and a dizzy sensation filled her head. She wasn't imagining his attraction to her this time. It was right there, firm and thrusting against her.

He wanted her.

Norah shut off the part of her brain that was screaming, "This is fake! Fake, fake, fake!" and just went along with what she felt. Todd squeezed her hip before sliding his hand up her side, gliding his chilled fingers across the exposed skin on her neck. She swallowed when he parted his lips, his tongue darting out to lick them. She craved for him to run his tongue along her lip, her neck, everywhere.

"Is this...okay?" he whispered.

"Mmmhmm," is all she could say, afraid that if she opened her mouth to speak, she'd tell him exactly what she wanted.

He clutched his hand around the back of her neck, guiding her mouth closer to his. Closer. Closer. Until a rush of hot breath wafted over her lips and a shiver convulsed through her. She licked her lips self-consciously and Todd's eyes darted there, staring, watching, studying.

"I really want to kiss you right now," he finally said, his long fingers stroking and kneading the back of her neck.

"What's stopping you?" she said, sounding desperate. Because that's exactly how she felt. Greedy and hungry for him. She gripped the collar of his coat, her lust for him blooming without control.

"You," he responded, breathlessly.

Norah reared back slightly and blinked at him. "Me?"

"I just want to make sure that you're sure. That you're okay with this."

Was he kidding her right now? All her childhood fantasies were about to come true. Todd Langston wanted to kiss her. Like, for real. Teen Norah would die.

She rocked her hips against him, and a rumbling groan escaped his throat. She lowered her chin and hovered her lips over his, speaking in a low, hushed voice, "I think it should be obvious by now, that I'm more than okay with this."

"Thank God," he said.

He tethered his fingers in her hair, and slowly guided her mouth to his, sliding his lips against hers. He kissed her gently, with the kind of carefulness that made her insides want to both melt and explode all at the same time. As his hand tugged on her hair, a quiet moan escaped her.

Sparks of desire lit inside of her as he deepened the kiss, shoving his tongue into her mouth and wrestling with hers. She let go of his collar and slid her hands around the back of his neck, her fingers itching to touch him anywhere and everywhere.

But making out on the cold, hard ice rink was much hotter in her mind than it was to experience in real life. Her fingertips trembled against his skin and her body shivered against him, the chill in the night air biting against her back. Regretfully, she pulled back from the intoxicating kissing, pressing one more soft peck to Todd's lips before exhaling a deep sigh.

"We should go," she said.

"What do you mean, isn't this romantic?" He chuckled.

It actually was.

Norah had probably never shared a more romantic kiss before. And despite how cold she was, it was probably also the hottest kiss she'd ever shared before too. That's why it was nearly killing her to end it. But really, how much further could their make-out session go, out here, in a public area, houses nearby?

She took her time, slowly pushing against his chest and climbing off him. Once steady on her feet, he propped on his elbows gazing up at her, his eyes dark and hungry. A smile tugged at her lips.

"C'mon, Mr. Langston," she teased, "let's go." She held her hands out to him and yanked him up.

Todd rubbed at the back of his neck. "What are the chances we'll be able to pick up where we just left off tomorrow?"

She pushed off the toe pick, before spinning around and

skating backward toward the edge of the rink. "I'd say, the chances are very good." She shot him a smile and he watched her, his eyes brimming with dark mischief.

CHAPTER 15

Todd

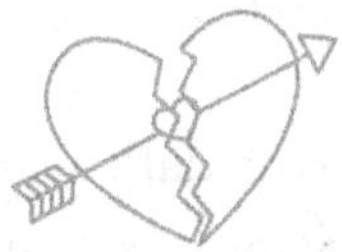

When Todd opened his eyes, the room glowed with the faint morning light of the new day. It wasn't bright enough to even be a decent hour, telling him it was way too early to be awake. He scrubbed his hands over his face, being extra careful to not make a sound and wake up Samson.

After kissing Norah at the rink the day before, the memory of her body pressed against his, her hips rocking into him, Todd had tossed and turned all night. To say he was sexually frustrated would've been an understatement. He'd never wanted to take a woman back home with him more badly than he had the night before.

Except he wasn't at home.

He was in this small, snowy town that reminded him more of what you'd see inside a snow globe rather than a real place. Not only that, but he was also staying at Norah's parent's house. And she was in the room next to his. Which had only made his desire for her increase tenfold. And in turn, making sleep that much more impossible.

He should be given a medal for the restraint he had the night before. Hell, a gold medal. The kind of control he'd had was surely Olympic Games medal-winning worthy.

Since he clearly wasn't going to get any more sleep, he kicked off the covers. He glanced at the kennel where Samson was already sitting up, wagging his tail. He chuckled to himself while he stood and stretched.

"Hold on, buddy."

He dressed in a pair of dark jeans, a long-sleeved white Henley, and a flannel. Samson sat up and whimpered while Todd buttoned the flannel.

Opening the kennel, Samson bounded out and Todd snuggled the puppy to his chest. He latched the leash to his collar. "Need to go potty?"

Samson wriggled to get out of his arms, but Todd carried him down the hall, not wanting to risk the puppy having an accident. He tiptoed down the stairs and slipped his feet into his boots before stepping outside and into the cold morning.

Samson pulled Todd down the front steps and across the snowy grass. Todd yanked the leash, directing the puppy toward the driveway. Samson pounced on a small pile of snow, amusing Todd. His puppy was awesome. Full of personality.

Margo may not have appreciated him, but Norah had already taken to him. She saw his potential and was already trying to teach him commands beyond *sit* and *lay down*.

Back inside the house, Todd found the Whitley's kitchen empty. He was relieved when he noticed the coffee pot full of the hot brew. He filled Samson's food dish before searching the cupboards for a mug.

"Morning," a sweet voice sounded behind him.

His stomach clenched as he whirled around.

Norah stood before him, hair pulled into a mess on top of her head, plastic-framed glasses perched on her upturned nose, and a matching set of pink thermal pajamas. She was a sight to behold. He wanted to snap a mental picture of her, standing there, looking absolutely adorable but in the sexiest way possible.

She blushed and hell, he'd been staring at her for far too long.

He cleared his throat. "Morning."

Norah shuffled around him, barefoot and tempting, he should stuff his hands into his pockets, so he didn't reach out and grab a hold of her.

She headed straight for a cupboard displaying a massive selection of mugs, choosing two and handing him one.

"You're up early," she mused.

"Couldn't sleep."

Todd studied the mug so he wouldn't be tempted to check her out further. It was white with a mountain scene and the words *Pineridge, Colorado* scrawled along the bottom.

Norah poured the steaming coffee into her mug first before gesturing for him to put his cup out and she filled his too. "Same here," she finally admitted.

Their eyes clicked for a brief moment—electricity shooting straight through his veins and waking up every single one of his body parts. Forget caffeine. All he needed was a shot of this woman. A simple look, a smile, a kiss. He'd take all of it.

He'd take all of *her*.

"Why? You got something on your mind?" he teased.

The corner of her mouth lifted, and a captivating blush crept across her cheeks.

She shrugged a shoulder. "Maybe."

After the kiss they shared, now she was going to play hard to get? He smirked. At some point, the two of them were going to pick up where they left off the night before. He had no doubt in his mind. It was obvious they were attracted to one another.

They either had to bang this out and get it out of their systems or it would help them discover if there was something more between them.

Todd wasn't sure which he was hoping for.

As long as their feelings didn't get in the way of the deal they made, he didn't see the harm in taking this fake relationship to the next level.

TODD HADN'T KNOWN EXACTLY WHAT HE'D AGREED TO until he was at the elementary school with Norah, staring down at the prehistoric cotton candy machine.

He studied it, brows furrowed. "Does this thing even work?"

The P.E. teacher, Mr. Brannon pushed off his ball cap and wiped his sweaty brow. It was maybe forty-five degrees out, but the man's perspiration gave Todd the indication of just how heavy this old machine was. He'd gotten it on a hand truck for them, but now it was clear he had finished his job.

"Oh yes, it works just fine. Better than fine." Mr. Brannon, a man in his late sixties returned the hat to his head. "As long as you follow the instructions, you'll have this baby purring and spinning up some beautiful fluffy candy."

"Thank you, Mr. Brannon. We really appreciate it."

Norah patted the older man's arm like he was fragile. She was always doing things like that—touching a person on the arm, giving someone a kiss on the cheek, patting their back. She was kind and gentle and it was obvious the people in Pineridge adored her.

"Just be sure to bring it back in one piece. The kids will need it for their carnival this spring," Mr. Brannon said.

Todd took that as their cue to leave.

He grabbed a hold of the handle on the dolly, tipped it back on its two wheels, and held the weight of it while Norah said goodbye.

"I'll bring it back right after the party. All intact. Promise." Norah gave Mr. Brannon a wave before they both turned to leave.

After loading the machine into the back of Leo's truck and tying it down, Todd jumped into the passenger seat. "It's a good thing Leo let you borrow his truck. I don't think that thing would fit in my Jeep."

"Or my SUV," Norah countered, buckling her seatbelt. "I told you it was old and heavy."

Norah started the engine and pulled away from the curb, heading back onto the main road. The guilt over leaving Samson with the Whitleys again rattled him. He knew Leo wouldn't want the puppy roaming free in the truck and it was way too cold to put him in the back. But Samson was his dog and his responsibility.

"So, Mr. Langston," Norah peered over her shoulder at him, her long lashes distracting him from the guilt he felt only seconds before. "Are you ready to get your mind blown?" She smiled and his eyes went to her mouth.

A nervous chuckle bubbled out of his throat. "Uh...what?"

"You said you wanted to know what put Pineridge on the map. Remember?" She'd already turned her attention back onto the road.

"Oh, right. Yes. The famous love lock bridge." He rubbed his palms down his jeans. "I'm ready."

"Trust me, you won't be disappointed."

"I trust you," the words slid out easily.

Todd didn't trust many people. He had trusted Margo and look where that had gotten him.

She glanced at him again, her pink lips curving into a smile and his heart drummed in his chest.

"Good," she said.

He hated that not only did he yearn to tear this woman's clothes off, but he wanted to get inside her head, and learn all her likes and dislikes, her dreams, and her fears. He craved to just be near her, to catch a hint of that cherry blossom-scented hair again.

After what felt like only moments, Norah cut the engine of the truck. Todd glanced around and found them parked near what looked like a park. The old, dirty snow had been shoveled into piles leaving the sidewalks clear. Tall pine trees surrounded the park and there was a bridge a couple hundred feet up ahead.

Sliding out of the truck, Todd zipped up his jacket. The snow might've been melting but there was a chill in the air that afternoon as the wind picked up. Norah moved around the front of the truck and shoved her hands into the pockets of her coat. She had on a gray beanie hat today, and her long, auburn hair hung down framing her face. Dressed in fitted jeans that hugged her curves and a pair of Timberland's, she looked like she could be posing for an ad for the brand of boots.

Todd met her in front of the truck, and he found her eyes lit up.

"C'mon, this way." She gestured with her chin, and he followed her.

He thought he might follow her anywhere—to this famous bridge, to a longer stay in Pineridge, heck, he'd probably follow her to the moon if given the chance.

Norah shuffled along the cleared sidewalk, and he walked next to her, the two not speaking. Since he wasn't sure how many more chances they'd get to be alone this week, he wanted to say something to her. Tell her how much he'd enjoyed spending time with her and getting to know her the past few days. And thank her for agreeing to be his fake girlfriend.

But then he saw it. The Love Lock Bridge stretched over a narrow section of the river. The water was beautiful, black, and wintry. Though he imagined it looked better when it was either covered in snow or clear in the summer. Right now, with the snow melting, the banks around it looked soggy.

"It's just up ahead. You ready?" Norah lifted her eyebrows.

Todd slid his phone from his pocket. If this was as famous as Norah had let on, he'd need pictures.

"Ready." He held up his phone.

They stepped off the sidewalk and onto the bridge. And then the locks came into full view. The metal railing stretching over the length of the bridge was put there for safety, but you could no longer see the fencing on most of the rail. Padlocks overlapped padlocks in most areas of the bridge, displaying all different colors. Some were your typical golden bronze, some silver, and others an assortment of colors ranging from blue to hot pink.

Norah was right about something—he had never seen anything like it.

"I gotta admit," Todd finally said, "I was not expecting so many."

"It's incredible, isn't it?"

Todd tore his eyes away from the locks and looked at her for a moment, taking in her demeanor. She was proud of this. It wasn't only because the landmark put Pineridge on the map. She took pride in it as a resident. It was a part of Pineridge's history. And too late, he realized, most likely it was part of *her* history.

"What's most fascinating to me is that there's so many

people who think they loved each other enough to go through this trouble," he said.

Sure, maybe he was a little bitter about love these days. But wasn't she? She'd been cheated on. And early in her marriage.

When she remained quiet next to him, he looked at her, studying her and trying to gauge her thoughts.

"If you love someone," she mumbled, shrugging, "it's not trouble. It's like that final declaration of commitment."

"Ha! Silly me, I thought that was what marriage was for," he said sarcastically.

"This is different. This is a symbol. And anyone from all over the United States, or the world even, could come here and see it."

Todd pursed his lips. "I guess."

He wasn't sure why he was playing off how cool this bridge was. Because he definitely found it fascinating. Maybe because he knew Norah most likely had a lock on this bridge. And he didn't like the jealousy that snaked in between his rib cage at the thought.

He held out his phone and took a few photos. Zooming in, he crouched down and tried to get a few shots of some of the locks with initials and names either scrawled with a Sharpie or etched into the metal. Todd lifted a few. One had a faded red ribbon tied to the top. And another had the words indicating that one of the lovers had died. There was a pang in his chest he couldn't explain even to himself. He didn't know this Dorothea and Ray and yet he felt the loss cut deep in his heart for these two by simply touching the cold metal lock.

He pushed himself to stand and cleared his throat. "You're right. This is different."

"Told ya," she said.

"And you were also right about something else."

"What's that?"

He set his fingertips on both sides of his head at his temples and then made the gesture for *mind-blown*.

She snorted a laugh.

"No, but I'm serious. This is pretty special. I get why people come to see it." He shoved his phone back into his front jeans pocket. "Thanks for showing it to me."

She tugged the beanie hat further over her ears. "You're welcome."

They were quiet for a moment, Todd still lost in thought over this bridge, over the locks and their meanings. These belonged to real people.

A young couple holding hands shuffled over the bridge. Todd stepped back, moving closer to Norah but he couldn't help from keeping an eye on the couple. They studied the fence and the locks for a good few minutes before they crouched and together, they hooked a gold lock around the fence, clasping it in place. They kissed and Todd glanced away rubbing at the back of his neck, feeling guilty for intruding on this intimate moment of theirs.

When the couple stood again, Todd rushed toward them, his feet having a mind of their own. "Hey, do you guys want me to take a picture of you?"

"Oh, really? Sure, that would be great. Thank you." The young woman gave him her phone.

"It's no problem." Todd took a few pictures for them before handing back the phone.

"These are perfect, thanks." The woman scrolled through the pictures he'd taken. "We just got married and we're on our honeymoon."

"And you came here? To Pineridge, Colorado? For your honeymoon?"

"Yep. We had to come here to the Love Lock Bridge."

"Wait. So you're telling me you planned your honeymoon around the Love Lock Bridge?"

The man shrugged. "I mean, it's our honeymoon. It doesn't matter where we are. It's not like we're leaving our room much anyway." He gazed down at his new bride, smiling.

Todd chuckled. "Right."

"Thanks again," the woman said, taking her husband's hand.

"Congratulations," Norah called.

After the couple was out of earshot, Norah elbowed him. "See, we're on the map."

Sticking his hands up in surrender, he said, "Hey, I'm a believer, you don't have to try to convince me any longer."

She smiled.

"So..." he began but hesitated. "Do you have a lock on this bridge?"

Her shoulders slumped and she dropped her chin to her chest. "I do," she muttered.

"Oh yeah?" He hoped his tone sounded nonchalant.

"Only one."

And he dreaded what she was about to say.

"Landon and I put one on."

His attention drew to her, hearing the emotion in her voice.

She pulled her bottom lip in between her teeth before finally releasing a shaky sigh. "This is where he proposed."

Oh hell. Well, that changed everything. He suddenly hated this place. Hated this bridge and everything it stood for.

But then he quickly wondered, why didn't she?

"You didn't have to bring me here. You know...if it makes you sad?"

"It does make me sad," she said, peering at the locks while she continued speaking, "but I'm not resentful. I still think this bridge is magical. Sure, there are probably a ton of silly locks, and some short-term high school relationships. But there are also ones that have been here for years, decades even." She swiped at the hair the wind pushed into her face. "This bridge and all these locks give me hope. My story isn't finished yet. And I'll get to put a lock on there again—this time that lasts forever."

She did look wistful, but she couldn't hide the sadness in her eyes and the pain. She probably thought of Landon and their failed marriage every time she passed this park, every time she thought of the bridge and the locks, every time the love lock bridge showed up in the news or someone mentioned it. He hated to think about it hurting her. He wanted to do something about it.

"I'm sure you will," was all he said.

She glanced his way, eyes watering, and her lips pulled into a small smile.

He needed to come up with a way to fix this for her.

CHAPTER 16
Norah

After the visit to the love lock bridge, Norah and Todd returned to the Whitley home. She'd invited Maddie to come over to help her pull off her brilliant idea of inviting everyone in Pineridge—despite having a date or not—to the Galentine's party. Why should it be exclusive to only couples when the theme had strayed so far from the original plan anyway?

It was clear Todd was hesitant, worried about upsetting Izzy. But Maddie was all in. The wrath of Norah's big sister not too worrisome apparently. She didn't want to admit to herself that she might've had an ulterior motive. Maddie's opinion was important to her. And even though Norah hadn't told her about the deal, she needed to know what Maddie thought of him. Norah had been blabbing about her crush on Todd since she was a young teenager. This would be a chance for Maddie to get to know him.

The three of them sat cross legged on the floor in Norah's room, Samson stretched out with his back resting against Norah's leg. The puppy had taken a liking to her, and she couldn't resist him either. She'd spent more time with Samson this week than with Netflix and that was saying something. She tried not to think about Todd and Samson leaving in a few days.

"We have to make sure Isabella doesn't see the invite," Norah said, petting Samson's side. "If she finds out, she'll freak."

Todd rubbed at the back of his neck, his legs stretched out in front of him, and feet crossed at the ankles. He had on a long-sleeved black shirt, Samson's light-colored hair clinging to it. Norah tried to focus, but his long body, those long fingers at the nape of his neck caused a distraction of longing to swoop low in her belly.

"You sure we can't just tell her?" Todd asked.

"What? No."

"Can't. She'd be pissed," Maddie said.

"But don't you think she'll be more pissed if we don't?"

Norah snorted. "Absolutely."

"I thought you and Isabella were friends? You know how she is, right?" Maddie asked.

"Oh yeah, I know how she is. I just feel bad. She's gone through a lot of trouble to plan this party." Todd plucked a few Samson hairs off the front of his shirt.

"Actually, *I've* gone through a lot of trouble," Norah corrected. "She's hardly done anything since she came up with this idea. And it was super sweet of her to want to throw this party for me, but after talking to a lot of people in town, they don't have a date or don't want one."

"I don't need a man to attend a party," Maddie said flatly.

Norah didn't *need* a man either.

But did she want a man to link arms with at the party so she wouldn't have to attend solo? Yes. Especially if that man was a tall, smart, and handsome man with unruly sexy hair. It sure beat her nights of solitude filled with yoga pants, wine, and Netflix.

And no, she'd never done a day of yoga in her life.

"Okay, tell me your genius plan of getting the word around without Isabella finding out," Todd said.

"Well lucky for us, she doesn't spend much time on social media. She's too busy with work and deadlines. The party is in two days, and we need to get the word out fast and social media is our safest bet," Norah explained.

"My idea was having everyone share it on their socials but block Isabella."

"I feel like someone will drop the ball somewhere in that plan." Todd brushed at the dog hair attached to the front of his shirt, which only seemed to draw in Norah's attention to his chest.

"Did you have a better idea?" Maddie asked, incredulous.

"Pineridge is a small town." He shrugged. "Why not just rely on word of mouth?"

Maddie fiddled with her earring. "So...like what? You suggest we go door to door like we're Girl Scouts selling cookies?"

"Something like that." Todd pet Samson.

"It's not a bad idea," Norah said.

Maddie's brows lifted in question at her.

"I'm off work for a couple days and Todd's schedule is wide open. We could go around town and invite some people. He's right, there aren't too many to invite that aren't already coming," Norah said.

"I mean, I guess it could work." Maddie tucked her hair behind an ear.

"We'll start today." Norah sounded a bit too eager. "We could knock a few out, then we'll have less to do tomorrow. Because I'll need most of tomorrow to decorate. Leo has agreed to work from home for the next two days, so I'll have free range of the studio."

"I guess it's settled then." Maddie sat back, leaning against her hands.

"You sure you don't mind helping?" Norah slid her gaze up to meet Todd's and she practically melted into a pile of goo when they locked eyes.

"What else do I have to do?" he asked. "You said it yourself; my schedule is wide open."

Her cheeks warmed.

Samson rolled to his front, lifting his head, and licking his jowls after a yawn.

Todd scratched behind Samson's ears. "Besides making sure this guy stays out of trouble."

"I'm sure he won't mind going for a walk," Norah said.

The dog looked at her and tilted his head at the word.

"You've done it now. You said the 'w' word."

Norah winced. "Sorry."

Samson jumped up and paraded around in circles.

Maddie stood and grabbed her coat. "Looks like my help is no longer needed here." She bent and pet Samson before crossing the room toward the open doorway. "I'll let you two get started. And Nor, let me know if you need any help with the setup before the party."

Samson trotted behind her, trying to sneak out of the room. But Todd was faster. He swooped in front of the door, blocking the exit. "I don't think so, pal."

Norah pushed off the floor to stand. "Wanna go now?"

"I don't think Samson is giving us a choice." He picked him up.

"Let's hit up all the people within walking distance and then we'll swing by the businesses near the studio tomorrow."

"Sounds like a plan." He shot her a grin over his shoulder as they headed down the stairs.

In the front entryway, Todd put his boots on and attached Samson's leash to his collar. Norah plucked her coat and scarf from off the coat rack.

"Ready?" she called absentmindedly as she flung open the front door and was bombarded with the familiar face of her ex.

"Hey, Nor," Landon's voice sliced through her center.

"What are you doing here?" she muttered.

His expression shifted and his jaw ticked. "You on your way out?"

Crossing her arms, she clenched her teeth, not speaking.

"Do you want some company?"

Was he joking? She pushed open the door further, revealing Todd as he stood next to her in the entryway. Landon's face fell. And she couldn't help but feel a bit of satisfaction.

"I already have company."

"Oh. Todd, right?"

Todd reached for Norah's hand and said, "Good to see you again."

Why did Todd have to be so friendly? So mature?

"What are you doing here?" she repeated.

"Right." Landon held up some kind of metal tool that looked heavy. "Just returning this crescent wrench your dad loaned me."

Dad was loaning out his tools to Landon? The act, though generous, felt like a betrayal. Dad quite possibly loved his tools more than his own children. And he was just, what? Handing them out to people? People meaning her ex-husband.

"Just leave it on the front porch."

"Uh," he hesitated, "I'd feel better if I left it inside. You know how your dad is about his tools."

She rolled her eyes, stepping aside and waving him in. "Fine," she muttered.

Landon strode past her, dressed in jeans and a thin winter coat. A few months ago, simply seeing him in those low-slung jeans would've sent her over the edge with desire. But now, she was blinded by the irritation of him. Blinded by his selfish actions and bad choices.

He set the wrench down just in the entryway.

"Okay, well, Dad's not home so I'm sure he'll be glad you brought his tool back to him in one piece."

"Bummer. I was hoping to get a chance to talk to him for a minute."

She furrowed her brows.

"What about Finn, is he around?"

"Nope, Finn isn't here either."

She didn't budge in her stance. She didn't want him to feel welcome there anymore. When he chose to sleep with someone else, he lost that privilege. And even though his brother, Leo was family, along with their dad, Howard, Landon no longer was.

"Ready to go, Buttercup?" Todd asked, squeezing her hand.

Landon's eyes danced back and forth between her and Todd.

"Sorry, we were just heading out."

"Ok, yeah...well, I'll see you around," Landon muttered.

She all but shoved him out of the house before she and Todd left as well. After Landon had climbed back into his truck, Todd set Samson on the ground, and he held the end of the leash.

"Does your ex come by often?" Todd asked as they walked down the shoveled sidewalk, Samson stopping to sniff nearly every bush.

"Not that often."

"That's good," Todd mumbled. "I mean, not good-good, but like it's probably good he doesn't come around often so you don't have to always see him."

"Right." She groaned.

"How long did you say you've been split up?"

"About a year."

The late afternoon air felt warmer than it had the past few days, and she unraveled the scarf from her neck, letting it hang.

"I think he's still in love with you."

She spun to look at him, her feet halting. "What?"

"If not in love, he's definitely regretting cheating on you."

"Pft," she muttered. "Yeah right. Him and his new perfect girlfriend are shacking up together in my house. I don't think he has any regrets."

Samson tugged on the leash, causing Todd to follow, and leading him toward a tree. "I don't think you can tell when a guy is jealous. Because that guy back there was clearly jealous."

"Jealous? Maybe. But only because he's threatened by you."

"Maybe I've reminded him what he's lost." Todd gazed at her intently, and she couldn't pull her attention away. "I know if I was him, I'd be kicking myself."

Norah sucked in a breath, welcoming the cool air to enter her lungs.

"Better yet, I'd be asking someone else to kick me. Straight in the balls."

She snorted.

"I'm serious. And my guess is I wouldn't have to even ask someone to do it. After meeting you once, my brother, Ryan would do it willingly."

"Your brother sounds like a handy guy to have around. Sort of like a conscience."

"That's a good way to describe him. Though sometimes I'm

the one who has to be *his* conscience." He shrugged. "I guess that's how siblings are, right?"

She thought about her relationship with Izzy. Even though there was a decent age difference between the two of them, they'd stayed close. Finn was even older, but he'd always lived nearby. During college and partially through his residency, Finn had lived at home. After he and Nina dated for a few months, he moved to Denver with her, but they never lost the bond they had.

"Yeah, if you're lucky," Norah said.

"Sorry if I made you feel uncomfortable."

"By what?"

"You know, about saying your ex is still in love with you. Didn't mean to make you question things," Todd said.

"It's fine. And believe me, you didn't make me question anything. Landon and I have been over for a while."

It was quiet between them. Norah peered up at the sky. The bright sun tried to break free from the clouds, pale yellow streaks shining.

"Can I ask you something?" Todd asked, his voice soft.

Norah glanced over at him, finding his gaze on her and her cheeks warmed. "Sure."

"Do you still love him?"

That was a loaded question. How was she supposed to answer? *Did* she still love Landon? Most days, it would be an instant *no*. But there were a few, rare, low days when she thought she did still love him. On days when she missed him. Missed *them*.

But today? No. She didn't love him.

Because today, she was spending the day with Todd. And being with him, talking and laughing with him, Landon didn't even cross her mind.

"I think..." she began, "I'm in love with the idea of him than actually in love with him. Does that make sense?"

"Perfect sense."

Studying her feet while they continued to walk down the sidewalk, she said, "What about you?"

"Me?"

"Yeah, do you still love Margo?"

"Uh...that feels like a trick question."

She nudged an elbow into his side. "C'mon, I told you."

"Fine. I guess my answer is similar. I'm in love with the old us. Past Margo. Not present-day Margo. She's changed a lot. But I guess more truthful," he paused, and it drew her attention, she watched his face, "We've both changed. And I can't really blame her for that." He shrugged.

"I guess not."

"Besides," he said, waggling his brows. "I'm not sure if you've heard the rumor, but I kinda have something going on with this hot redhead in a small town."

Elation bloomed in her chest, and she suddenly had a bounce in her step without intention. "Oh, yeah? Too bad my hair isn't red. It's burnt sienna. Now I'm curious—who is this hot redhead?"

Todd reached an arm around her back and pulled her snuggly into his side. The plane of his hard body pressed against hers. He ran his chin over her cheek, the rough stubble scraping against her skin and sending a zing of pleasure between her thighs.

A few weeks ago, her biggest problem was trying to land a date for the Galentine's Day party. Now that she had one, and one that she not only approved of, but was crushing on hard— her biggest problem was not wanting to let him go. During the past few days, she and Todd had become close. And no other guy turned her on quite so strongly as Todd did. Her hormones felt wild and reckless whenever she was with him.

Sure, they'd agreed on a fake relationship. She needed him almost as much as he needed her. But her feelings for him were growing stronger by the day. She needed to know if they were the manifestation of a childhood crush, or if they were real.

CHAPTER 17
Todd

It was early. Too early when Todd's phone skittered across the worn wood nightstand. He fumbled around for it without opening his eyes. After a few unsuccessful attempts, he finally located his vibrating phone.

"Hello?" he croaked out the greeting.

"Hey, it's me."

Todd's eyes sprang open, the shock of the voice on the other end of the line woke him instantly. He ran a hand down his wary face and sat up in the small bed.

"Did I wake you?" Margo whispered.

He held the phone away from him, checking the time. "It's barely six o'clock here."

"Oh gah, I'm sorry. I completely forgot about the time difference."

"It's fine." He glanced over at the kennel and found Samson stirring. "Samson will need to go out soon anyway."

"Samson?"

He rolled his eyes to himself. He'd moved out only a few

months ago and she'd already forgotten about the dog. The one that should've been theirs. "Yeah. My puppy."

"Ohhh, right. I didn't think you kept him."

"What the hell, Margo?" he barked.

"What?"

"Why wouldn't I keep him? You think just because you rejected me that I would do the same thing to an innocent dog?" He didn't wait for her to stick up for herself, he pressed on. "Why are you calling?"

"I'm sorry." She sounded vulnerable and he hated that he could hear it in her voice. "I just wanted to check in and see how you're doing?"

He wanted to let loose on her. But if he did that, she would mistake it as still caring. Still being hung up on her. And he wasn't.

Not really.

Maybe it was the same as what Norah had said about Landon. He was still in love with the idea of her—of them. But being away from her, in a different town, and state, he was realizing he hadn't been in love with Margo in quite some time.

He groaned loudly into the phone. "I'm fine."

"Good. That's good."

"Yeah. It's been great being here. Catching up with Isabella. And getting to know her family."

"I'm glad," she answered softly.

He could hear the smile in her voice, picture it, the sweet, full lips pouting, and he hated it. He didn't want to know that about her anymore and he especially didn't want to imagine it. Maybe in time, he'd forget. But not if she was going to still call him. It would be hard enough when he got back home and returned to work. When he'd have to see her in the office every day.

And see her with Aaron Brown.

"How's Aaron?" he bit out.

There was a pause on the other end of the phone.

"That isn't why I called."

"Then why did you?"

"Never mind. Just forget it." She sighed into the phone. "I thought...I don't know, I guess I thought we could at least be friends." He could hear her deep breaths that followed. "I miss our friendship."

He'd be lying to himself if he said he didn't miss it too. They'd been friends so long before they'd ever began dating. But he didn't know if they'd ever get back to that place again.

"Me too. But Margo...it's gonna be a while before we can be friends again."

"Okay. I understand," she whispered. "I just wanted to make sure you're still trying for the promotion."

He stiffened. "Why wouldn't I try? I think you know me better than that. I'm not a quitter."

"Right, I know." There was a long pause on the phone before Margo finally spoke again. "And Norah, Isabella's sister...she's what? Your girlfriend now?"

Ignoring the question, he asked, "Why are you whispering?

"Oh, uh—it's early."

"It's not that early there. And you live alone." His stomach churned, a sick dread filling it with concrete. "Are you not alone?"

An even longer pause followed.

"Please don't ask me that," she mumbled.

The dread turned to anger. "How about next time you don't call me when you've got another guy at your place. And yeah, to answer your question, Norah is my girlfriend." He ended the call and tossed his phone onto the floor before pressing the heels of his hands into his eyes and groaning out loud.

Todd was now beginning to see that the day Margo confessed to him that their futures were headed in two different directions was a very good day. His eyes were opened that day and even more since then. He'd been delusional in thinking he and Margo were perfect for one another, trying to disregard the red flags waving and warning him of issues between them. Even ignoring his brother, Ryan's advice. If she hadn't ended things with him that day, who knows how long they would've lasted before their relationship blew up.

There was a light, slow knock on his door before it pushed open.

Norah stood there, hair piled in a messy high ponytail, a long-sleeved thermal shirt with hearts on it and a pair of plaid flannel shorts. Very *short* shorts.

"What. Is. With. All. The. Noise?" she groaned.

"Sorry. Phone call from New York. Time change." He hoped that said it all.

Her eyes widened and her mouth made an O shape. "New York?" Her voice sounded softer, quieter now.

"Yep." He sighed. "It seems our fake relationship has passed at least one test."

Her brows lifted and her lips transitioned into an *oooo* shape. He very much appreciated the look of her lips. He suddenly didn't mind being woken up early since it meant being able to see those lips.

"Really?" she asked. "Margo?"

He pushed his hand through his hair. "Yeah. It's weird."

Norah trudged over to the bed and plopped down on top of it. Todd felt a bit exposed sitting there in only his boxer briefs, just the sheet and comforter covering him. But Norah didn't seem to notice. She pulled her knees up and leaned on a hand, her shorts riding up further and revealing even more bare skin.

It wasn't simply the short shorts that had his hormones

buzzing. With her hair tousled into a mess on top of her head, his mind went to places it shouldn't go—especially this early in the morning—like maybe this was how her hair looked in the morning or looked after sex.

"Okay, tell me everything." She smiled wide.

And he couldn't help but smile back at her. She had this *kid-on-Christmas-morning* look. She was sexy and hot, and he couldn't help but wonder, if he leaned in for a kiss, would she meet him halfway?

No. He was being stupid letting his lower extremities think for him.

This was fake.

Samson sat up and his wagging tail thumped against the side of the wired kennel wall. Todd wouldn't have a lot of time before the puppy started whining and barking. So he'd have to give Norah the condensed version of his phone conversation with Margo.

"She's still into you," she said.

But he didn't care about Margo. He'd forgotten all about her. All he could think about was how perfect Norah was and he wouldn't mind waking up to her every day.

Dammit. *This is fake, Todd.*

"What are you gonna do about it?" she pressed.

Feeling flustered, he tugged the covers further up his torso. He hoped he could stay hidden in the bed for the rest of the morning, or at least until Norah left the room. "I'm not going to do anything."

"What? You're gonna do nothing? She's clearly jealous. She probably saw the photos of the two of us together on Instagram and now she's jealous."

"How can she be jealous? She had another guy over."

She shook her head. "Women."

What did that even mean?

"Did I tell you that Margo was never one of my favorites of my sister's friends?"

A lump formed in his throat, and he was too afraid to ask. He swallowed. "No?"

"No. Now, let me help make this relationship look more real." Norah crawled over to him and snuggled in close to his chest.

He inhaled a frantic breath.

"Wh-what...are you doing?" he fumbled his words.

She had her warm body pressed against his now. She was so close he could smell her hair. He could see down the V-neck of her shirt.

At this rate, he'd never be getting out of this bed.

"Give me your phone," she demanded.

He fumbled for his phone on the bed next to him and slipped it into her awaiting hand without asking questions.

She took a few selfies of the two of them snuggled closely before handing the device back to him. "Here. Share these on Insta. Caption them something like, *just woke up.* Or, *waking up with you isn't so rough.* Something like that."

Studying the pics she'd taken, he said, "This gives off the impression of a committed relationship?"

Norah propped herself on an elbow, peeking up at him through sleepy eyelashes. "What shows committed more than the two of us in bed together?"

She had a point. This would show they were in a real relationship. If this was a one-nighter or a fling, they wouldn't be snuggling in bed the next morning.

"And maybe Landon will see it and get so jealous he'll leave the homewrecker and ask you to take him back?" He wasn't sure why he said it, but he regretted it instantly.

"I hope not. I don't want him back." She looked flustered,

pushing her fingers through her hair. "I want to move on. Be myself without him."

He needed to recover from this.

"I think you're doing just fine without him."

She gazed at him, leery. "Yeah? Because sometimes I worry, I relied on him too much."

"You come across as a successful, independent woman to me."

"Stop, you're just saying that because we're in a fake relationship." She shoved him playfully in the chest. "But secretly you wanna sleep with me." He took a hold of her hand and her expression shifted into surprise. He felt like being bold at that moment. He didn't have many days left here. He was running out of time.

They were running out of time.

"Maybe," his voice came out in a growl.

When she dipped her chin, an adorable blush swept across her cheeks, and he fell for her even harder. The definition of fake blurred in his mind while he fantasized all the places he wanted to kiss her.

Norah slid her hand from his grip and danced her fingers up his bare chest. "If you and I are gonna Pretty Woman this thing right, we need to learn more about each other." She smiled.

His brows pinched together. "Pretty Woman?"

She groaned, swatting his arm. "Richard Gere? Julia Roberts? It's only one of the best fake dating romcoms ever."

"I'll have to take your word for it." Grazing his hand over the bare skin on her thigh, he waggled his brows at her. "Or we can watch it together? Maybe have an entire movie day? In bed?" He cleared his throat. "You know, like a real girlfriend and boyfriend would do."

"That sounds perfect." She leaned further into him, her hands teasing his chest.

He was about to yank her on top of him when the bedroom door pushed open suddenly, loudly banging against the wall as Norah's niece bounded in the room.

"Auntie Norah!" She lunged for the bed and caused him and Norah to jolt.

"Ava? What are you doing up so early?" Norah tickled the girl's side and Ava rolled around on the bed and giggled.

"Daddy told me to go downstairs and watch cartoons but I'm too old to watch cartoons," she whined.

"You're seven."

"Cartoons are for babies. Sophia watches them."

"Hardly. Sophia isn't even one. A one-year-old's attention span doesn't last long."

Ava finally took notice of Todd in the bed, and she pushed up to her knees, staring him down. Now he felt even more indecent under the intense gaze of a child, his bare chest on display. He clutched the blanket.

Ava frowned. "Did you guys have a sleepover?"

Norah whipped her head in his direction, terror flashing in her eyes. "What? N-no."

Todd chuckled. He had to hand it to Ava, she was observant for a seven-year-old.

"I heard a noise in here. And I came to check it out. That's all," Norah said.

Samson released a loud puppy bark, and it stole Ava's attention away immediately. They were off the hook—at least for now.

Ava climbed off the bed and raced to the kennel. "Aww. Good morning, Samson. Did you have a good sleep?"

Norah slid Todd a look, biting her lower lip with a scandalous smile.

"Hey, kid?" he called to Ava.

She glanced up at him.

"You wanna take Samson out for his morning potty break?"

Her eyes went round and bright. "Can I?"

"Sure. But you have to hold his leash tight. And only in the backyard," Norah said.

"Yay!"

Norah handed the leash to Ava and helped her clip it onto Samson's collar after he bounded out of the kennel. Samson looked as happy as the girl did. He seemed to really like Ava. He'd be a good dog to have around with kids. If he ever had kids.

"Smooth move," Norah said once Ava and Samson had left the room. "Pawning off your responsibilities onto an innocent child."

He hunched a shoulder. "What? She was happy to do it. You saw."

"Yeah, yeah." Norah waved him off, heading back to the open doorway.

"Besides, it's not like I could've done it."

She turned to look at him, confused until he gestured at his crotch with both his head and eyes.

It took her a few seconds before realization set in. "Ohhh-hh." Her face flushed and she grinned. "Well, I'll leave you to... um, that, then. Guess our couples Q&A will have to wait." She stepped out of the room, her backside in the tiny pajama shorts in full display for him and she closed the door behind her.

He groaned and slid back underneath the covers.

Nope, he wouldn't be going anywhere for a while.

CHAPTER 18

Norah

Temps were warmer than they'd been all week so instead of bundling in her usual winter jacket and scarf, Norah dressed in a pair of black leggings, her Timberland's, a long-sleeved denim shirt and a puffy black vest. She pulled her hair into a messy topknot and grabbed her sunglasses.

On her way down the stairs, the voices of her family carried throughout the house, warming her heart. She allowed the sweet sounds of familiarity fill the crevices of her broken heart. She definitely didn't want to live with her parents forever, but as much as she hated to admit it, she desperately needed them.

She entered the dining room just as Todd was saying, "No joke, there were literal tears."

"I'm not surprised," Finn said, shoveling a bite of scrambled eggs into his mouth.

"Izzy was always our dramatic one," Dad added as he handed Norah a mug of filled coffee.

"Thanks," she muttered, still unsure what conversation she'd just walked in on.

"Here, sweetie, you can have my seat." Nina stood, hoisting baby Sophia up with her.

Norah took Sophia's hand and cooed at her before whispering to Nina, "What are they talking about?"

"Izzy. Her first time experiencing things in New York. This one is about the Statue of Liberty."

"Ahh." Norah slid into the chair and Todd winked at her from across the table. Flames licked at her cheeks, and she wanted to hide. What if her family had seen?

But she supposed in her family's eyes, they were a real couple.

Mom set a plate in front of her, piled with eggs and bacon and greasy hash browns.

"Thanks, Mom."

Mom patted her hand. "Of course, sweets."

"How'd she handle seeing Central Park? She was always a big fan of the show *F.R.I.E.N.D.S.*" Finn picked up his mug and drained the rest of his coffee.

"She skipped around the park like a lunatic." Todd chuckled. "We had to explain to those around us not to worry, she was perfectly sane."

"Aww, I wish I could've seen that." Mom stood at the kitchen island, eating a piece of bacon.

The way Todd got along with her family caused Norah's heart to squeeze. Landon had always seemed like he was trying too hard and even still—came in second place next to Leo. Even though no one had ever verbalized the competition, it was obvious who was the winning son-in-law in her parent's eyes.

"So, the big party is tomorrow," Dad began. "Y'all ready?"

"Almost." Norah held her steaming mug of coffee in both hands, elbows resting on the table. "Todd and I are going to spend the day decorating the studio."

Dad set his dishes in the sink. "Do you need me to pet sit Samson again? Because I don't mind."

"Thanks for the offer, but I'm going to bring along his leash and kennel and then he should be fine."

Norah's phone vibrated on the table next to her and she glanced at the screen.

MADDIE

Tell me everything.

As soon as Maddie saw the pics on Instagram of Norah and Todd, she'd been blowing up her phone. Norah didn't have a choice—she needed to come clean about the deal. Lying to Maddie was impossible.

Later.

MADDIE

You gotta give me something. How do you really feel about him? Are you into him?

I don't know.

MADDIE

What's not to know? He's hot. And he's clearly into you.

Jump his bones already.

But he's leaving.

MADDIE

Even better reason to jump his bones.

Stop saying jump his bones. No one says that.

MADDIE

Your best friend says that.

Norah snorted, then glanced around the room. The conversation had moved on from the party to dogs. And by the sounds of it, Dad was very close to looking for an English Mastiff rescue or breeder in Colorado. The look on Mom's face, said she wasn't as convinced.

> We're spending the day together. We'll see how it goes.

MADDIE

> Fiiiiiine. Keep me posted. Love ya!

> Love you too!

The thought of Todd leaving in a few days did something weird and achy in her chest. They'd spent so much time together this week, she didn't want to think about him leaving. Because after he did, she'd be left with what? Her few figure skating classes a day at the rink? Planning a party occasionally for a local resident looking for assistance? Her wine, yoga pants, and Netflix nights?

Her life sounded awfully pathetic.

The few things that put Pineridge on the map didn't seem like much compared to Central Park and The Statue of Liberty. There didn't seem to be enough to entice him to stay. Heck, there didn't seem to be enough to make *her* want to stick around.

IN TOWN, TODD TIED SAMSON TO THE BIKE RACK BEFORE they went inside The Daily Grind to grab a cup of coffee and to speak to the manager. Jeff was one of a handful of decent eligible bachelors in Pineridge. For one hot second after Norah and Landon split up, she considered going on a date with him when Hannah, one of The Daily Grind's barista's asked if she could hook the two of them up.

But Jeff had more interest in ice hockey than women.

"Hey, Norah," Hannah greeted from behind the bar. "Your usual?" But her brows quickly gestured toward Todd.

"Hi, Hannah, yeah, I'll take a medium caramel macchiato please. And, this is Todd Langston, a friend of Isabella's from New York. And...my boyfriend."

There, she'd finally said it out loud, and she was surprised by how easily it slid from her lips.

Daring a glance at him, she found him smiling that warm welcoming smile that made her insides turn to mush. She could only imagine what it was doing to Hannah.

"Boyfriend?" Hannah's brows shot up as her vision danced between Norah and Todd. "So the rumors are true?"

But Todd remained aloof, even drawing Norah in snuggly against his side. "Long distance is a bitch."

Hannah clamped her mouth shut, her lips twisting.

"It really is," Norah agreed.

When Hannah finally recovered from the shock, she said, "New York huh? I've always wanted to go there."

"You should. It's incredible." Wide smile again.

"And what can I get started for you?"

"Just a large black coffee."

"Sounds good, I'll have those ready for you at the end of the bar in a few." Hannah slid Norah a look that said, *holy begeezus, he's hot.*

Norah ignored her. "Hey, is Jeff here?"

"Uhh, he's around here somewhere." Hannah glanced over her shoulder. "Hey, Jeff, someone's here to see you."

In a moment, Jeff appeared rounding the corner from the

back of the shop. "Norah Hoffman," he greeted, flashing a bright smile.

"Whitley," she corrected him.

He winced. "Right. Sorry. What's up?" He passed a sideways glance in Todd's direction.

"I wanted to invite you to a party tomorrow night."

His brows lifted with interest. "Yeah? On Valentine's Day?"

"As I'm sure you've heard, Isabella is hosting a Galentine's Day party tomorrow night at Leo's studio and I just wanted to make sure you knew you were invited."

"Do you need a date? Because I'd gladly volunteer," he said, hope in his voice.

The heat radiated from Todd's body as he squeezed her tighter.

"That's sweet, but I actually have a date already."

As Jeff sized up Todd, he finally said, "I guess that sounds fun. I can probably swing by. I'll bring Garrett along too."

Garrett Vance was possibly Pineridge's most eligible, most attractive bachelor. But he was also one of the most conceited. It wasn't only the fame and fortune brought on by the exposure from his show Renovation Dudes on HGTV, he'd always been like that. Thankfully his twin brother, Davis was practically the polar opposite since he and Kelsey had been dating for the past few months.

"Um, I heard Garrett was going to be out of town?"

Jeff deadpanned. "Is he? Must've forgotten."

Norah narrowed her eyes.

"Drinks are ready." Hannah called.

"Thanks, Hannah. See you tomorrow night." Norah picked up both cups, handing Todd his, their fingers grazing for just a moment sending a zing through her core.

"See you, Jeff." The bell above the door chimed as they turned around with their drinks.

Vanessa, a friend of Izzy's, stood in the doorway, propping the door open for her husband Joey to roll his wheelchair inside.

"Hey, Vanessa. So glad I bumped into you."

"Norah, hey. How are you?" Vanessa smiled.

"Good. So, you're coming to Izzy's Galentine's Day party tomorrow, right?"

She slid a look at Joey.

"What?" He held up his hands.

"Yes, we'll be there. Much to Joey's chagrin."

"Oh, Joey, it's gonna be fun. We have the perfect playlist, lots of yummy food from Sweet Cakes Bakery, a photo booth, dancing—"

"And there it is," Joey interrupted.

"Fine, you don't have to dance," Norah said.

Vanessa squeezed his shoulder. "But your wife would really appreciate it if you did."

He rolled his eyes, relenting. "Fine."

Vanessa watched as Joey wheeled over to Jeff and they fist bumped. "Thanks for this. You don't even know. You've saved my Valentine's Day."

Norah smiled, the happiness blooming in the center of her chest.

"And you must be the mysterious boyfriend from New York I've heard about?" Vanessa eyed Todd as she held out an awaiting hand.

Good to see the Pineridge rumor mill was up and running. But she wasn't ready to discuss their relationship.

"Right, that's me." Todd shook her hand.

"Okay, we should get going. See you tomorrow night." Norah shoved Todd toward the door.

"It was nice meeting you," he called over his shoulder.

"Friends from high school?" Todd questioned once they were outside, and he began untying Samson's leash.

Norah crouched and petted the puppy as he wagged his entire butt with excitement. "They're mostly friends of Izzy's, but I guess mine too. When you stay in the same town you've always lived in, you sort of all become friends."

"I get that. Though, I haven't experienced it much myself."

She straightened and took a sip of her coffee, the caramel sweet on her tongue. "You don't run into many childhood friends in the city?"

He looked amused. "Contrary to what famous sitcoms like *F.R.I.E.N.D.S* might have shown, New York is big. And crowded. I couldn't even pick out my doctor if we happened to be in the same coffee shop."

The explanation of that felt odd to Norah. She couldn't imagine walking around a city, not knowing anyone, or not running into someone she knew. Though it also sounded intriguing. To have that kind of privacy seemed unfathomable. Here, she couldn't leave her house without bumping into someone who either used to change her diaper or who'd she'd spill her Christmas list to while sitting on their lap at Christmas. Mr. Olsen had always been Pineridge's best Santa.

"That kind of sounds incredible."

"Yeah, it has its perks that's for sure. But here, everyone knowing everyone, it's kinda nice. You're like one big family."

Hearing Todd talk about her town with such adoration caused her limbs to weaken. As much as she loved it, there were several times in the past year she felt like leaving Pineridge without looking back. But showing Todd around and introducing him to her friends was as if new life had been breathed into Pineridge again.

"I want to show you something." She took his hand, and he held steady eye contact with her, his pupils large.

"Okay." His smile was curious, and it sent goosebumps shooting down her arms.

With the pressure of his hand in hers, his fingers clasping tightly, it caused her heart to swell. The comfort of being in a man's presence was a new feeling to her. Rather than a sense of ownership, she felt cherished and protected.

"It's just up ahead about half a mile," she explained, the coolness of the late afternoon buzzed across her skin.

"That's about the perfect amount of walking for Samson." Todd slipped the leash around his wrist and held coffee cup in his free hand.

Up ahead, Norah could already spot their destination peeking above the tops of the pine trees. The abandoned treehouse on an old farmer's yard had become somewhat of a landmark for the teens in Pineridge. A rite of passage if you will. Every senior in high school brought a favorite picture or quote or trinket and stuck it to the wall or left it on the windowsills or under the floorboards.

When they reached the treehouse, Norah watched as Todd peered up at the neglected structure with lackluster in his eyes. He scooped Samson into his arms. "You sure it's safe?"

An amused smile spread on her lips. "It's fine, c'mon."

They climbed the rickety wood ladder to the top where a platform surrounded the treehouse and was enclosed with a railing. She ducked her head and entered inside first. Not much had changed since the last time she'd been there. Besides more photos and memorabilia that hadn't been there before. Several more years of seniors who had pinned their favorite things to the walls and left pieces of themselves behind.

Norah found the switch on the strand of battery-operated string lights that wrapped around the ceiling, a bit surprised when they lit up. Todd spun around, taking in his surroundings of aged photos overlapping, small pieces of paper, graduation tassels, and dried-up corsages, and she could see how this wouldn't be meaningful to him. He didn't know these people or their stories. His life didn't intertwine with theirs. But she knew them, and her life did.

"Each senior, before they graduate, comes here and leaves something behind. Either a favorite quote they've written down or a favorite picture. Maybe even an item that holds a special memory," Norah explained, her fingers grazing a wall of Pineridge's history.

"I gotta admit, I've never seen anything like this in New York City."

Her heart warmed at that thought. It was a reminder that this town was different, it was special.

Todd set Samson down to sniff the aged structure and its belongings. "Where's yours?"

She knew that question was coming and that's why she'd been searching through the hundreds of warped photos and crinkled scraps of paper trying to find it. In her search, she came across a hockey puck with Leo's name and high school jersey number on it he'd screwed to the wooden wall, and Izzy's item.

"Look, here's Izzy's." She pointed to a newspaper clipping with a picture of Izzy next to an article she'd written. "It was her final piece she wrote in the high school newspaper."

Todd chuckled. "What was with her hair?"

Norah mindlessly ignored him while she continued to search and finally, found hers. She'd scrawled her favorite quote onto a worn piece of paper. It seemed silly now as she read it with Todd standing so close to her. And yet, the meaning of that quote had changed over time.

"This is mine."

Todd leaned in, squinting his eyes as he read it out loud. "Never say goodbye, because saying goodbye means going away, and going away means forgetting." His voice rumbled in her chest and when he turned to look at her, her knees buckled. "Did you write that?"

She dipped her chin to her chest, her cheeks filling with slight indignity. "No...it's a quote by Peter Pan."

Todd's eyes twinkled with amusement and his lips twitched and instead of allowing humiliation to consume her she readied herself for the ridicule. But it didn't come. Instead, he surprised her when he rested his hands on her hips and urged her agonizingly slow toward him.

"It's painfully beautiful," he murmured.

He gifted her with a kiss to the forehead before he lowered his lips and hovered them above hers. He was so close, they shared the same breath, and her head felt woozy.

Norah was letting him get too close, the line between fake and reality blurring. And her heart was at stake here. She needed to be strong.

"We should go before it gets dark," she blurted, interrupting the impending kiss.

His eyes flew open. But with his lips pressed tight, he nodded in agreement. Sliding his hand away from her hip, he took a small step away from her, and she shuddered at their instant distance.

They climbed down from the treehouse and set off on foot back toward Main Street, Samson trotting in front of them and leading the way. Norah's insides exploded with a craving and desire so strong for Todd she wasn't sure she'd be able to contain it any longer. He was not only sexy with that wavy hair flopping in his face and a tattooed forearm, but he also caused her to snort laugh, something only Maddie seemed to bring out of her.

She hadn't realized she'd been staring at him with adoring and probably cartoon heart eyes until he said, "Are you okay?"

"W-what?" She swallowed, forcing her gaze to the ground. "Yep. I'm cool."

I'm cool?

Yeah, no. She definitely was *not* cool. She was hot. On fire, actually. And completely turned on. She was seriously considering jumping into the pile of dirty, slushy snow on the side of the road to cool herself off.

Once she gave her heart to him—fully—she knew there would be no getting it back.

CHAPTER 19

Todd

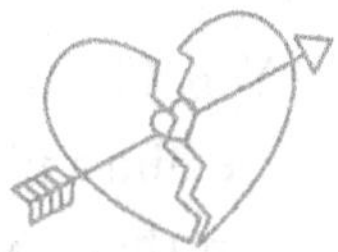

Todd was beginning to hate how much he loved this little town. Full of people who knew everyone. As he helped Norah decorate for the party, their chosen playlist for the party streaming through the Bluetooth speaker, he didn't want to think about leaving in a few more days.

"Where do you want this table?" he asked over his shoulder while Norah opened packages of balloons.

"Oh right. Let me find my design."

He quirked a brow. "You made a design?"

"Yes," she answered, incredulous. "I wouldn't be a very good party planner if I didn't have a plan, would I?" She pulled an iPad out of her bag. "I'll print this out."

It was just a couple tables; how hard could it be?

As she headed into the office in the back of the studio, he pulled out the legs of a table and set it off to the side in the wide-open studio. He grabbed a second table and set that one up alongside the other. He didn't know much about party planning, but he could set up a few tables. It wasn't rocket science.

"Okay," she said as she breezed back into the room and

tossed down a freshly printed sheet of paper on the table. "This is the main studio," she pointed at it. "Since we need room for dancing, and the small photo booth, the tables need to go here, and here."

He leaned over, observing the design of the room but her proximity distracted him from fully paying attention.

"See?"

He cleared his throat. "Yep. Got it."

She straightened and gave him a playful smile. "Good."

After he put the tables in their exact locations, he helped Norah fill the Mylar balloons in an assortment of pink shimmering letters. "What's this gonna say when it's done? Man Hater?"

She didn't hide her eye roll. "Do I need to show you the design again?" She smirked at him.

"You even included the balloons in the design?"

"I told you, I'm a planner." She tossed a balloon letter at him with little accuracy of hitting him with it. "Besides, Izzy made me go over the plans with her."

"Yeah, that sounds like Izzy. Wait. Is this a hashtag?" He quirked a brow.

"Yes. It's supposed to say: #*gals*." She shrugged. "This was originally going to be an all-girls party, remember?"

He pushed his lips into a thought. "I guess that makes sense. Okay, what else?"

Norah checked the paper. "*No Boys Allowed* and *Cupid is Stupid*."

He shook his head slowly, letting out a low whistle. "Gotta admit, it's gonna be awkward being at a party with all these anti-men decorations."

"Believe me, no one's gonna pay attention to the decorations once they start drinking."

"You're probably right."

Todd helped by filling the balloon letters with air while Norah strung them on a ribbon in the correct order. He climbed the ladder and held up an end of the ribbon as he glanced over his shoulder at her. "How about this?"

Norah stood back and pressed a hand to her jutted hip while she considered the placement of the balloon letters. "A little higher. Okay, now a little to the left. And just a smidge lower. Annnnd perfect."

"You sure?" he asked, his tone teasing.

"Yes. Now we just need the other side to match."

"That shouldn't be too hard."

Todd proceeded to go through the entire routine with the other side of the string. When he finished, the balloon letters read: *No Boys Allowed.* He studied the picture of the design, checking where the next string of letters would hang. He maneuvered the ladder to the right location in the room and climbed up.

"Part of me wishes I would've convinced Izzy not to change the plans from the Galentine's party," Norah said, peering up at him. "I mean, you're right, this is a lot of decorations."

Todd shrugged. "It's fine. And I gotta admit, I'm glad the plans changed. Otherwise, I wouldn't be here." He held up the end of the string, waiting for Norah's direction.

"Because then you would've missed out on the awesome party playlist and the cupcakes, right?" She grinned.

Honestly, he hadn't been able to stop thinking about those delicious cupcakes. But what he really wanted was to spend as much time with Norah as possible. He headed back to New York in just a few days, and he was going to miss her.

"Absolutely."

She dipped her chin to her chest. "Because there couldn't possibly be another reason," she muttered.

Did she want him to say it, to admit that he wanted to be

there because of her? To admit that he wanted to spend every second with her until he left?

"Besides also wanting to try one of those champagne glasses with the swirl of cotton candy on top that you have on the menu, I guess I also wouldn't mind seeing you in that dress I saw hanging on the back of your door."

Her chin lifted and if he wasn't mistaken, her cheeks blushed. "Yeah?"

"Did you see how low that dress dips in the back?"

She snorted into her hand. "Um, yeah. I am aware."

"Does that thing even cover your butt?"

"I guess you'll have to wait and see." She flashed him a coy gaze.

"Can't wait," he growled.

Her lips pulled into a dazzling closed mouth smile and a zing of desire shot through him.

In the matter of a few days, they would be separated by many miles. Even if she came to New York at least once to help convince the partners they were in a serious relationship, he wasn't sure that would be enough for him. He wanted more. More time. More *her*.

They might have agreed on a fake relationship, but there was definitely nothing fake about his feelings for her.

"Higher."

"Huh?" He shook his head, ridding his mind of the prior thoughts.

"That side needs to go higher." She pointed with her finger.

"Oh. Right."

"A little more to the right. Okay, there is good."

He fastened the string to the wall before climbing down from the ladder and stepping back to study his work. Despite the Galentine's Day bashing statement, he had to admit, it looked good. They only had one more to hang and then, he gazed down at the design laying on the table, about a million more things to hang and set up. A look at the decorations, and he realized they were going to be there all night.

But he didn't mind as long as he was spending it with her.

His phone chimed and he slid it out of his front pocket.

RYAN

What's the ETA on this thing?

What are you talking about?

RYAN

When are you gonna finally nail this girl?

The blood drained from his face and Todd hugged his phone to his chest. A quick glance at Norah and he saw she was distracted by a heart-shaped centerpiece. He still tried shielding his phone while he typed back a reply to his meddling brother.

What girl are you talking about?

RYAN

The hot girl in all your Instagram pics this week.

Todd groaned. He was surprised Ryan hadn't asked him about Norah before now.

RYAN:

Was she in your bed?

Technically, no.

RYAN

Obviously I'm not talking about technically.
It's either yes or no.

Then yes. But nothing happened.

RYAN

I ain't trying to hear that.

Give me something.

I like her.

RYAN

Bro! You cannot get emotionally attached.

I'm not.

He wasn't. Not really. Okay, not too emotionally attached. Maybe only a little. A little wasn't so bad.

RYAN

Mayday!

What?

RYAN

Abandon ship!

You're supposed to be pretending.

Why had he told Ryan about the stipulations of the promotion?

I gotta go.

He slid his phone back into his front pocket.

"Everything okay?" Norah asked.

He glanced up, feeling annoyed by his brother but forced a smile. "Yep. Everything is great. What's next?"

They hung several heart garlands, draped pink tulle from the ceiling, and curled ribbon. Together, they shook out white linen tablecloths and covered the tables with them. Then there were flute glasses to set out and balloons to hang.

A knock sounded on the door of the studio and Norah hustled to answer it.

"Kelsey." She held the door open and checked the time on her watch. "Right on time."

"Yeah, but barely." Kelsey entered, holding a large box pressed to her chest.

Todd rushed to help. "Need some help with that?"

"Actually, I've got this one. But do you mind grabbing the other boxes from the back of the van?"

"Not at all." Todd headed out to the van with Sweet Cakes Bakery in cursive on the side of it. He retrieved the boxes from the back and carried them inside the studio. "Where do you want these?"

"Just anywhere on the kitchen counter is fine," Norah said.

"I thought the baked goods were being delivered tomorrow?"

"They are. These are all the tiered trays and special boards. And some of the stuff that can be set up today." Kelsey was already at full speed, unloading the boxes.

"Thanks, Kelsey. Everything looks great."

"Thank me tomorrow when I somehow manage to make your delivery and still get ready in time for the party."

"What happened to Ashley? Why can't she make the delivery?"

"Because. She's coming to the party too. And she needs the entire day to get ready, and I quote, '*you wouldn't understand because you don't spend that much time on your appearance. You're lucky Davis doesn't care what you look like.*" Kelsey dropped a flat wooden board down on the table.

"What? She said that? I'm gonna kill her."

"Oh sweetie," Kelsey patted Norah's arm. "Thank you. But you're too sweet and not at all threatening. And believe me, I'm this close," she pinched her fingers in the air, "to taking her out myself."

"Can't your mom fire her?"

"She needs the help. There are more jobs than people in this town these days. Well, I gotta get going. I have two more deliveries before I need to be back at Tapp's to relieve Kai. He's been there all day. And hopefully Ashley will be the one picking everything back up the day after the party."

"Thanks, Kelsey."

Kelsey waved over her shoulder and left the studio, barely taking the time to shut the door behind her.

"That Ashley sounds like a piece of work," Todd mumbled.

"Right. That is so messed up. But she isn't wrong about one thing, Davis adores her. He's seen her at her worst."

"I mean, that's love right?" He set the boxes down.

Norah stopped fidgeting with the three-tiered tray she was putting together and looked at him. "I suppose. I guess...I wouldn't know."

His throat constricted and he shook his head, unable to find the words. It was unfair that Norah hadn't been shown the love she deserved. Unfair that the marriage vows her ex had pledged meant nothing to him.

"Have I told you how much I appreciate your help?"

He shrugged off her gratitude and swallowed the animosity he felt for Norah's ex. "I wouldn't mind hearing it again," he teased while studying the design again.

"Thank you. Seriously. There's no way I could've done this without you."

He proceeded to set out the champagne flutes, plates, and cutlery. "You would've managed."

"You're sweet. But that's doubtful."

Opening a package of hot pink paper napkins, he said,

"Have you ever thought about going into party planning as a profession?"

She waved him off, exhaling a laugh. "What? No. I couldn't. You've spent enough time with me to recognize my anxiety. I'm not organized enough to do this daily."

"I don't think you give yourself enough credit."

"About this?"

"About a lot of things." He lifted his arms, spanning them out. "Look at all of this. This is seriously impressive."

"Yeah, but Izzy helped."

"She confirmed everything. She didn't pick the menu, the decorations, give you the idea of the photo booth or these little cards." He picked one up and waved it in the air.

She hunched a shoulder, pink tinting her cheeks. "Yeah, I mean, I guess."

"What do you mean, *I guess*? You have a knack for this. And with your tight knit community, I'm sure they'd love to hire locally. Something tells me you'd stay pretty busy."

She ran her fingertips against her neck. "You're right, they are loyal to the locals."

"See."

"I don't know." She glanced down, shuffling her feet.

"You could keep doing the figure skating lessons. Because it's obvious that's where your heart is. And the students must love you. But this could be a side hustle. Something more to pay the bills, get you back on your feet and out of your parent's house." He shrugged. "Don't get me wrong, your family is great, but something tells me that occasionally they make you feel less than."

Her eyes went glossy, and he winced.

Crap. Did he say something wrong? Was she about to cry?

"Norah...I—"

"No one has ever really put all of that into those words before."

"Well, it's the truth."

"And you, Mr. Langston...are something else."

The look she gave him, full of yearning and desire, had his heart fluttering. The amount of self-control he had to force himself not to pull her into his arms was beginning to waver.

The deal.

The promotion.

He couldn't risk screwing everything up. They had to see this thing through. The proof of their relationship being real was the key to him getting the promotion. He couldn't let their feelings compromise the deal.

Which meant he couldn't be alone with her. He didn't trust himself. Keeping his distance was the only answer. If he was alone with her again, he wouldn't be able to restrain from acting on his feelings.

CHAPTER 20

Norah

Back at the house, Norah had somehow managed to tell Todd goodnight without throwing herself at him.

But she could think about very little else.

If Todd wasn't so hot or caring, if he didn't see her from the inside, would she still be as attracted to him? Because Landon had never encouraged her to try anything new. He'd never really understood her love for skating. Or party planning.

But Todd was not only telling her to go out and follow a dream—one which she'd never even told another soul about—he understood that figure skating still had a tight hold on her heart.

After Norah showered and dressed in a pair of jeans and a hoodie, she tiptoed back down the stairs. It took all her willpower to not knock on Todd's door. She needed to make the champagne Jell-O shots for the party, but she didn't want to ask for his help. She'd already consumed enough of his time. He had spent this evening with Samson before he'd called it an early night and headed to bed.

Was that code for: *come to my room?*

Nah, she was definitely reading into his words and actions too much. She needed to calm down.

In her parent's kitchen, she pulled out the ingredients and the small plastic cups. The familiar creak on the stairs sounded out and her fingers froze while she waited for whoever would come around the corner.

"Hey, sweets." Mom entered the kitchen.

Her shoulders relaxed. "Mom? It's late. You okay?"

"I'm fine. Just can't sleep. Figured I better make one of my special melatonin drinks." Mom pulled the carton of milk out of the fridge and poured some into a mug. "What are you making?"

Norah suddenly felt like a teenager again, sneaking alcohol into the house. Since she returned home after the separation, it sometimes felt like she'd reverted to those years.

"Uhh...champagne Jell-O shots."

"Yum. Save one for me, will you?" Mom grinned.

"Okay. Yeah, absolutely."

Mom put her mug into the microwave then crossed her arms and ankles, leaning against the counter. "Sooooo?"

Norah narrowed her eyes at her. "Sooooo what?"

"Norah sweetie, I wasn't born yesterday. What's going on with you and our houseguest?"

"What?" she gasped, her heart racing.

Mom gave her a knowing smile. "Don't think I haven't heard the rumors. Or saw your pictures on Instagram. You and Mr. New York have been spending a lot of time together."

"We just hit it off, that's all. He's a nice guy. But like you just said, he lives in New York. And he's leaving in a few days."

Mom patted her hand. "Take it from me, there aren't many people out there that you just *hit it off with*. When you find them, you grab on tight."

Norah tilted her head, pursing her lips. Why would Mom

say, *take it from me?* Had there been someone else before Dad? "Mom?"

The microwave beeped. "Ah, milk is ready." She spun around and carefully removed the hot mug. She sprinkled in the cardamom and gave it a stir. "I sure hope this does the trick. Otherwise I might have to break into your dad's stash of whiskey."

Norah was surprised Mom knew about dad's whiskey. But then again, why was she surprised? That's how a marriage was supposed to be. They thought they had secrets but didn't actually, and to keep things exciting, they let the other person think they did.

"All right, night, sweetie. Don't stay up too late. You know Ava and Sophia will be up early."

Before Mom breezed out of the kitchen, Norah called, "Hey, Mom?"

"Mmm?" Mom half-turned, holding the brim of the mug up to her nose to catch a whiff of the spicy scent.

"You know with all of this planning I've been doing for Izzy's party, and all the decorating, I've been thinking." She hesitated to get the words out, worried Mom wouldn't get it in the way Todd had. And maybe holding this tight to her chest would be better, safer. But no, she needed someone else's opinion. And Moms had always mattered to her. "I think I want to do it again."

Mom smiled. "That's nice. I'm glad you're enjoying it. And I gotta admit, it's been nice seeing you have a project to distract you."

"No, I mean, I think I want to keep doing it. Like as a job."

Mom's brows shot up. "Oh."

"Is that an, *oh, this is a bad idea?* Or, *oh, this is a great idea?*"

A wide smile spread on Mom's face. "Sweetie, this is amazing. I think you'd be great as a party planner. There's a lot involved in a business like that, but I trust you'd do all the research before jumping in."

Norah smiled. "Thanks, Mom." It wasn't the one hundred percent supportive response she'd hoped for, but she supposed it was enough.

"But remember, it doesn't matter what I say. This is your life. Your dad and I will support you in whatever you choose to do."

And there it was. There was the one hundred percent supportive response Norah needed. She fought back the emotion crawling up her throat.

She sniffed. "Thanks."

Mom tiptoed out of the room and Norah got to work on the Jell-O shots.

After only a few minutes, the same stair creaked again. It was probably Dad, his turn at grabbing a night cap, most likely his not-so-secret stash of whiskey. But her heart lunged into her chest when she Todd rounded the corner into the kitchen.

"Hey," her voice croaked out.

"I thought you were going to try to get to bed early tonight?"

"I thought *you* were?"

"Nah, Samson is finally settled so I figured I'd head down here and...okay, full disclosure?"

She looked at him, her body heating under his intense gaze. She couldn't speak so she simply nodded.

"I knocked on your door," he confessed. "When there wasn't a response, I peeked my head in and saw your bed was empty. I figured one of two things, you either lied to me and ditched me to go out with your friends or you lied to me and had more prep work for the party." He gestured at the spread of ingredients across the counter. "Surprise, surprise."

She breathed out a laugh and held up her palms in surrender. "Guilty."

"So, what can I help with?" He sidled up next to her, so close she could smell his familiar scent.

"Um...how about pouring the packages of Jell-O into this pan?"

While he proceeded to do so, she had one thing on her mind, playing on loop in her head, *I knocked on your door.*

"Why did you knock on my door?" she finally got the nerve to ask.

He gave her a look, eyes darkened and heavy-lidded.

Caught in the look shared between them, she inhaled a sharp breath when he put both hands on either side of the counter around her.

"I think you know why," he whispered.

She held her breath when he suddenly clutched her waist, lifting her up and placing her gently on the counter. He spread open her legs and moved in between them, running his hands up her back.

A shiver of longing slid through her entire body.

He leaned in close to her. "I'm trying to resist," he mumbled, his hot words rushing at her neck causing her insides to tingle.

"Resist what?" she whispered.

"You, Buttercup." He gave a gentle tug on a strand of her hair and pressed a tender kiss to her exposed neck.

A quiet moan escaped her throat, and she bit her lower lip. Unable to keep her betraying hands from finding their way inside the back of his shirt. She explored his hot, bare skin, dancing her fingers up and down the sides of his torso. His body convulsed at her touch.

He pressed his forehead to hers, willing her to look at him. "I don't want to screw up this...arrangement we have."

The mention of the deal stilled her exploring fingers. He wasn't wrong. If they acted on these impulses, these feelings, it could interfere with everything. Sure, he had a lot more at stake to lose than she did, but was she willing to risk their fake relationship being exposed? If Landon found out, she'd be humiliated.

With his fingers intertwined in her hair he said, "I also don't know where you're at with the whole healing process after your split with your ex. I don't want to push you. But I'm leaving. In three days. And..." his voice lagged while he began spreading kisses, starting at her forehead, and trailing down to her nose, where he stopped and hovered just above her lips, his breath sweet and humid. "I don't want to have any regrets when I leave."

The apprehension she'd felt moments ago slipped away at his words. The very thought of him leaving before she could kiss him again had her heart racing with urgency. She knew, without a doubt she would definitely regret it.

She tilted her mouth in an invitation and his lips slid over hers in acceptance, gifting her with a delicious kiss full of need and want. Her mouth answered in response, her tongue sweeping over his with vigor. Without thinking, she hooked her legs around his back, urging him even closer to her. She could feel all of him against her, immediately causing a deep ache for him. Digging her heels into his back, he gripped her backside as she rocked her hips into him.

She tossed her head back, the dizzying sensation making her feel delirious as he pressed kisses to the bare skin of her neck.

"Hey, Nor? I..." Nina shuffled into the kitchen.

Norah jerked her head up and released her spider-monkey hold on Todd, her entire body stiffening.

He released his hold on her but only backed away slightly.

"Nina? Hey, what's up?" Norah slid her hand against her swollen lips.

"Uh...sorry...never mind. It was nothing." Nina tip-toed backward, slipping a mischievous grin in Norah's direction.

"Are you sure?"

"Yep. I'll check back in with you tomorrow. You two just go back to...uh...whatever it was that you were doing." She whipped around and hustled out of the kitchen. She threw a, "Goodnight," over her shoulder in singsong.

Todd now had the counter gripped in each hand on either side of her body, bending slightly at the waist. She set a hand to his firm chest where his heart thumped, and she gave him a gentle shove, dipping her head and laughing.

He chuckled and backed up, running both hands through his hair.

"I'm sorry," she said.

"No, no. *I'm* sorry. That was...obviously not thought out real well."

"This house is always full of too many people." She groaned as she hopped off the counter, adjusting her clothing. "It's usually the thing I love most about it. *Usually.*"

He exhaled a long, low breath. "I bet."

She picked up the pan. "It's comforting. All the bodies. The voices. The warmth." She shrugged. "It's kinda silly, I know."

His fingers cinched around her wrist, a gentle touch sending goosebumps shooting up her arms. "It's not silly. I agree, it's nice."

She smiled at him, and he opened the Jell-O, pouring it into the saucepan. "Is your family close?"

"Yeah. But there's just the four of us. Mom, Dad, Ryan, and me. Mom is bugging Ryan and I to settle down and give her some grandbabies. But at the rate the two of us are going, it's not likely to happen in her lifetime."

Her fingers froze while they worked, stirring the water and Jell-O while it heated over the stove. It was none of her business, but it didn't mean she wanted to know his stance on kids any less. Before she and Landon got married, they'd talked about having kids. Lots of kids. That was the plan. But soon after the excitement died down following the wedding and the honeymoon, she discovered that Landon wasn't interested in having babies any time soon. And maybe not ever.

"So, you don't see kids in your future?"

"I don't know. Maybe."

She shouldn't care. What did it matter if Todd wanted kids or didn't?

"I mean, I hope so. If I meet the right person and if it works out for us to have kids. If I'm not too old by then."

She couldn't restrain from smiling, her insides bubbling.

"There are a lot of *if's*."

It was true.

"What about you?" he asked.

"Me?"

"Yeah. Kids? Babies? A family?"

"Yes," she answered promptly.

He quirked a brow at her. "Yes...to what?"

"All of the above." She shrugged. "You should know by now; I love a loud house full of people."

He nodded and smiled.

Their conversation petered out and an unexpected tension filled the space between them. Their evening had taken a turn. From passionate make-out session to serious. And she wasn't sure what was causing the tension.

"So?" Todd finally broke the silence. "How many of these

Jell-O shots do I need to do to get a little buzzed?" He waggled his eyebrows, holding up a plastic cup in each hand.

She snorted a laugh. He was a true pro at lightening the mood and it was a talent about him she admired. It was only *one* of his talents that she admired. He was talented in many other aspects—physical aspects, knowing exactly what to do with those soft lips of his, and those long, confident fingers. She could only imagine what other talented body parts he had and what they could do.

To her body, more specifically.

CHAPTER 21

Todd

By the time V-day rolled around, Todd was tired of the color pink. And he was currently up to his eyeballs in an assortment of pink balloons. Norah wanted a lot of balloons scattered across the floor of the studio. She said it would add to the ambiance while also adding to the fun.

But until Todd dropped Samson off with the Whitley's to babysit for the night, all balloons that weren't filled with helium had to remain in the back storage room. It was too much temptation for a puppy. Samson was somehow finding other ways to get into trouble and distract Todd from being more helpful.

Kelsey stopped by in the afternoon, delivering the cookies, macaroons, and cupcakes they had chosen from Sweet Cakes Bakery. Norah had planned for them to set the baked goods on display right before they returned to the Whitley's to get ready for the party. The second to last item on the to-do list was to make the cotton candy.

"I think everything is ready," Todd said, scanning over the design sheet he'd practically memorized by now.

"You made sure the photo booth is all set?"

Todd nodded. "Yep."

She tapped a finger on her chin, thinking.

"How offended was Leo when you told him you wanted one of those photo booths set ups instead of having him take the pictures?"

"You'd be surprised, but not that offended. He hates taking wedding and party pics. Not since he became this amazing landscape photographer."

"I don't blame him."

Todd maneuvered some of the helium filled heart balloons, setting them closer to the outside brick walls rather than in the middle of the room. Imagining someone getting tangled up in the strings while dancing looked much funnier in his head than it probably was in person.

"Is it almost time to make the cotton candy?"

"Is that all you care about?" she teased.

"Truthfully? Yes." He grinned.

She checked the time on her phone. "I think that might be the last thing we need to do. It's getting late and I need time to get ready."

"You could show up to the party wearing that and no one would care."

She glanced down at herself. She was dressed in an oversized *F.R.I.E.N.D.S* sweatshirt and a pair of worn jeans, tattered holes down the fronts of both legs, and barefoot. "Yeah, right. While all the other women are wearing fancy outfits, I'm gonna show up like this?"

He shrugged. "I wouldn't mind." And he wouldn't. Because all he could think about was what was underneath the clothing. Since their make-out session the night before in the Whitley's kitchen, he couldn't think about anything else.

"And let that pretty dress hanging on my door go to waste? I don't think so."

"Ohhhh right. The dress with the sexy low back. Yeah, we definitely don't want that to go to waste," he growled.

She rolled her eyes playfully and waved him toward the storage room where they'd been storing the cotton candy machine. But he forgot to warn her about the balloons he'd also shoved in there until she was already opening the door. She squealed and ducked while the balloons poured out, billowing at their feet in the hallway.

"Oops." He winced, chuckling.

Samson rounded the corner, bounding straight for the fun. But instead of attacking the balloons like Todd imagined he would, he was cautious. He stood away from the threatening balloons and barked.

"Okay, buddy. That's enough. These guys won't hurt you." Todd bent and petted the puppy.

"Did you forget to tell me about something?" Norah teased.

Pushing a finger against his chest, he said, "Me? Nah, don't think so."

"Well, I guess we better get the machine out before we collect the balloons." She stepped inside the small storage room and pulled on the dolly that held the cotton candy machine.

"Let me get that for you." He rushed over and took a hold of it, beginning to push it out of the room and into the main area of the studio. "How long does this stuff take to make?"

"Not sure. Hopefully not long." She studied the user manual, chewing on her bottom lip. "I would've done it yesterday, but you know how day-old cotton candy looks."

"Do I?" He rubbed at the back of his neck.

"It shrinks. It's no longer fluffy. And the fluffiness is the whole point of these drinks," she answered, annoyance in her tone.

She looked flustered.

"You do know that most people won't notice the consistency of the cotton candy, right?" He raised his brows at her while she flipped through the machine's user manual with more force than necessary. "They won't even notice if you don't serve the drinks at all."

She lifted her gaze to him, and her chin wobbled. "I know that."

There was a pinch in his chest. He wanted to be helpful and supportive.

"Everything doesn't have to be perfect, ya know?"

She narrowed her eyes. "I didn't spend every free minute over the last several weeks working on every detail of this party to have things not be perfect."

He held up his palms and backed away. "You're right. Everything will be perfect. I'll finish up in the kitchen. Let me know if you need help."

The last thing he wanted to do with Norah when he only had three days left with her, was argue. He had much better ideas for their time together. Ideas that required less talking and way more touching.

BACK AT THE WHITLEY'S, TODD TOOK SAMSON IN THE back and let him roam around free in the fenced in yard. The puppy investigated the trees and perimeter, marking his territory, before bounding over to check out the swing set. Todd sat on the top step of the deck, simultaneously watching Samson, and catching up on Instagram.

Unable to help himself, he tapped on Margo's profile. She'd

posted a couple stories in the last twenty-four hours. One of her sushi dinner, one of her legs outstretched and propped on the coffee table with her coffee mug in her lap, one of her leaning over the balcony, with a view of the city, an extra set of hands visible—man hands. His gut tightened. The last story was a selfie of Margo standing in front of a full-length mirror wearing a black, low-cut dress, and heels. With the caption: *Ready for Valentine's Day*.

"Hey," Finn called from behind him.

Todd quickly turned his phone off and set it in his lap.

Finn dropped down next to him on the step. "What's this rumor I hear about singles crashing the party?"

He exhaled a tiny sigh of relief; he'd expected Finn to give him a hard time about Norah. Asking what his intentions were. And honestly, Todd didn't know what his intentions were. Only that he wanted to spend every waking second with her while he was here and if he was lucky enough, see her soon in New York.

"Rumor is true. Norah's idea. But Isabella doesn't know."

"I figured. Sometimes it's best to not tell Izzy everything." He gave him a wry smile.

This was the first time he and Finn had been alone. Todd hadn't had a chance to get to know him much over the past few days since he'd been busy helping Norah. And Finn was busy with his two kids.

The silence stretched heavily between them.

Finn finally cleared his throat. "But Norah on the other hand, she's a straight shooter. Ya know?"

Todd felt Finn looking at him, so he glanced over his shoulder. He wasn't sure what to say to that. Was he even expecting a response?

"You gotta tell her how it is. Otherwise, she gets all anxious and worked up." Finn gazed out at the backyard. Samson dug his nose in the snow while he pranced through it. "There's a reason why we give Izzy a hard time. She's tough, she can handle it. But Norah, they just aren't built the same. She's always been softer, her heart just a little too big."

"Huh, didn't know someone could have too big of a heart," Todd said, trying to make light of the conversation but failing miserably he realized when Finn shot him an incredulous look.

"All I'm saying is, what happened to her—that bastard, Landon—she didn't deserve that."

Todd nodded. "I agree."

"Good. She's a good kid. I just don't want to see her get hurt again." Finn pushed off his knees to stand. "I guess I'll probably see you tonight at the party." He turned to head back into the house.

Todd watched him go, before finally saying, "You know she's not a kid anymore? She's smart. Accomplished. Has some incredible ideas. But you guys treat her like a child."

Had he really said all of that out loud? And to Norah's big brother? What should he expect next? A fist to the face? Todd didn't have a sister, so he didn't know the protocol here.

"She may not be a kid, but she'll always be my little sister. And she doesn't have the best track record with men. We're just looking out for her," Finn countered.

Todd stood and shoved his hands into the front pockets of his coat. "I get that. But maybe let her know that you trust her to make her own decisions. That you're proud of her. Instead of holding her back."

Finn deadpanned. "You got any sisters?"

"No, just a younger brother."

"Well then, I don't expect you to understand." Finn returned inside the house.

Todd shook his head slowly, releasing a low whistle under his breath. Samson bounded up the deck steps and went to the back door. "I guess you've had your fill of snow, huh, buddy? Me too."

Maybe he'd even had his fill of Pineridge.

Heading up the stairs, Todd put Samson in the kennel for a nap so he could focus on getting ready for the party. He hoped he wouldn't be overdressed, in the tailored black pants, and black suit jacket, the white long-sleeved button-down shirt and the skinny black tie. He debated taking the tie off, he kind of looked like he was attending a funeral, but without it, he'd feel like the look wasn't complete.

There was a soft knock on his door, so quiet he almost thought he'd imagined it. When he opened the door, Norah stood on the other side, *the* dress hugging every inch of her body. She was breathtaking.

"Wow," he said, before exhaling a shaky breath.

Her cheeks blushed and she dipped her chin to her chest. "Thanks."

He should say more. He *wanted* to say more. But all words seemed to have vanished from his vocabulary.

When she spun before him, his gaze drank her in like a fine wine, deliberately appreciating the dangerously low-cut back and slinky fabric clinging to her curves. He instinctively clutched a hand to his chest. With her auburn hair cascading over her shoulders in waves, she was a welcomed distraction.

"You," she said, gesticulating a hand toward him, "wow, too." She grinned.

Her words brought him back to reality.

He chuckled. "You're absolutely stunning."

"Thank you. Now, c'mon, you ready to put this fake dating to the ultimate test?"

He cleared his throat before finally releasing a raspy, "Ready."

Truthfully, he wasn't ready to leave. He wanted to pull her

the rest of the way into his room and shut the door and spend the rest of the evening here.

In his bed.

Forget the evening, he wanted to keep her all to himself for the rest of eternity.

CHAPTER 22

Norah

The only way to appear as a couple, would be to act like one. Norah wasn't ready to come clean with Izzy or Finn. And which would she be coming clean about? The fake relationship or the real one? But to make the plan work, they really had no choice.

It was a sacrifice she needed to make.

But after Norah took one look at Todd in that fitted black suit, that freshly washed tousled hair of his, and hint of facial scruff on his chiseled jaw—it wouldn't be much of a sacrifice. She wanted to sidle up next to him, grab on, and stake her claim.

Part of her regretted inviting everyone to the party. The single women in this town were going to eat him alive. With enough drinks in them, they had no shame. They would throw themselves at him, proposition him, you name it. She only hoped the rest of the eligible men in this town would arrive soon.

Norah was well aware of how possessive that made her sound. It wasn't as if she'd called dibs on him. He wasn't some prize. He was more than that. Over the past week, he'd morphed from her childhood crush to becoming a close friend.

Norah slid one last look in Todd's direction as they walked up to the door of Leo's photography studio. He looked like he could be featured as Sexiest Man in People Magazine. So, what was he doing with her; a cute girl in a small town who lived so far away? She hated to think about him leaving in two days and taking all that sexiness with him.

And Samson. Gahhh, she'd miss that sweet puppy so much.

Todd opened the door and escorted Norah inside, his warm hand at the small of her back where her skin was exposed. The skin-on-skin contact caused a sensation to rush between her thighs. He was simply being a gentleman but all she could think of was how it would feel to have those large hands caressing her entire body.

He leaned in close, and his hot breath tickled her neck. "Your skin feels as smooth as silk."

And then she melted.

Literally, her knees weakened, and she hoped he would catch her. No, she *wanted* him to catch her, lift her up and carry her—anywhere—as long as they were alone.

For an entire week, the sexual tension between them had been so constant, so strong and she decided right then and there—she wouldn't let him leave Pineridge without doing something to alleviate it.

Tonight, she was ripping off the Band-Aid.

Or in Maddie's words, she was going to *jump his bones*.

"Hey, you two," Isabella called, waving, and shuffling toward them. "Finally."

"Finally? We're early."

"Hardly. The party starts in ten minutes."

"See, early." Norah nodded.

Todd slid his fingers down the inside of her arm and held

her hand, giving it a gentle squeeze. It felt like a reminder that he was here to support her. That he was here with her. She exhaled a shaky breath.

"Not to worry, everything is done. We were here until just a few hours ago getting set up," Todd said.

All Norah's hard work felt unnoticed as Izzy resituated a few things on the table, re-fanning out the napkins, and repositioning some of the heart-shaped macaroons on the tiered tray.

"You just go and relax. I've got it all covered." Norah shooed her sister away.

Isabella bit her lip. "Are you sure?"

"Take a look around," Todd said, spanning an arm across the main room of the studio. "Everything is perfect. Whitley, Norah worked her ass off on this party, a little gratitude would be nice."

Clutching at her chest, Izzy said, "Oh my goodness, you're right. I'm so sorry, Nor. You did an amazing job at pulling all this together. I couldn't have imagined it would look this good. Thank you."

Norah pursed her lips. "Well, Todd was a huge help."

"C'mon now, she's just being modest. She designed all of this. I was just a workhorse." He slid Norah a crooked smile.

She choked. The way he said *workhorse,* came out sounding like sexual innuendo and she cringed hoping Izzy wouldn't pick up on it.

"Well, thank you to you too, Langston."

He let go of her hand and put an arm around her shoulder. "Don't you think Norah would make an awesome party planner?"

Norah shot him a look. Even though she'd been giving it some serious thought the past day or two, she wasn't ready to talk to Izzy about it. Izzy was the planner. The wildest thing she ever did was leave New York and risk everything for a future with Leo. But she'd always wanted Norah to think things through before jumping into anything. And a new career —a business, she'd surely want to give her two cents.

"Oh yeah, definitely. And after this party, you'd get a lot of business, I'm sure."

Norah's eyes widened and she glanced back and forth between Isabella and Todd, shock rippling through her. "Really?"

"What do you mean, *really?* This place is spectacular. And I've always known you had a talent for this stuff. You should really look into it."

She had—barely, but now it suddenly felt like she'd been given Izzy's blessing to go for it. To at least try. To do some serious research and maybe make an actual attempt at this thing. Her throat thickened with emotion and her words lodged there. She smiled at her sister, taking her by the hand and squeezing it. Isabella wasn't a touchy-feely person so Norah had to take these rare moments when she could.

The door of the studio opened, and Kelsey popped her head inside. "Am I early?"

"Nope, c'mon in," Izzy said, happily but to Norah she hissed, "Get the music going, will you?"

"Right, music."

Todd took a hold of her shoulders. "No, I'm on it. You go have a good time."

"You sure?"

He nodded, smiling and her skin tingled. She watched him strut away, sucking her lower lip in between her teeth.

"Mmm-hmm," Kelsey groaned next to her, causing Norah to startle. "That is one fine piece right there."

"Uh...yeah, I hadn't really noticed."

Kelsey deadpanned. "Right. As if it wasn't obvious you were just picturing him fathering your babies."

"What? I wasn't. I..."

Kelsey bumped her shoulder into her. "Don't worry, your secret is safe with me." She smiled wickedly.

And Norah didn't believe her one bit.

"You two can keep parading this charade of dating but I know heart-eyes when I see them."

Guilty.

"You look smoking hot, by the way. That dress? It's so sexy I almost want to do you." She laughed.

"Kelsey," Norah shrieked, feeling her cheeks burn.

"Get a grip, girl. You're so tense, have you forgot my sense of humor?"

Norah ignored her comment. "Well, you look hot yourself. That skirt looks great on you."

"Aw thanks. I'm no Barbie but this body hasn't let me down yet." Kelsey fiddled with the waistline of the red floor-length skirt.

"Where's Davis?" Norah asked, glancing over both shoulders.

"Parking the truck. Cars are already lined down the street." Kelsey tucked her dark hair behind her ear.

Norah winced. Maybe inviting the entire town wasn't such a great idea after all.

"I'm here," a voice called in singsong. "Time to get this party started."

Norah spun around to find Maddie, dancing her way inside before striking a pose. She wasn't wrong. Now that Maddie had arrived, the party had officially begun.

It didn't take long for more single people to arrive. And Isabella was not only disappointed, but she also looked genuinely confused. It took some explaining of why Norah and Maddie thought they should have an open invitation to everyone in town.

"It's fine. We'll chat later," Izzy said to her.

Something told Norah it wasn't fine.

After watching her walk away, Norah picked up a glass of the champagne with the cotton candy on top.

Todd reached for one at the same time.

"These seem to be a huge success," he said, flashing her a closed mouth smile that sent heat traveling through her veins.

"Thanks to you." She held out her glass to him and he clinked his own into hers.

He shrugged. "I only read the manual. You made the cotton candy," he said before taking a sip.

Unable to resist, she admired his Adam's apple as he drank. She swallowed her own champagne, the bubbles tingling her tongue.

"So?" He raised his brows. "How bad do you think Isabella is gonna go off on us after everyone leaves?"

"Hopefully she forgets all about it. Look at her," she gestured with her glass in Izzy's direction. "She looks so happy dancing with her husband."

"There's a relief."

She watched Isabella for a moment longer before Todd spoke.

"Sooooo..." he stretched out the word and Norah looked at him, waiting for him to continue.

Todd scratched at his jaw, drawing her attention there—to the light-colored scruff, to his tempting mouth, to his soft lips. Her body buzzed as her mind traveled back to the kiss they'd shared the night before in her parent's kitchen. How his lips melted against her bare skin, how his fingers tangled in her hair and then his hands gripped her backside.

"Norah?" The somewhat familiar voice behind her interrupted her fantasy.

She spun around and found Garrett Vance. *The* Garrett

Vance that made up half of the Vance twins and the Renovation Dudes. And the same Garrett Vance that wasn't supposed to be here.

"Wanna dance?"

"Uh," she said hesitating.

Her vision slid to Todd, her eyes pleading for him to help her out. She wanted to dance with Todd not Garrett. The only thing she wanted to do with Garrett was give her a piece of her mind for lying to her best friend.

"Don't let me stop you." Todd stepped backward. "These glasses aren't going to fill themselves."

She glanced back at Garrett, who held an open palm out to her. He had large hands, rough from his carpentry work. Something she normally would find attractive. But since she'd had a chance at the feeling of Todd's smooth hands on her skin, the rough hands were no longer a turn on.

When she looked back over her shoulder, Todd was gone. She pushed her lips into a pout of disappointment and then slipped her hand in Garrett's awaiting one. Garrett had a wide back and muscular arms she could feel through his suit jacket. There was no denying he wasn't fit and attractive, with his dark hair, straight jawline, blah blah blah.

But his cocky, egotistical personality was far from attractive. And the stunts he'd pulled on Maddie were unforgivable.

Garrett's hand slid down her back, so far it threatened to reach the point of no return and she wouldn't let him get that far. She broke free from his embrace, before the song had even come to an end.

Punching a soft fist into his shoulder, she said, "What the hell, Garrett?"

"What?" He frowned.

"You show up here, asking me to dance, after lying to Maddie about being out of town," she bellowed.

"I didn't mean to lie." He scratched at his chin, gaze flicking around. "I just...I just didn't want to let her down again."

She glared at him. "But you did. When you lied to her."

"I like her, Norah, I do. But I'm a screw up. I have a reputation. And honestly, she deserves better."

Norah reared back her fist and punched him again, harder this time.

"Ow, shit, stop doing that, would ya?" he whined, rubbing at his shoulder.

"She deserves an explanation. So, march your butt right over to her and give it to her. Now." Norah maneuvered herself behind him and shoved him through the crowd.

"Fine, fine," he muttered. "I got this."

She watched him go in search of Maddie before she spun around and headed in the opposite direction. Some of the trays needed to be refilled with the heart-shaped cookies that had the anti-men-valentine's-hater sayings.

Instinctively, her eyes drifted around the room searching for Todd. She spotted him dancing with Izzy while *Here I Go Again* by Whitesnake played through the Bluetooth speaker. She smiled as the memory of her and Todd's impromptu dance session in her room came to her mind. She knew she'd always think of him when she heard that song from now on.

It was *their* song.

The front door of the studio opened and in walked Landon, hand in hand with Mia Mosley. Norah groaned inwardly. Why were they here? Shouldn't they be out celebrating their first Valentine's Day together? It was the reason Mia had declined the invitation to the party in the first place. Not that Norah had even wanted to invite her. But Isabella and Kelsey both thought she at least deserved an invitation. They didn't want to leave a single lady out.

The two shuffled through the crowd before splitting off,

Mia heading toward a group of women by the food table and Landon—*oh crap*—headed straight for *her*. She turned and took a step to the left, but there were too many people, so she spun around and took a step to the right and bumped into the back of a guy she didn't recognize. By the time she turned back around, Landon was standing there, his firm chest visible in the stretched material of his black sweater.

"Hey, Nor."

"Don't call me that," she muttered the reminder for the thousandth time, rolling her eyes.

"I've always called you that."

"Yeah well, you used to also see me naked. Things changed when you cheated on me."

He studied his feet while they shuffled against the hardwood floor. "How long are you gonna make me feel guilty for that?"

She gasped, folding her arms in front of her. "You're kidding right?"

"Look, Nor—Norah, however long it takes, I'll take the blame. Because you're right, I messed up. I'll probably spend every day of the rest of my life regretting what I did. I just need you to forgive me."

"I have forgiven you, Landon. But that doesn't mean we need to be friends." She whipped around, snatching a full glass of champagne off the table before she rushed to the back of the studio and into the small kitchen. Norah braced her hand on the counter and downed her glass of champagne before leaning over the sink. She needed to pull herself together and stop letting the sight of Landon crawl under her skin.

The sound of footsteps behind her caused her to stiffen, she glanced over her shoulder. And thank God, she was rewarded with the sight of Todd. He strutted toward her, and she drank him in fully, all long legs and arms in the tailored suit. He came up behind her, pressing his body into hers and bracing both hands on either side of the counter. With the quick movement, the feel of the pressure against her, she sucked in a sharp breath.

And *oh my*, she wanted him.

"I've been waiting to dance with you," his voice growled into her hair, hot and muffled in her ear, a shiver shooting through her core.

"So why didn't you ask?" she whispered.

"I'm trying to give you your space."

"And this is giving me my space?" She laughed through the tingling traveling down her limbs.

"I'm growing impatient." He looped an arm around her middle, bringing her in closer to him.

She spun around in his embrace and gripped the counter behind her, not trusting herself to touch him. "Then stop trying to give me space I didn't ask for." She drew her lower lip in between her teeth.

His lips pulled into a wicked smile. He released her, but took a hold of one hand, walking backwards while taking her with him, enticing her with his darkening green eyes. She went willingly. At this point, she felt the attraction for him so strongly, so deeply, she'd allow him to take her anywhere.

He guided her through a crowd of people, some calling to her as they went by, but she ignored them, feeling as if in a trance by this charismatic man. When they reached the dance floor, he held up their adjoined hands and wrapped the other around her back, pressing it low and firm.

The reality of the fact that the studio was packed full of people who were most likely watching them itched underneath her skin. These were people she knew, people who knew her situation, and people she'd have to answer to after Todd headed back to New York. While he held her close and they swayed to the music sounding through the speakers, her worries of everyone began to slip away. She hardly paid attention to the song that played, and she slowly lost herself in the heat radiating between them, the craving for one another so electric.

"Who are we making jealous tonight?" she whispered in his ear.

"Everyone, Norah. Everyone," he growled.

He slid his hand further down her back, the skin-on-skin friction causing her body to hum in all the right places.

And she was in serious trouble. Her longing for him was morphing from a lustful desire to a more permanent need. A hope a dream for something more. Something long-term.

But the reality was; he was leaving, and she was staying.

CHAPTER 23
Todd

If he suggested they leave the party and head somewhere to be alone, Todd had a strong inclination Norah would agree. There was no denying that the sexual tension between them had been there, swirling between them all week. But the urgency to do something about it felt too strong tonight to ignore.

The reality that he would be leaving in just two days hit him like a sucker punch to the gut. Not only was he not ready to leave and return to New York, he wasn't ready to say goodbye to this woman. Norah was unlike anyone he'd ever met; fun, lively, energetic, kind, and despite all she'd been through the past year, optimistic.

Todd wanted to spend the rest of the evening with only her, ignoring the ogling eyes he was getting from a couple of the women. But how could he steal Norah away when she was the host of the party? She was constantly getting interrupted from the fun to answer questions, talk to people, and refill snacks.

He stood back, leaning against the brick wall of the studio, sipping another glass of champagne, and watching Norah talk to her ex. From where he stood, it appeared to be a casual conversation. Norah was distant, her fingers fidgeting at her sides. When her ex reached out and nudged her hair behind her ear, Todd pushed against the wall, readying to interrupt their conversation.

Maddie approached him. "Their chemistry is undeniable."

He shot her an incredulous look. "Excuse me?"

"I mean some couples got it and some don't. And them, they definitely got it."

He tilted his head as he narrowed his gaze at her. "I don't know what game you're playing here, but—"

"No, I don't know what game you're playing," she interrupted. "It seems awfully convenient that you suddenly popped up on Norah's Instagram the week of Valentine's Day."

His brows drew together.

She pointed at Norah and her ex with her glass. "Your little plan seems to have worked."

"I don't follow."

"I know Izzy invited you to come here to be Norah's date. And I know you and Norah faked this whole thing so Landon and your ex would get jealous. But she deserves much better. And she thinks you're better."

His gaze dropped to the floor.

"So be better," she said softly.

He glanced up at her.

"Don't disappear on her. She loves you." Maddie gave him a half-smile before she left him and crossed the room.

Todd wanted to be better for Norah than her ex was. He snatched another champagne glass from the table and shuffled through the crowd toward Norah. By the time he reached her, she was standing dangerously close to her ex. A jealous feeling coiled in his gut.

"Hey," Norah brightened.

"Brought you another drink." He handed her the glass she didn't ask for.

"Um, thanks." Her eyes shifted from him to Landon, and she appeared flustered.

He wasn't an intimidating guy, even though he was taller than her ex. But he needed to show Landon that she was no longer interested in getting her heart broken by him again.

Besides, if these two were too close for comfort, how would he and Norah look convincing as a couple?

"Hey, Mr. Lawyer, right?" Landon said, attempting to be funny.

Todd clenched his jaw.

"I was just trying to convince Nor to save a dance for me. You don't mind, do you?" He patted Todd on the arm.

"Actually, I do mind you wanting to dance with *my* girl-friend." He held his hand out to Norah. "C'mon, Buttercup, let's go take our turn in the photo booth." He smiled, wiggling his brows suggestively.

"Ohhh, okay." She slipped her hand in his and he exhaled a relieved breath.

"We'll catch you around," he mumbled to Norah's ex, and squeezed her hand.

Todd led her through the dancing crowd and toward the area where one of those remodeled travel trailers had been turned into a makeshift photo booth had been set up. They were the big thing at parties. Once Pinterest showed something to the world, that's all it took.

"If you wanted to get me alone, why didn't you just say so," she whispered when they reached the line for the photo booth.

"You looked like you needed saving." He hadn't dropped her hand, instead held it tighter, putting pressure in her palm.

"For the record, I didn't. I can save myself."

Pressure landed in his gut, and he cleared his throat. "Okay, you're right. But what if I *wanted* to save you?"

Her cheeks flushed as her smile grew and it was captivating.

They moved up, only one more couple waited ahead of them. There were things he wanted to say. But he wasn't exactly sure what. Something like, *I need to know you'll be fine after I leave. I worry about you. I want you to come with me.* Okay, that last thought hadn't occurred to him until just that moment. *Did* he want her to come with him? Back to New York?

He had absolutely nothing to offer her. What would he say, *leave your family, your job, your hometown and come shack up with me at my parent's house?*

The couple spilled out of the photo booth and the woman approached Norah. "This party is so much fun. Isabella said you planned the whole thing. You think I could hire you to plan my daughter's first birthday?"

"I...um...yeah, maybe."

"Great. I'll be in touch." The woman sauntered away with her husband.

Norah turned to Todd, and he raised his brows, giving her a knowing smile and squeezing her hand.

She squealed. "Okay, maybe you were right. Maybe I could actually attempt this party planning thing."

He pulled her close to his side and pressed a kiss to her temple and if felt so natural. No prompt necessary. No selfie or ex around. And it felt right.

"It's our turn." She tugged him inside the photo booth.

After he closed the door behind them, they followed the instructions attached to the wall next to the screen where the camera lens was. Norah waited on the refurbished leather seat, sorting through an assortment of photo props resting on a tabletop. Lots of various mustaches attached to wooden sticks, hearts, lips, funny glasses, black quote bubbles with sayings like: *Will you be my Galentine, #single, fries before guys, no boys allowed, Cupid is stupid.*

"We only get four poses, so we better make them count." He joined her on the seat.

"Okay, here, you use these, and I'll use these." She handed him large red glasses with the saying: *Hers.* With an arrow pointing in Norah's direction. He looked at her, brows raised. "Really?"

She hunched a shoulder, tilting her head toward it sheepishly, holding up her own; Glasses with an arrow and the saying: *His.* "These are perfect couple photo opportunities."

"Right."

Because this wasn't real. They weren't a real couple. She wasn't wrong—these would be great for posting on all his socials. If his bosses and the partners saw them, they would help make their relationship look even more credible.

Still, the disappointment sat heavy in his chest.

Norah handed him a thick curling black mustache while she held big red lips in front of her. Regardless if this was all for show or not, he wouldn't waste the opportunity to hold her, to pull her in tight, to feel her warmth against him.

They smiled and the first flash went off. With only about ten seconds in between each picture, they had to be quick in choosing their next pose. For the second picture, he chose the quote bubble with the words: *Fries before guys.*

Norah giggled and held up the quote bubble: *Cupid is stupid.*

Seemed fitting.

They tilted their heads close together and smiled, waiting for the flash.

For the third picture, they dropped the props and Todd

pinched a strand of Norah's hair, bringing it toward him and underneath his nose to act as a mustache. She laughed and did the same, pulling a separate strand of her hair and holding it underneath her own nose and they made a funny face until the camera flashed.

For the fourth picture, Todd was taken by surprise when Norah looped her hands around his neck, spreading her fingers through his hair, drawing him in toward her neck. He breathed in her intoxicating scent, and he pressed a kiss to her neck. A throaty moan escaped and caused his hormones to kick in high gear as he kissed her stupid, their mouths crashing together in a frenzied way. He wanted to devour her, right then and there. His mind shut out everything else—the people and the noise— gliding a hand underneath her dress, he gripped her smooth thigh.

"There are people waiting," she whispered, kissing him again and tugging on his lower lip as she pulled back.

"I don't care," he panted, kissing a trail from her neck and down to her collarbone. "You started it."

She giggled. "I know. But not now. Not like this."

He lifted his gaze, peering into her heavy-lidded eyes and recognizing the craving there.

He could be patient. "Okay. You're right." He pressed his lips to the tip of her nose.

Standing, she took both of his hands in hers and yanked him up with her. He adjusted his pants and pulled her in front of him so her body would block him from questioning eyes when they stepped out of the booth.

"Just stay in front of me."

Norah snorted a giggle and pushed open the curtain, they stepped out and practically ran smack into Isabella, hands propped on her hips and a scowl on her face.

"Izzy?" Norah exclaimed.

Isabella narrowed her eyes. "Just what in the hell do you two think you're doing?"

CHAPTER 24
Norah

It had been a long time since Norah had seen the look Izzy was giving her now. It was a mixture of disappointment and anger.

"What's up?" Norah's voice cracked.

Izzy snatched Norah by the wrist and yanked her toward the small kitchen. "What's up?" she mimicked. "What is going on with you two?"

Norah flattened her lips and peered up at Todd who had his hands clasped in front of him. She wanted to giggle but clearly that was not the right response, Izzy was upset.

"Chill out, Izzy. What are you even talking about? We're friends."

Her brows shot up into her hairline. "Friends?"

"Yeah, friends."

"You hardly know each other."

"I'd beg to differ." Todd smirked.

Oh, they knew one another better than Izzy could imagine. Norah knew what his mouth on her skin felt like, what his lips on hers felt like, she knew the rhythm of his tongue, she knew how those large hands felt gripping her backside.

Her cheeks burned at the thought.

But she also knew about his family. About his hope to one day settle down, give his mom grandbabies. She knew about his relationship with his brother, Ryan. And about his quiet unhappiness with his job and maybe he didn't want to be a lawyer forever. She knew how much he loved New York.

"You know, Izzy, while you've been busy working this week, Todd and I have been preparing for this party. We did all the decorating. Which means we've been getting to know each other. You can't spend an entire week with someone and not get to know them."

"Yes, but one week is nothing."

Todd cleared his throat and both women looked at him. "We're just having some fun. There's nothing to worry about."

Norah blinked at him. Is that all it was? Is that all they'd been doing? Having *fun*? Sure, it's not as if she thought they had a future together, but weren't they doing more than having fun?

"Right," she blurted.

He slid her an uneasy smile. Almost as if he hadn't expected her to agree with him. But what else was she supposed to do?

"Regardless," Izzy said. "Both of you just got your hearts broken. Neither of you are going to be the other's rebound." She pointed a finger in their faces. "Got it?"

Norah nodded.

"Got it," Todd said.

"Good." Isabella flattened her dress. "Now, no more of these rumors that the two of you are a real couple. I'm gonna go and try to have a good time. I suggest you two do the same." She spun around and left them standing there.

"I guess we should go mingle?" Norah suggested, even though it was the very last thing she wanted to do.

"I guess," he relinquished. "But, you—me, later?" His brows rose in question as he stepped backward slowly.

Even if his intention was just to have fun with her, she had the burning desire to finish what they'd started. The rebound idea didn't sound too bad. She could do that. No commitment. No attachment.

Besides, she didn't have a choice. Like it or not, Todd was leaving in two days.

She nodded and bit her lower lip.

He clutched at his chest. "Don't do that," he growled, his attention on her mouth.

"What?" She grinned, knowing exactly what she was doing to him and loving it.

AFTER ABOUT AN HOUR, THE CROWD HAD DIMINISHED substantially, and only close friends remained. Todd seemed to mingle well with Norah's Pineridge friends which only warmed her heart more. But her attention had mostly been on Maddie and Garrett. The two had been practically inseparable all evening. She wanted to be happy for her friend, but not only had Garrett lied to her about going out of town tonight and broke off their date, he had a bad reputation. And it had only gotten worse since he and his brother Davis had signed the contract for their show.

Norah had to distract herself from hovering over the two while they sat next to one another flirting and touching. She stepped away and headed for the photo booth. No one was waiting in line anymore and the door was open. She saw several strips of photos scattered on the small table next to it—abandoned photos of the party goers. Her interest piqued and she sorted through them, finding one of Maddie and Garrett and she smiled, shaking her head. Two of the biggest flirts in this town. They were trouble. The two hadn't even used any of the props, but rather used themselves as props. Her on his lap, kissing, him with a handful of her boobs.

Okay, maybe she'd toss these.

But then her eyes drew toward another set of pictures. Landon and Mia. Her stomach flipped and all the champagne she'd drunk suddenly went to her head causing her to feel off kilter. Each of the four pics looked...fine. Not inappropriate at all. They used the photo props, they smiled, but she had to admit, she couldn't see a spark between them.

This is what Landon had ruined their marriage for?

Somehow, seeing their lack of intimacy made her feel worse.

"Whatcha looking at so intently?" Maddie said, suddenly standing next to her, peering over her shoulder.

Norah dropped the slide of pictures. "Huh? Mhmm nothing."

Maddie narrowed her eyes at her before glancing down at the pictures. She picked up the ones of Landon. "Huh."

"What?"

"These are...well, they're boring."

"You think?"

"Oh yeah, no sexual attraction between these two whatsoever."

Norah rubbed at the back of her neck.

"Now these two," Maddie said, picking up another set of

slides. "Wowzers, the attraction is blinding." She hid her eyes, turning her head away dramatically.

Norah giggled and snatched the pictures from her. "Whatever. We were just having fun." She studied the slide of pictures of her and Todd, her skin warming at the memory of their time in the booth.

"You go ahead and tell yourself that. But the Norah I know, doesn't do fun. I mean, you're fun. But you don't do rebound sex. You don't do one-night stands. You're the forever kind of person. You're looking for your lobster."

Norah rolled her eyes. "Wrong. I found my lobster and he left me for a new, perkier lobster."

"Then obviously, Landon wasn't your lobster," Maddie countered.

Norah pursed her lips and stuck her chin out defiantly. "I can do a one-night stand." She didn't even sound convincing to her own ears.

"It's okay, Norah. It's not for everyone."

"But I can. And I will. Tonight."

Maddie's eyebrows shot up unconvincingly. "Sweetie, don't you do it on my account. I know I've been bugging you to get back out there and have a few flings. But this isn't what I was meaning. This one," she paused, tapping at Todd in the pictures still clutched in Norah's hand, "isn't a fling."

Norah glared at her friend.

"There's more there. And I know you know it too."

Garrett appeared at the room's opening. "Mads, ready?"

Norah mouthed, *Mads?*

They were on a nickname basis already?

"One second." Maddie held up a finger to him before turning back to Norah. "Please promise me you won't do anything you'll regret in the morning."

"You too," Norah countered.

Maddie glanced at Garrett again and shrugged.

Norah rolled her eyes while she watched her best friend saunter toward the town's biggest player. She looked down at the scattered pictures again. She gathered them into a pile but picked up the one of her and Todd. Studying it, she felt a swoop low in her belly. Regardless if there was a longing for something more between them, the reality was, she couldn't have more.

So she'd have to take what she could get.

ONCE THE STUDIO HAD EMPTIED, NORAH BEGAN gathering empty glasses, and plates. She moved around the studio dragging a large black trash bag behind her and filling it. Todd picked up balloons from off the floor, using scissors to release the air.

"Are you sure you don't want us to help?" Izzy asked.

Norah took one look at her sister, paying attention to the dark circles underneath her eyes, and the slump in her shoulders.

"I'm sure." She squeezed her hand. "Leo, get my sister home and to bed."

"You got it." He waggled his eyebrows, snaking his arm around Izzy's waist.

"Eww." Norah looked away but smiled.

"And you make sure to clean this place up and lock the doors behind you."

"Yeah, yeah, I know."

"I mean it. My studio better look exactly as it did a week ago," Leo said pointedly.

"Norah, you should head home, and I can come by in the morning and help clean up."

"Nope. I got this." Norah nudged the two of them toward the door. "Now, go."

"Fine, fine. Goodnight. See you tomorrow."

"Yep, tomorrow."

Norah shut the door behind them, locking it and pressing her back against it, squeezing her eyes closed.

Finally.

She exhaled and went back to cleaning up, clearing away the leftover treats and more empty glasses. Todd brought another trash bag to her, and together they filled it full. The playlist of love songs and anti-love songs still played on repeat through the space of the studio.

The sound of the music hummed throughout her body while the champagne still worked through her veins. Todd sang some of the lyrics to *Keep on Loving You* by REO Speedwagon underneath his breath. It was sexy and wished she wasn't still so turned on from their make out session in the photo booth.

Okay, maybe it was the result of every single encounter they'd had throughout the entire week, building. At this point, she felt as if she might explode. This was the lengthiest foreplay she'd ever experienced.

When Todd began singing the lyrics to another song, she glanced at him. "Do you know every song?"

He shrugged. "No but I guess I know a lot of songs. My dad is a huge music buff. Used to take me to concerts, made me sit for hours on Friday night's listening to loud base-filled songs."

"That sounds nice."

"Yeah, it used to annoy me and Ryan when we were kids. But now, I'm grateful he shared something he loved with us. It gave me the opportunity to get to know him on a different level."

Norah's chest warmed. She liked learning another thing about Todd. But was then reminded that the more she knew about him, the harder it would be to say goodbye to him.

"I get it. My dad loves Country music. Got us hooked early on."

He quirked a brow. "Country?"

"Yep. I can't help it. I'm a sucker for the genre now."

"Really? Country?"

"Shush." She giggled. "It's all about love and finding love and being in love."

"I guess," he mumbled.

Heat crawled up her neck and her cheeks flushed. Here she was, wanting to seduce this guy and try the whole *one-night stand thing* and she was going on and on about love.

"There're some break-up songs too, obviously. But there's also some hot ones. You know...about sex and one-night stands."

"Yeah?" Disbelief shone in his eyes.

"There are." Her voice went up. "You don't believe me?"

"It's not that I don't believe you, I just think maybe you're confused by the content."

What was that supposed to mean?

"Fine. I'll show you." She walked to the computer that was set up on a table for the music. She sorted through her playlists on Spotify. When she found the song, she was looking for, she added it to their playlist and hit *play.*

The voice of Chase Rice began with the lyrics she found familiar. The ones that caused her body to hum in all the right places. She peered up at Todd who stood back, hands on his hips while he listened. He glanced at her, the two of them making eye contact and she was grateful he couldn't read her mind. If he could, he'd discover all her racy thoughts of dragging her fingernails up his back, of putting her mouth on all the dips of his body, of feeling the weight of his body on top of hers.

The song ended and the air between them was thick with sexual tension. Another love song began, and she cleared her throat. "See, told you."

At first, it looked like that tough exterior of trying to keep this thing between them pretend might break. The usual bright green hue in his eyes darkened and his jaw ticked. But he cocked a brow at her and bowed dramatically. "I am not worthy."

She snorted a laugh and exhaled a shaky breath, relief filling her lungs at his ease to break the tension. Because honestly, someone had to. She sure as heck wouldn't. All her childhood fantasies of being with her crush felt within reach and yet at the same time, felt so far away.

Forcing her legs to move, she returned to their clean-up work. With her arms full of dirty tablecloths, she walked past him, but he reached for her, taking a hold of her wrist and the tablecloths dropped to the floor. He whirled her into him, looping both arms around her back and pulling her in close to him purposefully so she could feel *everything*. All of him. Every hard plane and crevice of his body.

His lips hovered over hers and she focused on steadying her breaths, resisting from sweeping her tongue out.

"You honestly thought you were gonna play that song and then we were gonna just go back to cleaning?" His words growled against her lips.

"I...I don't know...I guess I thought..." She stopped speaking. Honestly? She was hoping if she played him that song, that he wouldn't be able to resist her. That he would want her. And finally do something about the tension they'd been dancing around all week.

"Say it?" he growled, demanding. "I want to hear it."

"I want you to do something about this tension between us," she whispered.

A wicked smile played on his lips as he maneuvered his hands from her back and into her hair. He finally kissed her then, relieving at least some of the craving that had been building. His mouth was needy at first, but she hoped he'd slow it down so they could take their time. If this would be their only night together, she wanted to explore everything.

He fingered her hair, drawing her closer into him, their mouths connected. As he smoothed his hands down the length of her body, across her bare back and over her butt, she tugged at the knot of the tie around his neck. She gave it a good yank before using both hands, her fingers working quickly to loosen it and pull it over his head. His palms squeezed while he kissed her neck, her collarbone, her shoulder, and she began working at the buttons of his shirt, her breathing thin.

"Maybe," he whispered, panting in her ear, "we should head back to the house. You know, where there are beds?" He planted a trail of delicate kisses from her neck down to her collarbone.

"And have someone interrupt us? Not a chance." She shoved his shirt off his shoulders. But he had a white tee underneath she'd have to work on next.

Lifting his head, he gazed down at her, his thumbs grazing her cheeks. "Are you sure about this? Because we don't have to. We can just go back to pretending. It's okay."

His mossy green eyes pierced into her soul. The connection between them went deep. This was more than a physical attraction and she knew it. But did he know it too?

She wouldn't allow herself to second guess it. This could be their only opportunity and she wouldn't let it slip them by.

She nodded. "I'm sure. I don't want to pretend anymore."

"Pretty sure we weren't fooling anyone, anyway."

She grinned and he devoured her lips, sinking his tongue further into her open mouth. With meticulous care, he slid her dress off her bare shoulders, allowing the material to fall and stop at her hips. When he gazed down at her, she felt less exposed and more conscious about the weird nude backless bra she had to spend a fortune on at Victoria's Secret to wear with the dress. Instead of waiting for him to try and figure it out, she carefully released her breasts from the adhesive cups and tossed the bra to the floor.

Relief reflected in his eyes, and he smiled appreciatively at her. She drew her lip in between her teeth. The only other man to ever see her naked was Landon. The two of their bodies had practically grown up together so she hadn't felt as exposed with Landon. But now, under the intense gaze of Todd, her skin tingled with worriment. What if he didn't like what he saw? What if he had been with so many women, she was nothing in comparison.

But when he reached both of his sturdy arms around her, pressing his hands into her back, and drawing her in close against his broad chest, she felt the protection from him. Almost as if he could feel her vulnerability and was trying to put it to ease. This small act only made her crave him more.

"There's the couch," she mumbled through the heady feeling of the champagne mixed with desire. "In the photo booth."

Todd didn't waste any time, he released her, but took her hand in his and led her toward the photo booth in the studio. The streetlamp outside shining through the cracked blinds illuminated the studio with a romantic glow.

Inside the photo booth, he closed the door before he stood in front of her. He dragged her dress slowly down her hips, allowing the satiny material to pool at her feet and leaving her standing there in only her underwear and heels. Feeling less exposed in the nearly darkened small booth, an unexpected confidence she hadn't had in quite some time filled her. After Landon had cheated on her, left her for another woman, she'd felt less-than. But tonight, with Todd's attentiveness, she felt beautiful and sexy.

And wanted.

Gathering the hem of his white tee, she slowly slid it up his solid chest before finally yanking it over his head. She took him in, biting her lower lip. His physique was lean but strong. The perfect V, somewhat hidden at the waistline of his pants, teased and urged her to continue undressing him so she could get a full view of his naked form.

And then he was standing before her, solid, and breathtaking.

The resistance was hopeless. She leaned into him and smashed her lips against his, sensually, then earnestly, and then they were kissing in a frenzy. Like they'd been waiting their entire lives to finally be with one another. She kicked off her shoes and her fingers made quick work at his belt. Once undone, he helped by wriggling out of the suit pants. He thrust her backward until she collided with the loveseat, being less careful with her now.

And it turned her on even more.

When he hovered over her, she danced her fingertips up the smoothness of his chest and back down again, his muscles tensing underneath her touch. His hands and mouth worked over her entire body with precision, while she pushed her fingers through his hair and dug her nails into his back.

Spreading her legs open, he dragged his tongue down the inside of her thigh causing her to shiver and inch up the sofa. He took her hands in his, fingers joining and clasping around each other's while his tongue went to work, circling her navel before moving south, licking and teasing. Pressing their hands back and resting them next to either side of her head, she wrapped her legs around his shoulders, moaning and rocking her hips to guide his mouth to just the right spot.

"Langston," she said, breathless, "I'm ready."

He released her hands and propped himself over her, gazing down at her as if drinking her in. "Are you sure?"

"Please." She bit her lip and grinned.

Todd produced a condom as if out of nowhere, sliding it on quickly before easing himself into her, gently and taking his time so she ached for him even more. While he moved them together in a meticulous rhythm, her hands explored his body, the hard muscle, and his strong shoulders. He continued to ravage her mouth with his while he slid his hands over her tender breasts, taunting and teasing.

Until at last, she couldn't hold on any longer and teetered on the edge of pleasure.

"Finally," he groaned in her ear, and exhaled a gruff laugh.

She pinched her eyes closed while he consumed her mouth with intense kisses and tiny fireworks splintered off before exploding. And then she was plunging, melting into him, and whispering all kinds of wild things in his ear like, "I think I'm falling for you."

Panting and having a difficult time catching her breath, he pressed a kiss to her lips, her neck, and then the crevice of her collarbone, which seemed to be his favorite place. She wanted him to camp there, keep his lips there for the rest of her life.

She threw her arm over her face. *What was she saying—the rest of her life?* He was leaving in two days. Maybe she should just hope he would stay with her for the night. He laid his head on her chest, in between her exposed breasts, wrapping his long arms and legs around her like he was an octopus.

"If you don't mind, I'm just gonna live right here from now on."

She snorted a laugh while her eyes watered.

"Charge me rent if you must," he mumbled.

Swallowing, she said, "I should warn you, it's not gonna be cheap."

"I'd expect nothing less, Buttercup." He pressed a gentle kiss to the side of her breast.

Her eyes burned at the corners while she continued to thread her fingers through his hair.

CHAPTER 25
Todd

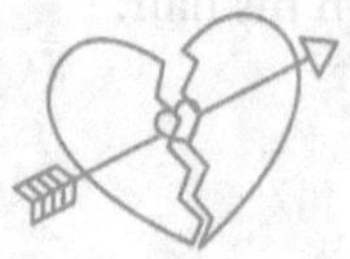

aylight streamed through the slits around the door of the photo booth, rousing Todd to wake. Feeling the rise and fall of Norah's chest pressed against his arms that were wrapped around her, satisfaction filled him.

The two had only gone two rounds before she'd curled into him on the small sofa. He'd draped his suit jacket over them and pulled her in close, his hands gripping her waist and chest, his nose so close, he inhaled the faint scent of her cherry blossom hair. The rhythm of her heartbeat had lulled him to sleep.

Now, pins and needles shot down the length of his arm that had fallen asleep at some point caused by the pressure of her head laying there. With the softness of her backside pushed into his crotch, he was tempted to wake her. But she looked so peaceful in his arms, he couldn't bear the thought.

Last night was everything.

Since that first kiss, he had wanted more. And each day after that, spending so much time together, being in close proximity, had felt like torture. But the wait had been worth it.

Norah had surprised him with her openness, her directness, her assertiveness. The people who called her cute obviously didn't know what she was capable of.

The blood began pounding in his hand and he couldn't take it any longer, he carefully slid his arm out from underneath the weight of her head. The way he figured, if she awoke, they could go another round. But if she continued to sleep, he could sneak away and see if the studio had any coffee.

She stirred, but coiled into herself even more so, causing her butt to push into him further. He groaned. Okay, she was clearly not getting up. He climbed out from behind her and stepped into his pants. Shoving his phone into his pocket, he glanced at Norah, curled up on the sofa, unashamed and beautifully naked. He covered her with his suit jacket.

Padding across the wood floor in his bare feet, Todd went into the small kitchen and found a single-serving coffee machine and pods in a carousel next to it. Score. He rubbed his hands together before filling the vat with water and choosing a coffee blend. He popped it in, found two mugs in the cupboard, and pressed the button before searching the small fridge for cream or milk.

As the second cup of coffee finished brewing, footsteps sounded out behind him. He sucked in a breath and spun around. His gaze found Norah, barefoot and dressed in his white button-down dress shirt, the sleeves rolled up.

And dang, he'd never seen her look more beautiful.

"Morning," she said sweetly.

But that mouth was anything but sweet.

"Morning," he growled, rubbing at the back of his neck and unable to take his eyes off this sexy woman as she advanced toward him.

"Coffee?" She peered around him.

"Uh...yes. Coffee." He turned back around, snatching one of the mugs and handing it to her.

She smiled and her lashes fluttered sleepily as she accepted the mug. "Thanks."

"I couldn't find much to put in it. Only some whipped cream." He waggled his eyebrows at her but suddenly felt nervous. He felt off his game. This was all new territory for him. He'd slept with his fair share of women. But last night meant something to him. More than something.

And he needed to tell her.

"Whipped cream sounds perfect."

Shaking the can first, he popped the top off before pushing the nozzle into her mug, only he must not have had it pointed down enough because air shot out, causing whipped cream to spray in all directions.

"Ahhh," she squealed.

He winced. "Sorry."

She snorted a laugh and used her finger to wipe some whipped cream off her eyebrow.

"Wait, there's more. Let me help you." Todd swiped at some on her cheek.

When he felt her eyes fixated on him, he gazed down at her, and his concern melted away. He leaned into her and sucked some whipped cream off her nose.

"When I woke up alone, I thought you'd left," she whispered like a confession.

He grazed his thumbs over her neck and her cheeks. "I'm not great at this morning after stuff. But this morning, with you, it felt...easy."

"I'm not great at any of this stuff," she admitted.

"I think you're doing just fine."

Going on tiptoe, she pressed a kiss to his lips. When she swept her tongue into his mouth, brushing it against his, the memories of the night before tipped his craving for her over the edge. He took charge of the moment, sliding his hands down her back and gripping her bare backside. He picked her up and she wrapped her legs around his torso as he carried her toward the counter, setting her down and unbuttoning the shirt—*his* shirt, but it looked so much better on her. He'd let her keep it. He could get another.

With her fingers tangled in his hair and her mouth on his chest, he pushed in between her legs.

"I guess I'll be your caffeine this morning," he mumbled.

"Coffee after. This now," she panted before taking his earlobe in between her teeth.

"What the hell?" a shrill voice cut through the air behind them.

Both Todd and Norah froze, their previously frenzied hands and mouths halted, and their breathing accelerated.

"Izzy!" Norah wiped her hand over her mouth and closed her shirt, crossing her arms over her chest.

Isabella stood at the front door. From there, she had a perfect straight shot into the kitchen.

"Hey," was all Todd could find to say, while he attempted to zip up his pants.

"*Hey? Hey?*" Isabella barked. "Is that all you have to say?"

Norah hopped off the counter, still clutching at the shirt. "What are you doing here?"

"Yeah, I mean we told you we would clean up from the party." Todd checked the time on his watch. "It's still early."

"I'm not here for clean-up." She stepped inside, slamming the door behind her, and stomping toward them.

Todd and Norah shared an uneasy look.

When she reached them, her eyes were wide and watering. "Is it true?"

Dread filled his legs. He had a sinking feeling he knew

what she was asking, but like any guilty person, he played dumb for as long as possible. "Is what true?"

"You two?" Isabella pointed an accusing finger back and forth between him and Norah. "Was this all fake? You two came up with a plan to...I don't know...fake date each other?"

"Why would you even ask that? Who told you?" Norah gave him a wobbly glance.

"Margo."

That answer was not what Todd had been expecting. "Margo?" he repeated.

Isabella crossed her arms. "She called me this morning. Told me all about your boss's stipulations for making partner. Which honestly, made a lot of sense. Her moving on with Aaron so quickly, and you two..." her words died off.

"But how did Margo find out?"

"So, it's true? This was all fake?" Isabella ignored his question.

"Yes?" Norah said, dragging out the word so it sounded like a question.

But at the same time, Todd said, "No."

They looked at each other. "What? I mean, yes, but no, not all of it," he stammered over his words.

"Right," Norah confirmed, and Todd's heart slid back down his throat in relief. "The feelings no, but the relationship and dating long distance, yes."

Isabella glared. "What were you guys thinking?"

"It's fine, Izzy. I don't know what you're getting all worked up about it."

"You don't know what I'm getting worked up about? Okay, gee, well I don't know." She paced in the small space in the kitchen. "Maybe that you guys lied. To everyone. And for what? A promotion at work? A—" Isabella paused, looking at Norah. "What did you even get out of this deal? Besides more of a broken heart? Nor, you just got divorced. And Todd just ended a serious relationship. This couldn't have been more than just rebound sex."

"Hey," Todd ground out. "That's not what this is." He turned to look at Norah, finding apprehension in her expression and his heart cracked slightly. He took her hand in his and squeezed it. "You know that's not what this is."

Norah gave him a half-smile.

"Sure, Todd. Now tell her your plans for a future with her. Tell her she's more important than your job, and you'd move here to make it work if you had to," Isabella challenged him.

He slid a look at her, his eyes narrowing.

But she glared right back at him. "Can't do it, can you? Because everyone knows your job is most important. Making partner at thirty is all you care about. It's all you've talked about since you passed the bar exam. Isn't that right? I bet right now, all you're thinking about is how Margo found out? And who else has she told."

Panic rumbled in his chest. He'd been trying to push that issue to the side while he dealt with Isabella. It was important to assure her that his intentions with Norah were genuine. But all those accusations were true. It was almost *all* he could think about.

Lying to his bosses, when they were a business built on ethics, would not go over well.

"I love you, Langston, but you are who you are. And you're no good for my sister."

"Izzy," Norah breathed out, looking tired as she rubbed at her forehead. "That's not your call."

"But Norah—"

"No," Norah interrupted. "You wanna know why I agreed to this plan with Todd? Because I was so sick and tired of being treated like I was fragile. Everywhere I went, I could see the way people looked at me. I wanted to flip the narrative. Have the rumors be about me and a handsome stranger, me moving on and not pining after Landon anymore. And yeah, maybe I wanted Landon to get a little jealous. To finally see what he'd lost."

"Oh, Nor."

"But not to get back together with him. Because despite what you think, I'm doing okay on my own. I know now that Landon wasn't for me. And I'm okay with that. I don't know what's going to happen between Todd and I after today, but it's not your choice to make. It's mine."

Todd glanced at the floor.

"I am sorry for lying to you. And to everyone."

"Me too," Todd said.

Isabella pouted her lips. If he thought Norah was stubborn, Isabella was ten times more. "I just love you. Both of you."

"We know," Norah answered for them both. "And we love you."

"Fine, whatever. I'm gonna go. But this mess better be cleaned up when I come back. And by mess, I'm not just referring to the studio." She turned and stormed out the front door, leaving the two of them alone once again.

They stood there awkwardly for a moment. He gazed at Norah while she fidgeted with the buttons on the dress shirt. He was conflicted. While they needed to discuss their relationship, all he could think about was checking his phone. If Margo knew about everything, there was no telling who else knew.

He raised his brows. "I need to get my phone and find out how much damage has been done. Then, do you want to finish our coffee?"

She shook her head. "You should go take care of that. I'm gonna stay and clean up here and then grab some coffee after I leave."

"I'll stay and help."

"No, it's okay. Just go." She waved him away and started gathering empty glasses off a table.

Todd hesitated before jogging to the photo booth and finding his phone lying on the floor. His stomach dropped. He had several missed texts and phone calls. Some from his boss and a few from Margo and Ryan.

Ryan.

Lead filled his feet. It was Ryan. He was the only one Todd had told. But why? He'd trusted his brother.

"Noooooo," Norah groaned loudly.

Todd spun around and jogged back out to where he'd left her in the middle of the studio. He found her staring at her own phone. Tears welled up in her eyes.

On instinct, he rested his hand on her back. "What is it, what's wrong?"

"It's not just Margo and Izzy who know," she mumbled. "It's...everyone."

The air whooshed from his lungs.

"Landon...Mia...everyone in Pineridge. They all know we weren't really dating. But how? How did they find out?" she glanced up at him, eyes still watering and her lower lip sticking out.

"I think it was Ryan," he muttered.

She furrowed her brows. "Ryan? But how? How would he —" she paused. He knew the moment she realized based on her expression. "You told him?" her voice wobbled.

"I'm sorry, I honestly never would've told him if I thought he would spill to Margo, of all people."

"We promised we wouldn't tell anyone. I didn't even tell Maddie. When she finds out, she's going to be so hurt."

"Imagine how I feel?" He held up his phone. "My bosses

obviously know. Forget the promotion, I'm probably gonna get fired."

"Is that all you care about? Your job? The promotion? This is my life we're talking about. I lied to my family and friends."

"So what? They'll get over it. They'll forgive you and move on. I've worked for over a decade for this dream—for this promotion. Don't you get that?"

She stiffened and crossed her arms. "Yeah, I get it. I get that Izzy was right, you do only care about your job."

Anger swirled in his stomach. He wanted to argue with her, but she was right. While he did think he loved her, he needed to save his career if he could.

His phone buzzed in his hand.

Jack Santos.

"I gotta take this."

Norah shrugged while she sniffed and swiped at her nose. "We're done here anyway."

"I know you don't mean that."

"Last night was fun. So was this week. But in the end, we were both pretending. So, let's chalk it up to a Valentine's Day one-night stand."

Her words caused his heart to crack. He glared at her. "If that's what you want?"

"It is," she whispered.

He glared at her while he put his phone up to his ear and rushed out the door of the studio. "This is Todd."

CHAPTER 26

Norah

Of course, she couldn't very well go into The Daily Grind in last night's party outfit, could she? No. She'd never taken the walk of shame before, but she'd seen enough movies to know to avoid it at all costs if possible.

Hauling several black trash bags full out to her car, her ankle wobbled in the heels from the night before. She shoved the bags into her trunk and hurried to slide behind the wheel. The thought of the other shop owners down the street seeing her caused a shiver of worry to travel underneath her skin.

She had a one-track mind: keep pushing through the motions so she didn't feel anything. Clean up the studio, take out the trash, drive home, and fall apart in the shower.

A quick glance across the street caused her to pause and do a double take while a lump formed in her throat. Maddie's car. If Maddie's car was still here, but she wasn't...the lump quickly turned into a giant boulder because that meant she must've gone home with Garrett.

"Oh, Maddie," Norah ground out.

Well, Norah knew what she'd be doing today. Instead of wallowing and licking her own wounds, she'd be rescuing Maddie. It was just as well. She owed it to her after lying to her. At least then she wouldn't have to think about a certain hot lawyer with mossy green eyes that had the power to set fire to her lady parts in seconds. She shook her head, attempting to rattle the growing craving for a guy she may never even see again.

When she pulled her car into her parent's driveway, her heart sank a little when she didn't spot Todd's car parked out on the road. What if he'd gone without even saying goodbye? Or was that their goodbye?

Norah slipped inside the house, hoping her parents wouldn't hear her come home. By now, they'd surely heard the rumor of her fake boyfriend and she didn't feel up to explaining quite yet. When she saw one of Samson's toys lying on the bottom step, her shoulders eased.

Stupid one-night stand.

Her throat thickened and she blinked back the tears threatening to build. She would not break down. Not here. Not yet.

Once safely upstairs, she removed the dress and Todd's shirt from the night before and allowed it to fall to the floor, not even bothering to hang it up. She carefully peeled off the adhesive bra and tossed it on top of the dress, her underwear came next, all of it in a heap on the floor. Her eyes tunneled at the sight; she felt a lot like that heap.

In the shower, as the beads of hot water pelted her back, she finally released the unbridled tears that had been building since she'd spoken those words out loud in the studio to Todd. She'd regretted them instantly, and wanted to take them back. But when Todd had agreed, had tossed her to the side like she meant nothing—it did something in her chest, her newly pieced-together heart had cracked again.

Maybe the worst part of all of this—Izzy was right. Norah didn't do one-night stands. It might be typical for people her age, for Maddie, for Garrett Vance, and for Todd. But it wasn't typical for her. Call her a hopeless romantic, but she'd always had this idea that there was one person for everyone, a lobster if you will.

Mom and Dad had been together since they were eighteen and were still happily in love. Isabella and Leo had found their way back to one another. And if she and Landon weren't meant to be, then that had to mean he wasn't her lobster. Hers still had to be out there. And something told her, it wasn't Todd Langston.

Disappointment rippled through her core, her breath hitching and her hot tears mixing with the water pouring over her face. She'd been such an idiot. Todd hadn't hidden his agenda from her. And she had agreed to it. Even if he had been truthful in his confession of having no intentions of getting back together with Margo, he also had no intention of pursuing her.

The reality was, she had to let him go. Along with the illusion they would have a future together. Who ended up with their childhood crush anyway? Besides, they'd only spent one week together. Surely that wasn't long enough to decide on forever.

When Norah stepped out of the shower and dried off, wrapping a fluffy white towel around her body, she wiped the fog from the mirror and gazed at her reflection. Puffy eyes from crying, swollen lips from all the kissing the night before, pink blotchy skin from the hot water, and the shadow of a hickey on her collarbone.

Just great.

Her eyes watered again, and she squeezed them shut, willing the tears away. She'd just had the best night of her life and was now a hot mess, grieving what was and what could've been.

Her phone vibrated against the bathroom counter and her heart skittered along with it. She sucked in a breath, picking it up, and then her shoulders slumped.

> **MADDIE**
> Soooooo I screwed up.

> What did you do?

> **MADDIE**
> Please don't lecture me. It's too early and I'm too hungover.

> Maddie!

> **MADDIE**
> I slept with Garrett

> WHAT?

> **MADDIE**
> That's not even the worst part.

> How could it get any worse?

> **MADDIE**
> I accidentally slept over.

Norah's mind skipped back to how her own morning began, waking up on the couch alone, Todd's suit jacket covering her naked body. For a moment, she'd panicked, thinking at some point in the night, Todd had snuck out and left her alone in the studio. Only, she found his clothes still strewn on the floor and caught the scent of coffee wafting through the air.

She'd dressed in his white button-down shirt, bunching the material, and bringing it to her nose. Drawing in a deep breath, her eyes fluttered shut as she inhaled his piney-musk scent. Vivid flashbacks from their passionate lovemaking assaulted her. She'd been thrilled he stayed. Had thought about making them coffee. She'd been full of so much unrestrained hope.

MADDIE

Hello? Are you there?

So what's the problem?

MADDIE

I wasn't supposed to stay over. We're just keeping things casual. Can you please come get me?

On my way.

MADDIE

Hurry

NORAH WAS RIGHT. BEING MADDIE'S KNIGHT IN SHINING armor distracted her from having a pity party herself. She pulled up to the curb outside of Garrett's home. Maddie waited there, wearing the dress from the party from the night before, her sling-back heels dangling from her fingers.

Poor Maddie. She was tough and she could fool most people. But she had never been very good at fooling her best friend.

Maddie slipped into the passenger seat and buckled her seatbelt without looking at Norah.

Deciding not to make things worse, Norah pulled away from the curb, staying quiet. She tried to watch Maddie from the corner of her eye, hoping she wasn't going to cry.

Finally, Norah broke the deafening silence, "So Garrett, huh?"

"Yep," Maddie said, a *pop* at the end of the word.

There was a long pause before Norah spoke again. "I just want to make sure I get this right. What's the term for a two or three-night stand?"

"Damn, Norah, that was harsh," Maddie bit out.

"I'm sorry, I was trying to be funny. Ya know, lighten the mood?"

"It's fine." Maddie smoothed her fingertips underneath her eyes, wiping away streaked mascara. "It was funny. I guess I shouldn't be so emotional about this."

Norah hunched a shoulder. "I mean, you've always had a thing for him. It would be okay if you were a little emotional about it." She felt the intense gaze on her as she studied the road.

Maddie sucked in a deep breath before exhaling it. "You were right."

Norah whirled her attention onto Maddie, her eyes widening. "*I* was right?"

"Don't sound so shocked," Maddie muttered. "About Garrett. Sleeping with him again was a bad idea. I still have a thing for him."

"Aw, Mads, I don't want to be right."

"I know, but it's the truth." Maddie sniffed.

"Did you tell him how you felt?"

"What? No, of course not. He's always made it perfectly clear he isn't looking for anything serious."

"Yeah, well, maybe if you tell him you are..." Norah suggested.

Wiping at her eyes, Maddie said, "I can't. He admitted to me last night that that's why he broke off our date to begin with. He lied about having work out of town because he said he was worried I was still into him and he's not sure if he's ready for a relationship."

"But you *are* still into him," Norah said flatly.

"Yes, but he doesn't know that."

"Oh, Mads, I wish you would've told him. I hate that he hurt you...again."

Maddie faced the passenger window. "Me too. But I'll be fine. Maybe I'll use your new life's motto." She shrugged. "I don't need a man."

Tears burned Norah's eyes and she swallowed. "Right." She focused on the road even as her vision clouded.

"Norah?"

"Mmm hmm?"

She couldn't look at her friend. One questioning brow and Norah would spill everything. Then she'd be sobbing right along with Maddie. And she was afraid once she started, she wouldn't stop.

"What exactly happened last night between you and Mr. New York?"

"Nothing," Norah's voice strained through thickened emotion, squinting her eyes from the sun glaring against the wet asphalt road.

"Why are you lying to me?"

"What? I'm not...I..." What was the use of trying? Maddie knew her better than anyone else in the world. "I finally did it. I ripped off the Band-Aid. I jumped his bones."

Maddie gasped. "You're kidding?"

"Nope." Norah pulled up alongside the curb behind Maddie's car.

"You actually did it?"

"Twice." Despite being heartbroken, she couldn't restrain the smile tugging at her lips. Last night spent with Todd was incredible. The kind of night that a person never forgot.

Maddie flung back in her seat, half-giggling, half-crying into her hands before finally facing Norah. "OMG. This is awesome. Norah! I can't believe this."

Except it didn't feel awesome.

Sorrow burrowed in her gut, her chest tightening with building anguish. She was about to cry. Again.

"Whoa, whoa, Nor. What is it? What's wrong?" Maddie reached for her hand.

Tears pooled in Norah's eyes and broke free, streaming down her face. "I can't do this. I'm not built for one-night stands."

"Oh, sweetie." Caressing her hand, Maddie said, "I gotta be honest with you, I don't know if anyone is *built* for one-night stands. Some people are just better about compartmentalizing their feelings. But when you're in love with someone, it's a super bad idea."

Norah reeled back, yanking her hand from Maddie's grip, and wiping at her eyes. "I never said I was in love with Todd. That would be completely bananas. I barely know him. And you're the one who told me to *jump his bones already*," she said the last part mimicking Maddie.

Maddie winced. "I know, and I'm sorry. But I never would've said that if I knew you had real feelings for him." She shrugged a shoulder. "I thought you just needed to get it out of your system, bang one out, so you could get over Landon once and for all."

"I mean," Norah began, before shifting her train of thought, "I kind of thought that too. We were having so much fun together and the sexual tension was definitely there. But I just assumed nothing would happen between us and he'd go on his way. Then something did happen. And now...ugh." She flung her head back, resting it against the headrest and groaning loudly.

"Besides the long-distance thing, I don't see what the issue is. You like him and I think it's safe to say, he likes you too."

"That's just it, though. He doesn't. It was all fake. Me, Todd, dating." Norah winced, waiting for the blow-up from Maddie.

"I know," she admitted.

She turned in her seat. "What do you mean, you know?"

"I'm your best friend, Norah, I know when you're lying."

"So why didn't you say anything?"

Maddie pursed her lips. "I don't know. I guess I figured you'd tell me when you were ready."

"I'm sorry."

"I forgive you." She reached across the center console and hugged Norah tightly.

"Let's hope everyone else is just as forgiving. So far Izzy is pissed."

Maddie gave a flick of her wrist. "She'll get over it, don't sweat it. But most important, what's happening now? With you and Todd?"

"He's leaving, I guess. I'm sure he's anxious to get back home to try to smooth things over with his boss."

"You need to tell him how you feel before he leaves."

Norah shook her head. "I don't even know how I feel. All he cares about is his job. And that stupid promotion. That stupid dream of making partner by thirty."

Maddie patted Norah's hand. "Everyone has dreams. Most of the time they don't make sense to anyone else. Even you have dreams." Maddie twisted her lips to the side. "Don't give up on him. You never know what could happen between you two in the future."

"Yeah, I guess."

But Norah felt less optimistic than Maddie. A relationship with Todd—long-distance or otherwise—felt hopeless. It had been hours since they parted ways that morning and she hadn't heard from him. At this point, she didn't know if it would be harder if he left without saying goodbye, or if she had to say it face to face.

Because she didn't want to ever say goodbye to him.

CHAPTER 27

Todd

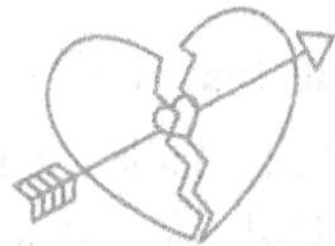

Todd sat in his Jeep while the world continued going on without him. The workers at the floral shop and Sweet Cakes Bakery shuffled out to the sidewalk to put up their sandwich boards and flip their signs from CLOSED to OPEN. Cars moved up and down the street, and people ducked into the shops. All while his life crashed down around him.

After his phone call with his boss, he'd been in a paralyzed state. Jack fired him over the phone. No chance to explain, no opportunity to wait until he was back in the office, no warnings or second chances.

He'd been terminated.

His first reaction was to call Ryan. To yell at him for ruining everything. But what would be the point now? Not only had he lost the promotion—and to Margo—he'd lost his job.

And maybe worse—okay definitely worse—he'd lost Norah too.

Out of the corner of his eye, Todd caught the sight of Norah as she dragged giant black trash bags out of the studio. Even though he was parked several yards away, he ducked in his seat. His heart gave small punches against his chest.

He was an idiot.

Without a doubt, he loved this woman. But what did he have to offer her? He lived with his parents. He didn't even have a job. He couldn't very well expect her to move all the way to New York. And he'd hurt her. Would she even forgive him?

It was Todd's last full day in Pineridge. He and Samson would hit the road in the morning and head for home. After his blow-up with Norah and his termination at Santos and Cho over the phone, he was anxious to get out of town. But he did have one place he wanted to visit before leaving.

By the looks of Margo's Instagram, she and Aaron were still a couple. Which meant Margo would be promoted to partner. Todd left her texts unanswered on his phone. No explanation she gave him would undo what she'd done. Eventually, he'd forgive her, but not today.

As Todd walked Samson through the sunlit park, over

soggy grass where the snow had melted, an ache continued to nag in his chest. It was becoming more and more difficult to differentiate between what he was most disappointed over; not making partner, or not having a future with Norah.

Samson bounded onto the bridge just as an older couple walking hand in hand came over the archway. They stopped to pet Samson and ask about his breed and age before they continued on their way. They looked so in love Todd wasn't sure if he was going to be sick or if he found it sweet.

Locks on top of locks stretched across both sides of the bridge. His chest tightened. He wasn't exactly sure why he'd even come here.

Maybe he wanted to punish himself some more.

He felt a nagging fascination to look for Norah and Landon's lock. He wanted to see it for reasons he couldn't explain. Possibly just to read it, to hold it, to feel the weight of it in his hand. Deep down, he felt the urge to find it, cut it off from the bridge, and dispose of it. It didn't seem fair, that there was a lock on this bridge with her name attached to someone else's.

He wasn't jealous.

At least that's what he chanted to himself over and over, the closer he got to the locks and the more his vision scanned over them wildly. While Todd searched through endless padlocks, Samson grew restless. He wanted to keep walking, keep finding patches of snow that hadn't melted yet, play in it, and most likely, eat it.

But Todd had this crazed throbbing in his chest. He couldn't leave this bridge without finding Norah's lock. He wasn't exactly sure what he was going to do when he found it, but that didn't matter.

After searching for what felt like forever, Todd finally came across it. A red padlock. He should've found it sooner. It stood out. It was newer, with bright unchipped paint. He couldn't stop himself from imagining cutting the lock off and chucking it into the swiftly moving water beneath the bridge.

But he wouldn't.

Todd had the tiny inkling that Norah might get upset by that. So he let go of it, allowing it to clatter back down against the other locks. To get lost amongst the sea of others once again.

A set of couples approached the bridge, each carrying locks of their own. They looked happy and a bit of jealousy snaked through him. He needed to get out of there. Away from the bridge. And out of Pineridge altogether.

Todd yanked on Samson's leash before one of the women, who was already eyeing the puppy came over to see him. Samson bounded across the bridge and Todd tucked his chin to his chest, following behind him. His phone vibrated in his front pocket, and he slid it out.

ISABELLA

Can you meet up before you leave town?

He sighed and tapped out a reply while rounding a corner in the paved pathway, passing more tourists and towering pine trees.

Sure.

ISABELLA

Tapp's in 30 min.

See ya then.

Back in his Jeep, Todd wiped Samson's feet with the towel on the passenger seat and set him down. The puppy shook his entire body and then wagged his tail, peering out the windshield. After their long road trip, Samson already loved riding shotgun. He was a decent co-pilot. Though his tiny puppy bladder meant numerous pit-stops that Todd didn't appreciate. He wasn't looking forward to the extra-long trip home.

Just a day ago, Pineridge and its residents had gotten a hold of his heart and he didn't want to leave. Okay, mainly one resident. Now, he couldn't even fathom staying in this town for another minute, never mind another night.

Once Todd reached the Whitley home, his chest heaved, his lungs expanding against his ribs. Norah's SUV was parked in the driveway. Of course, he knew he shouldn't leave without saying goodbye to her. She'd agreed to a plan most wouldn't have. He at least owed her a decent goodbye. What he would say to her exactly, he still wasn't sure. Even though he'd thought about it pretty much non-stop since he'd left the studio.

How do you say goodbye to a woman that you have a bond with? Have an emotional connection with? A physical attraction to? A deep love that didn't feel like it would ever quit?

How do you say goodbye to someone you don't want to say goodbye to?

Todd scooped Samson into his arms, not willing to waste time by allowing the puppy to wander around the yard scoping out the best spot to take a piss. He needed to make this quick. Load up all his and Samson's things into his Jeep, thank the Whitleys for their hospitality, and say a brief goodbye to Norah.

Quick, easy, painless.

At least that was his plan.

The front door of the house was unlocked so he didn't have to use the spare key Mrs. Whitley had given him. He stepped inside, instantly bombarded with the heady scent of baked cookies and melted chocolate. The television in the living room was on, giving off the impression it was Norah's niece Ava watching a children's show. He toed off his boots and tucked Samson close to his chest, tiptoeing up the stairs two at a time.

Heading straight into the room he'd been calling his own for the past week, he noticed from the corner of his eye that Norah's door was shut. His throat thickened.

He put Samson into his kennel, whispering, "Sorry, buddy. It will only be for a little bit."

Todd tossed the puppy toys and treats into a bag and zipped up his duffel that he'd already had mostly packed. At the soft sound of a light knocking on his door, he spun around.

The sight of Norah standing in the open doorway caused every one of his nerve endings to tingle. Immediately his mouth went dry. The room went still. Even the sound of Samson's tail wagging against the kennel faded into the background. Todd's desire to be near her propelled him forward, an urge to reach out and touch her, pull her into his arms.

But when he reached her, she stood rigid in the doorway, her hands stuffed in the front pockets of her jeans. When he gazed into her eyes, she dropped her chin and stared down at her feet.

"Hey?" she finally said, her voice small but still as sugary as ever.

"Hey," was all he managed to say in response.

She lifted her chin finally, pushing her hair out of her face with a shaky hand. "Were you gonna leave without saying goodbye?"

There was a piercing stab near his heart, and he tried to rub the pain away. Only it remained and seemed to build and permeate into a throbbing sensation.

"Wasn't planning to. But...didn't know you'd be around before I left."

Crossing her arms, she said, "Are you leaving now?"

"In the morning. I was just heading out to meet Isabella."

"Oh." She chewed on her lower lip, gazing up at him and nearly killing him at the same time.

Todd scratched at his stubbly chin. "Since I'll be leaving early, I guess this is goodbye."

"Right." She cleared her throat. "Probably a good idea," she said, rubbing the tops of her arms.

Taking a risk, he moved a bit closer to her. He heard her intake of breath, and felt the heat radiate off her body. "Listen," he said, pushing up his glasses, "I want you to know, our night together...meant something to me."

Norah nodded. "Me too," her voice was small and quiet.

"If you ever want to talk or something, or need anything, you have my number."

"Okay, yeah. You too."

He resisted the urge to question her. To ask her if she really meant that. Or if she was simply being polite.

He feared it was the latter.

She stared down at her feet again and he couldn't handle how adorable she looked, her feet inside thick socks, her toes curling. If he let her know, she'd hate it. But to him, she'd always be both—beautiful and cute.

Her adorableness made her sexy. He craved to tell her so, whisper it into her ear, mumble it across her bare skin, rush out the words over a hum against her lips.

But as much as he wanted to tell her, he resisted, running a hand against the back of his head. Instead, he said, "Thanks for the fun week. And showing me all the sights of Pineridge. It was exactly what I needed."

However in the end, the only thing in Pineridge worth seeing was her.

"Of course. Anytime. It was fun." She tucked her hair behind her ear.

"And if you ever find yourself in New York, I'll show you all the sights."

Norah smiled and nodded slightly. "Sounds fun."

"Right. Fun."

She laughed, though it sounded forced and harsh.

"Guess I better go."

"Oh...right. Okay." She stumbled forward, lifting her arms as if she was about to hug him but then rethought it and stuck out a hand.

Glancing at it, his chest tightened. That's what their relationship had come to? After being together the entire week and spending an amazing night together, they were going to end things with a handshake?

Not a chance.

Todd drew her in for a hug, squeezing her so tight he worried they'd need the Jaws of Life to cut them apart. He felt her shudder in his arms and it sent a pang shooting through his heart. His mind snagged on a memory from their time together. Without overthinking it, he whispered into her neck, "I'm not saying goodbye."

She deflated in his arms before at last stiffening and tearing herself away. With a quick swipe at a tear on her cheek, she said, "Okay, then...until next time."

Without meaning to, hope flickered in his chest at her words. She wasn't saying goodbye either. Which meant, she wouldn't forget him or their time together. "Until next time," he repeated.

She slipped past him into the room, knelt in front of Samson's kennel, and told him goodbye.

And then she was gone.

The flash of her auburn hair tumbled behind her as she bolted out of the room in a rush.

His chest felt heavy, and he scrubbed a hand over his face.

Sucking in a deep breath, he filled his cheeks with air before releasing it in a long and low sigh.

Letting Norah walk out that door had been harder than he'd imagined. He debated for a few moments if he should chase after her. But what would be the point? What did he have to offer her? Both she and Isabella had been right; his priorities had gotten out of control and he'd let work take precedence over everything else.

CHAPTER 28
Norah

Norah snuck out of the house early. There was a fresh dusting of snow on the ground that had fallen in the night, covering the trees and roofs. It glistened across the windshield of her SUV until the wipers cleared it. She cranked the heat as she drove out of her neighborhood. The moon shone, illuminating the glittering snow in the dim light of the early morning.

Getting out of the house and heading to the ice rink was the best plan. Norah couldn't be there when Todd left. Watching him load his Jeep, along with Samson would be too hard. Then watching him slip behind the steering wheel and pull away. Her heart squeezed in her chest at the image in her mind.

She couldn't do it.

Inside the building, Norah sat on a bench near the rink and yanked on her skates. She took her time lacing them, her fingers working meticulously. The weight of the memories shared between her and Todd that past week bogged her down. Her body ached in places it had never ached before. It made her feel as if she were getting the flu. But she knew this wasn't a viral sickness. This was a sickness of the heart. She'd felt it before. After she knew she and Landon were truly over. After they split. After the divorce was final.

But she'd never felt it quite like this.

She pulled out her phone, queued Spotify to the Galentine's playlist *Cupid is Stupid*, and pressed play. It was a sort of wretched punishment. But she couldn't resist.

Dressed in a pair of black, fitted fleece practice pants and a matching zip-up jacket, Norah took the ice gracefully. The rink was quietest at this time. Before the Olympic skaters and classes began. Only the sound of the Zamboni while it resurfaced the ice and Alison Krauss's voice singing *When You Say Nothing at All* echoed through the building.

Closing her eyes, Norah inhaled a heavy breath before she allowed her body to move. She shuffled her feet against the ice, studying her skates. If she could just force herself to go through the motions, she would be fine. Then she wouldn't think about Todd and the gaping hole in the center of her heart.

With her shoulders slumped, her body felt the music and reacted to it. She glided across the ice, her skates lifting and toes pointing in the air. Raising her arms at her sides, she stretched her hands above her head. Flashes of Todd's handsome smile and hooded green eyes assaulted her mind. So visual and clear as if he were standing before her now.

An image of him hovering over her, his straight, stubbly jawline tickling her neck. His hot lips pressed against her bare skin and his gentle hands and precise fingers on her body. Eventually, Norah grew momentum and maneuvered into a layback spin, bending backward while spinning on one foot and the other extended and pointed behind her. The sound of Todd's laugh was so familiar it felt as if it vibrated in her ears now. His nickname for her—Buttercup, and the way he said her name, without shortening it and speaking it as if it was a gift. As if *she* were a gift. Something to be treasured.

Norah spun until she couldn't spin anymore. Until she was breathless, and tears streamed down her face. She straightened and panted while she wiped at her wet cheeks.

"Hey, there, Miss Norah. You alright?" Ray, the Zamboni driver called, startling her.

She whirled around and found him peering over his shoulder, the Zamboni headed in the opposite direction.

"Hi, Ray." She sniffed. "I'm fine."

"You sure? Worked up a pretty good sweat there I imagine." He lifted his hat and wiped at his own brow.

"I'm sure. Nothing a good skating session can't fix." She forced a smile.

He tipped his hat at her. "Well, all right then. If you're sure, guess I'll get back to it."

"Thanks."

With slumped shoulders, she sluggishly skated off the ice and dropped onto the bleachers. She picked up her water bottle and took a long swig of it, cooling her hot and dry throat.

Eventually, it wouldn't be a lie. Eventually, she *would* be fine.

Norah had survived after Landon broke her heart. She would survive this too.

Wouldn't she?

It was difficult to believe when it felt as if the painful throbbing in her chest threatened to collapse her lungs. That didn't feel like a symptom of someone who was going to be okay anytime soon. What if her heart couldn't take another beating and she was never okay again?

Norah and Maddie had made plans to meet at Tapp's that afternoon. But there was something that had been nagging at Norah's heart and she needed to take care of it first. She drove to the river, parked her SUV in the lot, and climbed out, tethering her arms through her backpack. She shielded her eyes from the glowing sun that was about to dip below the horizon of trees along the bank.

People scattered along the curved, paved path, some on foot and others on bikes. While some headed toward the shops, Norah followed the path until she reached the edge of the love lock bridge. It was more crowded this early than she'd expected, and her heart sat a bit heavy in her chest. She'd hoped for some privacy. Maybe a last chance to say goodbye to Landon, to their marriage, to their love.

But maybe not dwelling on it would be best.

While she sorted through several padlocks, Norah felt as if she had an audience. Three couples stood on the bridge taking selfies while two more couples crouched and clasped their own locks on the wired fence.

Finally, she found the lock she was looking for. The one she and Landon had attached years ago. The one she assumed would be here forever. Some people left theirs on, regardless of relationship status. But something about that didn't sit well with Norah. Since her heart belonged to someone else, she couldn't leave this lock here.

Glancing over both shoulders, Norah slipped her backpack off and rested it on the bridge while she knelt and unzipped it.

Only a few people remained. She stood and offered to take pictures for one couple for a quicker departure.

With fewer people around, Norah returned to her backpack, pulling out the bolt cutters she'd found in Dad's toolbox in the garage. Thankfully the padlock Landon had used was a cheap, thin metal one from Dollar or Less. She placed the shackle between the blades and squeezed the grips of the bolt cutters together until they cut all the way through, the relief of the cutters jolting in her hands.

With it came a satisfaction stirring in her gut and blooming into warmth in her chest. It was odd to feel such alleviation but that only reminded her she'd done the right thing; in not only cutting off the padlock, but divorcing Landon.

Ignoring the gasps and gawking she felt burning into her back, she slipped the bolt cutters into her backpack and closed her fist around the broken padlock. She gazed out at the rushing river, the ground at the banks marshy and snow further back and winding around it. With tears burning her eyes, Norah's heart gave a heave as she withdrew her hand and chucked the lock into the racing water below.

The cheap metal sank and disappeared into the depths of the river, the icy water consuming it instantly. She couldn't help but smile. She'd always have her memories, some of them she'd clutch close to her heart. But her old life was gone. And she was ready for what this new life had in store for her.

Bending, she reached for her backpack, freezing in the process when something caught her eye. But not just *something*. A lock. Bright red so it stood out against the other faded ones. She crouched, getting a closer look. And when she did, her fingers hesitated to graze the cool metal. The words written in black Sharpie sent a shocking intake of breath into her lungs and caused a shiver to race down her spine.

Cupid is Stupid.

The tears Norah fought back previously returned with a vengeance, rolling down her cheeks while she proceeded to flip the lock over. The inscription on the backside of the padlock read:

Norah—Where my heart lives.

Love, Todd

In an instant, her mind was assaulted with the memory from their night together. When he'd told her he was going to stay living with his head pressed to her chest. Her heart had swelled in her chest, ready to invite him in fully. She supposed she had. But it had taken until now—in this moment—for her to realize it.

Her heart belonged to him.

Her heart lived with him too.

So why was she still here? She needed to be with him. She needed to go to him.

A building smile spread on her lips, and she sniffed, swiping at her tear-stained face. She slid her phone from her back pocket, snapping a few pics of the front and back of the lock. If Todd didn't need proof she'd seen it, her nosy sister and best friend would definitely want to see this.

Norah snatched her backpack off the bridge and took off in a jog, texting Maddie on her way.

> Raincheck for this afternoon? Something came up.

She attached the picture of the lock before putting the directions for New York in her Maps app. Todd had only been on the road for a few hours. She needed to find his exact location and to do that, she'd need the help of Izzy, Ryan, and possibly Margo.

The way Norah saw it, she had nothing to lose. She'd find Todd, apologize, and offer him the most valuable thing she owned; her heart.

Todd

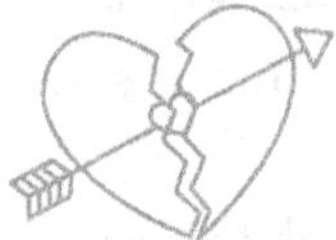

Being on the road headed for home should have brought Todd some kind of comfort. And it did. Some. But he hated saying goodbye to Norah. He hated leaving her even more.

Samson was happy to be riding shotgun again. Little did he know, he wouldn't be seeing Norah anymore. The dog had already fallen for her. He loved licking her cheek and sleeping next to her leg.

Todd reached over and petted Samson on the head while the puppy's drool flapped out the open window. "I liked her too, buddy. I liked her too."

Knowing how things had turned out, if Todd could rewind time, he wouldn't change a thing. He valued the week he and Norah spent together. Being with her opened his eyes to things about himself and his own life. He'd been inspired by her perseverance. The way she picked herself up and put her life back together after her divorce. Her dedication to plan the Galentine's party exactly how Isabella had requested, even though the very last thing on her mind was anything love-related.

He'd come to terms with being fired. If he was being honest, he deserved it. He lied to his bosses. If he'd been given the promotion, he never would've felt as if he earned it.

Thirty years old, back at home with his parents, and losing the promotion—his life was nowhere near where he thought it would be. He needed to make some changes. But where to start?

His phone rang through his Jeep's speakers.

Todd groaned before answering. "What's up, Scott?"

"Man, I've got some news. You back in town yet?"

Taking in the sights of the snowy Rockies, he sighed. "Not even close."

"Can you meet me at Marco's tomorrow night?"

"I can meet you at Marco's in about three days. I'm still in Colorado. On the road as we speak."

Scott gasped into the phone. "Seriously?"

"Can't you just tell me now?"

"It's too big. I wanted to do it in person.

He hated to admit it, but he was intrigued.

"Can you at least pull over? I'll Facetime you."

"Fine," Todd drew out on a breath. "There's a diner about five miles up the road. I'll talk to you in a few."

Todd took the exit for the diner and pulled into the parking lot. Samson practically jumped out the window before he'd even parked the Jeep.

"Hold on, Samson, let me find your leash."

He rummaged around behind him and attached it to his collar once he'd found it. It was cold being so close to the mountains, but the full sun took away the bite in the air. He'd barely made it a few feet before his phone started buzzing.

"Okay, what's up?" Todd answered, holding his phone out while Samson dragged him around the parking lot.

Scott hunkered down in a booth at what looked to be a hustling bar, acting as if he was about to fill Todd in on a secret. "It sucks about Margo and the promotion. I'm sorry. But...I think I have a better offer. One you won't be able to refuse." Scott waggled his eyebrows conspiratorially.

Todd chuckled, tugging Samson's leash from going into the bushes. "Yeah? And what could *you* possibly have to offer *me*?"

"Okay, smart ass. But after I tell you, I'm gonna be the one laughing. As in *haha, I told you so*."

Todd tilted his head, curious now. "Fine. What is it?"

Sitting up taller, pushing out his chest, Scott said, "For starters, you're looking at the newest associate of Miller and Schmidt."

Todd nearly choked. He swallowed and set his glass back onto the cardboard coaster. "BS? Wow, you weren't kidding when you said you had big news."

"I may be a jokester around the office, but that's because I knew I had no future there." Scott crumpled a napkin in his fist and tossed it onto the table. "Those guys had no intention of ever promoting me."

"You don't know that." Though Todd did know. Promotions were few and far between at Santos and Cho, the opportunity only arising once every several years. Which was why the one he'd been hoping for had been so important.

"At least at Miller and Schmidt, I'm not the underdog. I'm not a nobody in a row of cubicles in a sea of associates and paralegal faces. I actually have an office."

Todd filled his cheeks with air before blowing it out. "That's awesome. Can't beat that."

"And," Scott said, leaning forward, "I talked to the partners about you."

Straightening, Todd raised his brows. "Me? What about me?"

"Miller and Schmidt heard about the Pepperwood case you won earlier this year. They were impressed by your skills."

The Pepperwood case had been Todd's biggest win of his career to date. He'd put a substantial amount of time into that one. But the payoff had been worth it. And now, it had been the case to put him on the mark with Miller and Schmidt?

He wasn't sure what to say.

"There's no official offer. But I think it's safe to say, there will be."

Todd scratched at the rough stubble on his chin and walked back to his Jeep. "What exactly are you saying?"

A proud smile curved on Scott's lips; his shoulders pushed back. "They wanted me to wine and dine you and convince you to meet with them next week. They're gonna offer you a position." He held his hands up. "Now it's not for partner...yet, but it's pretty damn close. And you'd be respected at Miller and Schmidt. None of this, proving you're some kind of a do-gooder Boy Scout with a bleeding heart. You can be who you are, man. No strings attached."

It all sounded tempting. Todd thought of himself as a nice guy. A humanitarian if you will. But being backed into a corner, an ultimatum set, just for a shot at making partner at Santos and Cho, felt a bit unethical.

On the other hand, he'd worked diligently to get where he was at. He'd sacrificed, worked countless hours, and stayed at the same firm since he'd got his foot in the door right after law school. Switching firms now would feel like a step backward or like changing careers altogether. Was he ready to start over?

"It's a big decision," Todd finally said, picking up Samson and putting him on the passenger seat.

"It is," Scott agreed, nodding his head. "But it should be an easy one. C'mon, don't you want to be somewhere you're appreciated? Where your opinions matter? Where *you* matter?"

"It sounds good. It really does. I just don't know." Todd gave Samson a treat and petted him on his head.

"Hold on," Scott said, putting their FaceTime on hold.

A second later Todd's own phone lying on the table chimed.

"Here's Miller and Schmidt's contact info. They want you to call and set up a meeting."

Todd furrowed his brow. He supposed there wouldn't be any harm in at least meeting with Miller and Schmidt. He could appease them by listening to their offer.

"Man, if not for yourself; do it for me," Scott pleaded.

Todd exhaled. "Fine," he said, drawing out the word. "I'll set up the meeting."

"Yes!" Scott fist bumped in the air.

"But I'm not making any promises."

"I think this calls for a celebration. Text me when you're back in the city." Scott flashed him a peace sign before ending their Facetime.

It might've been too early to celebrate. But he supposed this offer could be something.

"Think it's time for a bathroom break and food." He pet Samson. "Be right back."

CHAPTER 30

Norah

It took some serious Nancy Drew-ing, but Norah tracked down Todd. His Jeep was parked at the diner off the highway exactly where Ryan said he'd be. Except she found Samson alone when she rushed to his Jeep, her heart hammering in her chest.

The window was cracked, and the puppy jumped up and wagged his tail when he saw her.

"Hey, Sammy, where's your daddy?" she asked, glancing around the parking lot and toward the diner. "Be right back."

With her legs trembling, she took a deep breath and walked inside the diner. Her gaze bounced around the inside of the diner until she caught sight of him. It only took a second for him to notice her too. And when their eyes locked, emotion flooded her body.

He stood and she advanced slowly.

"Hi," was all she could manage to say, tucking her hair behind her ears, and trying and so obviously failing at not crying. Tears built in her eyes, threatening to spill. But she hadn't come all this way to blubber like an idiot and not even be able to say the words she'd been rehearsing.

The entire drive from Pineridge to here, she'd contemplated what she would say. But standing before him now, gazing into his mossy green eyes, a streak of worry shot through her.

Had she made a terrible mistake?

Todd's hands fisted at his sides, and she wanted them to be on her instead. She needed him to hold her and give her the assurance that she hadn't chased after him for nothing.

"Wh-what are you doing here?" Todd asked, his voice low and rumbly.

Even though it came out sounding sincere, she couldn't help but waiver in her uncertainty of rushing here to see him. But it was a legitimate question. One she'd been prepared to answer. At least until he had asked it.

She cleared her throat. "I found the lock...on the bridge. *Our* lock."

Todd reached for her hand and stroked his thumb across the top of it while he stared into her eyes. Her chest heaved at his touch.

"Norah," his whisper growled but no other words followed as he continued to gaze at her.

"I'm sorry. I shouldn't have said all that stuff. I didn't mean any of it. And I shouldn't have let you leave. I was just...scared." She cautiously inched closer to him and pressed her palm to his chest, her hand already feeling the hammering of his heart.

Todd reached his free arm around her back, dragging her in closer to him and she sucked in a breath. "I'm scared too."

"You?" she scoffed, peering into his eyes. "What are you afraid of?"

"Besides my heart being crushed into a thousand pieces

again? Everything. Logistics. Do you know how far apart Colorado and New York are?"

Norah was all too familiar with the miles separating New York and Colorado. When Isabella had been contemplating a long-distance relationship with Leo, the distance had been an issue. The two of them had spent many conversations discussing it.

"I'm aware." Norah shrugged, tucking her chin to her chest. "But I guess I just assumed your heart wasn't in it."

He dropped her hand, placing a finger underneath her chin and lifting it until they made eye contact. "The job, the promotion, it means nothing in comparison to you. I'm sorry, I should've made my priorities clear. So, let me do it now." He tethered both hands around her waist. "Norah, I didn't just fall for you, I fell *hard* for you. I am in love with you."

Her throat thickened, and she tried to ignore their audience in the diner.

Squeezing her hips, Todd tugged her firmly against him. "So, the question is, do you love me?" he asked quietly, his voice so low it sent a vibration trembling in her depths.

Tears pricked her eyes once again. "It's always been you, dummy. Since I first met you at fifteen and you took me to Les Misérables."

Todd's lips curled at the corner, and he enveloped her in an embrace, as he pressed his hands against her back. "I'm sorry, but I think I'm gonna need to hear you say it."

Her cheeks warmed. "Fine. I love you, okay?" She gave him a playful shove in the chest. "There, you satisfied now?"

"Oh, I think you know me well enough to know when I'm satisfied," he said, his whisper rumbled out of his throat, a wide cheesy smile plastered on his face.

Desire swooped low in her belly.

"So, what now? You're on your way back to New York and I live here. How are we going to do this?"

"We'll figure all that out later. But right now, there is a more pressing matter I'd like to tend to." A slow grin spread on his mouth as he stared into her eyes with so much intensity her heartbeat quickened.

"And what's that?"

"Kissing you."

Blush crept into her cheeks as her smile deepened.

His hand traveled to the back of her neck, and he dipped his head, drawing his lips closer to hers ever so slowly her stomach clenched with urgency. When his mouth finally reached her lips, his own sliding against hers, heat rushed through her body, warmth pooling between her thighs.

Caught in the moment, she felt lightheaded and blissfully overjoyed. It had been so long since she'd been this elated, this carefree, this exhilarated. She wouldn't allow herself to question it. Because when she was with Todd, she didn't have to overthink her feelings. The rush of joy, passion, and love she felt each time she was with him was enough.

It had taken a short-term marriage that ended in devastation and brokenness for Norah to pick up the pieces of herself and learn how to rebuild her life again. With each piece, she'd dug deep, tried something new, and learned more about herself. Somewhere along the way, after she'd met Todd, he helped her stretch herself further and she'd grown even more.

A light-sounding applause sounded out around them. They'd apparently put on quite the show for the diner.

Drawing back from her, Todd pressed his forehead against hers and they both laughed a little. "What would you say if I asked you to go on a road trip with me?"

"I'd say, I was hoping you'd ask me."

Todd pressed a gentle kiss to her forehead. "I should warn

you though, I'm pretty sure I won't be able to let you go back. Pineridge will just have to find a way to survive without you."

"Oh, I don't think they'll be able to." She giggled.

He squeezed her sides, tickling her and causing her to laugh even harder before wrapping his arms around her and hugging her tight. The moment stretched between them, growing serious suddenly. She inhaled, clinging to him. He rested his palm against her chest.

"Remember, I live here. I promise I'm good for the rent," he mumbled, the raspy rumble shooting through her entire body.

The reminder of his words spoken that night after they'd made love was like a jolt of electricity to her heart. And her hormones.

Lifting his head, he waggled his eyebrows suggestively. "Otherwise, I can find other ways to pay."

"What did you have in mind?"

He dropped a $20 bill onto the table and draped his arm over her shoulder. "Let me tell you all about it on our drive."

Putting her arm around his waist, Norah held him tight while they walked out of the diner. She liked the person she was when she and Todd were together. She liked the prospect of this new life she was rebuilding. And having Todd in it only made it sweeter. Better. She was excited about her future.

Their future.

Maybe Cupid wasn't so stupid after all.

Acknowledgments

First, and foremost, I want to thank God for the ability, drive, and talent to be a writer. I am especially grateful for His grace. So, so much grace.

To my husband, Jeremy. Thank you for giving me space to chase my dreams and for being supportive of wherever they might take me. Thank you for being cool with me creating book boyfriends to swoon over. Even though you're my forever boyfriend and my best friend. Thanks for loving me and always making me laugh. And most importantly not caring how late we eat dinner and if it's frozen pizza.

Thanks to my amazing kids, who show their support and tell others about my books. I'm so proud of each of you and I'm so blessed to be your mom. I hope you always know I'll support your dreams.

To my talented artist Stephanie Henigen @stephsbook-therapy who designed the perfect cover characters when I shared my inspo as Zoe Deutch and Glen Powell. Thank you for taking this project on a little last minute and when I was beyond overwhelmed with this book. You are wonderful! Thank you for creating adorable bookmarks and making them available in your Etsy shop for my readers.

Thank you to my dad for instilling in me the importance of being a dreamer. Thanks for being my cheerleader and bragging about me to everyone you met. You were so proud of me and I knew that. I know you're still cheering me on. I love you and miss you every single day!

To my mom, I'm grateful for your encouragement and support. Thank you for loving me in the best way a mom can. Love you!

Thanks to my in-laws, siblings, and extended family, for the support, love, and prayers.

Thank you to my ride or die beta readers, (you know who you are), my CP's, and my ARC readers. Thank you for being patient with me and so giving of your time. Thank you to my online support system, the friends, connections, bookstagrammers—I will be forever grateful for you.

Thank you to every reader in advance, for purchasing, reading on KU, sharing on your socials, and most importantly, leaving reviews. You are the reason we authors, (especially indie authors) can keep doing what we love. Thank you!

About the Author

 Starla DeKruyf writes swoony love stories with a happily ever after. Her love of romance novels began when she borrowed her friend's copy of Tiger Eyes by Judy Blume and kept it hidden from her mom. When she's not working the day job or hanging out with her family, you can find her jamming out to her book playlists and writing her next swoony romance, usually by hand. She lives in Spring, Texas, with her husband, three children, and a rescue pup.

Also by Starla De Kruyf

Pineridge series—book 1:

Eight Days of Christmas

Pineridge series—book 2:

We Fell in Love in October

Juniper Ridge series—book 1:

A Pumpkin Patch and A Fling

A Standalone Romantic Comedy:

The Heart Rehab Experiment

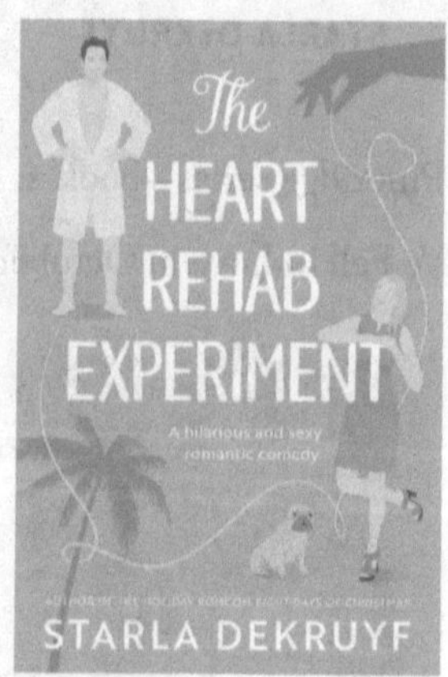